CRITICS ARE SINGING

RESERVATION BLUES

"QUIET, POWERFUL . . . SHERMAN ALEXIE CREATES STING-ING COMMENTARY, AND HE SHOWS HIS DETERMINATION TO MAKE YOU UNCERTAIN WHETHER YOU WANT TO LAUGH OR CRY. . . . He is funny, he is perceptive, and he knows how to stir us in large and small ways. The talent is real, and it is very large, and I will gratefully read whatever he writes, in whatever form."
—Frederick Busch, *New York Times Book Review*

"SHERMAN ALEXIE IS WILDLY TALENTED."
—*USA Today*

"HIGH-FLYING, HUMOR SPIKED . . . POIGNANT AND POET-IC. . . . EXPLORES THE PLACE WHERE DREAMS AND DOWN-AND-DIRTY REALITY COLLIDE."
—*People*

"THE MYSTICAL COMPLEXITY OF *RESERVATION BLUES* IS AS MESMERIZING AS THE POETIC POWER OF ALEXIE'S WRIT-ING. Alexie makes his story credible while playing fast and loose with the conventions of time. . . . Generously laced with bleak and sometimes wacky humor, but none of that detracts from the book's poignant theme."
—*San Francisco Chronicle*

"SCATHINGLY FUNNY. . . . *RESERVATION BLUES* NEVER MISSES A BEAT, NEVER SOUNDS A FALSE NOTE."
—*Los Angeles Times*

more . . .

"HILARIOUS AND HEARTBREAKING IN EQUAL MEASURE [WITH] THE TRUE TEXTURE AND RESONANCE OF THE BLUES. . . . Alexie's writing flows smoothly, carrying you smoothly into the story. It's only when you stop laughing that you're aware of the depth of both Alexie's talent and his tale. HIS IS A VOICE WE NEED TO HEAR."
—*Capitol Times*

"UNFLINCHING. . . . ALEXIE OWNS HUMOR AND THE POWER OF THE IMAGINATION IN SPADES. [He is] a tough and important chronicler of Contemporary American Indian Culture."
—*Oregonian*

"REMARKABLE . . . DELIGHTFULLY WHIMSICAL. . . . The narrative surprises at every turn, transcending the familiar tragedy of reservation life with humor and lyricism. HIGHLY RECOMMENDED."
—*Library Journal* (starred review)

"UNFORGETTABLE . . . SOARS LIKE THE ELUSIVE FIFTH CHORD. . . . Alexie mixes biting black humor, a healthy dose of magic, and sparkling lyricism to produce A REMARKABLY POWERFUL STORY."
—*Booklist* (starred review)

"VISIONARY. . . . LYRICAL AND HUMOROUS. It educates and enlightens a broad audience about the diversity of life on American Indian reservations."
—*Book Page*

RESERVATION BLUES

SHERMAN ALEXIE

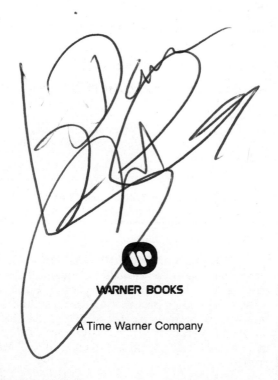

WARNER BOOKS

A Time Warner Company

"Cross Road Blues" and "Preachin' Blues" ("Up Jumped the Devil"). Words and music by Robert Johnson. Copyright © (1978) 1991 King of Spades Music. All rights reserved. Used by permission.

All of Coyote Spring's song lyrics have been reprinted by permission of Jim Boyd and Sherman Alexie.

Warner Books Edition
Copyright © 1995 by Sherman Alexie
All rights reserved.

This Warner Books edition is published by arrangement with The Atlantic Monthly Press, 841 Broadway, New York NY 10003

Warner Books, Inc., 1271 Avenue of the Americas, New York, NY 10020

Visit our Web site at http://warnerbooks.com

W A Time Warner Company

Printed in the United States of America

First Warner Books Printing: September 1996
20 19 18 17 16 15 14

Library of Congress Cataloging-in-Publication Data
Alexie, Sherman
            Reservation blues / Sherman Alexie.
            p.   cm.
        ISBN 0-446-67235-1
            1. Indians of North America — Washington (State) — Fiction.
2. Spokane Indians — Fiction.   3. Washington (State) — Fiction.   I. Title.
[PS3551.L35774R74   1996]
813'.54—dc20   96-33838
                                                                          CIP

            Cover design by Rachel McClain
            Cover illustration by Wendell Minor

for Diane

for Etta Adams

Acknowledgments

With thanks to Donna Brook, David James Duncan, and Dick Lourie for their editorial help, and Nancy Stauffer for her continued support and friendship. Special thanks to Jim Boyd, my Colville Indian songwriting partner. I want to acknowledge Christiane Bird's *The Jazz and Blues Lover's Guide to the U.S.*, Carl P. Schlicke's *General George Wright: Guardian of the Pacific Coast*, Benjamin Manning's *Conquest of the Coeur d'Alenes, Spokanes, & Palouses*, Robert H. Ruby's and John A. Brown's *The Spokane Indians: Children of the Sun*, and Mari Sandoz's *Crazy Horse: The Strange Man of the Oglalas* for valuable historical material. I want to especially acknowledge the influence of the Columbia Pictures film *Crossroads*, directed by Walter Hill and written by John Fusco, which was released to a very quiet reception in 1985. Most of all, I want to honor the memory of the real Robert Johnson. Without his music, none of the music contained in this book would exist.

God's old lady, she sure is a big chick.

—Charles Mingus

I went to the crossroad

fell down on my knees

I went to the crossroad

fell down on my knees

—Robert Johnson

I

Reservation Blues

Dancing all alone, feeling nothing good
It's been so long since someone understood
All I've seen is, is why I weep
And all I had for dinner was some sleep

You know I'm lonely, I'm so lonely
My heart is empty and I've been so hungry
All I need for my hunger to ease
Is anything that you can give me please

chorus:
I ain't got nothing, I heard no good news
I fill my pockets with those reservation blues
Those old, those old rez blues, those old reservation blues
And if you ain't got choices
What else do you choose?

(repeat chorus twice)

And if you ain't got choices
Ain't got much to lose

In the one hundred and eleven years since the creation of the Spokane Indian Reservation in 1881, not one person, Indian or otherwise, had ever arrived there by accident. Wellpinit, the only town on the reservation, did not exist on most maps, so the black stranger surprised the whole tribe when he appeared with nothing more than the suit he wore and the guitar slung over his back. As Simon drove backward into town, he first noticed the black man standing beside the faded WELCOME TO WELLPINIT, POPULATION: VARIABLE sign. Lester FallsApart slept under that sign and dreamed about the stranger before anyone else had a chance. That black man walked past the Assembly of God Church, the Catholic Church and Cemetery, the Presbyterian Church and Cemetery. He strolled to the crossroads near the softball diamond, with its solitary grave hidden in deep center field. The black man leaned his guitar against a stop sign but stood himself straight and waited.

The entire reservation knew about the black man five minutes after he showed up at the crossroads. All the Spokanes thought up reasons to leave work or home so they could drive down to look the stranger over. A small man with very dark skin and huge hands, he wore a brown suit that looked good from a distance but grew more ragged, frayed at the cuffs, as he came into focus. The black man waved at every Indian that drove by, but nobody had the courage to stop, until Thomas Builds-the-Fire pulled up in his old blue van.

"Ya-hey," Thomas called out.

"Hey," the black man said.

"Are you lost?"

"Been lost a while, I suppose."

"You know where you're at?"

"At the crossroad," the black man said, but his words sounded like stones in his mouth and coals in his stomach.

"This is the Spokane Indian Reservation," Thomas said.

"Indians? I ain't seen many Indians."

Thomas parked his van and jumped out. Although the Spokanes were mostly a light-skinned tribe, Thomas tanned to a deep brown, nearly dark as the black man. With his long, black hair pulled into braids, he looked like an old-time salmon fisherman: short, muscular legs for the low center of gravity, long torso and arms for the leverage to throw the spear. Just a few days past thirty-two, he carried a slightly protruding belly that he'd had when he was eight years old and would still have when he was eighty. He wasn't ugly, though, just marked by loneliness, like some red *L* was tattooed on his forehead. Indian women had never paid much attention to him, because he didn't pretend to be some twentieth-century warrior, alternating between blind rage and feigned disinterest. He was neither loud nor aggressive, neither calm nor silent. He walked up to the black man and offered his hand, but the stranger kept his hands at his sides, out of view, hidden.

"I'm careful with my hands," the black man said. "He might hear me if I use my hands."

"Who might hear you?"

"The Gentleman."

Thomas wanted to know more about the Gentleman, but he was too polite and traditional to ask and refused to offend the black man with personal questions that early in the relationship. Traditional Spokanes believe in rules of conduct that aren't collected into any book and have been forgotten by most of the tribe. For thousands of years, the Spokanes feasted, danced, conducted conversations, and courted each other in certain ways. Most Indians don't follow those rules anymore, but Thomas made the attempt.

"What's your name?" the black man asked after a long silence.

"Thomas Builds-the-Fire."

"That a good name?"

"I don't know. I think so."

"My name's Johnson," the black man said. "Robert Johnson."

"It's good to meet you, Mr. Johnson. Who's your traveling partner?"

Johnson picked up his guitar, held it close to his body.

"My best friend," Johnson said. "But I ain't gonna tell y'all his name. The Gentleman might hear and come runnin'. He gets into the strings, you hear?"

Thomas saw that Robert Johnson looked scared and tired, in need of a shower, a good night's rest, and a few stories to fill his stomach.

"How'd you end up here?" Thomas asked. A crowd of Indian kids had gathered, because crowds of Indian kids are always gathering somewhere, to watch Thomas Builds-the-Fire, the misfit storyteller of the Spokane Tribe, talk to a strange black man and his guitar. The whole event required the construction of another historical monument. The reservation had filled with those monuments years ago, but the Tribal Council still looked to build more, because they received government grants to do exactly that.

"Been lookin' for a woman," Johnson said. "I dream 'bout her."

"What woman?"

"Old woman lives on a hill. I think she can fix what's wrong with me."

"What's wrong with you?" Thomas asked.

"Made a bad deal years ago. Caught a sickness I can't get rid of."

Thomas knew about sickness. He'd caught some disease in the womb that forced him to tell stories. The weight of those stories bowed his legs and bent his spine a bit. Robert Johnson looked bowed, bent, and more fragile with each word. Those Indian kids were ready to pounce on the black man with questions and requests. The adults wouldn't be too far behind their kids.

"Listen," Thomas said, "we should get out of the sun. I'll take you up to my house."

Johnson considered his options. Old and tired, he had walked from crossroads to crossroads in search of the woman in his dreams. That woman might save him. A big woman, she arrived in shadows, riding a horse. She rode into his dreams as a shadow on a shadowy horse, with songs that he loved but could not sing because the Gentleman might hear. The Gentleman held the majority of stock in Robert Johnson's soul and had chased Robert Johnson for decades. Since 1938, the year he faked his death by poisoning and made his escape, Johnson had been running from the Gentleman, who narrowly missed him at every stop.

"Come on," Thomas said. "Hop in the van. You can crash at my place. Maybe you can play some songs."

"I can't play nothin'," Johnson said. "Not ever."

Robert Johnson raised his hands, palms open, to Thomas. Burned, scarred, those hands frightened Thomas.

"This is what happens," Johnson said. "This is how it happens sometimes. Things work like this. They really do."

Thomas wanted to take Johnson to the Indian Health Service Clinic, for a checkup and the exact diagnosis of his illness, but he knew that wouldn't work. Indian Health only gave out dental floss and condoms, and Thomas spent his whole life trying to figure out the connection between the two. More than anything, he wanted a story to heal the wounds, but he knew that his stories never healed anything.

"I know somebody who might be able to help you," Thomas said.

"Who?"

"Big Mom. She lives on top of Wellpinit Mountain."

Thomas pointed up through the clouds. Robert Johnson looked toward the peak of Wellpinit Mountain, where Big Mom kept her home. Pine trees blanketed the mountain and the rest of the reservation. The town of Wellpinit sat in a little clearing below the mountain. Cougars strolled through the middle of town; a bear once staggered out of hibernation too early, climbed onto the roof of the Catholic Church, and fell back asleep. A few older Indians still lived out in the deep woods in tipis and shacks, venturing into town for funerals and powwows. Those elders told stories about the gentle Bigfoot and the Stick Indians, banished from the tribe generations ago, who had turned into evil spirits that haunted the forests now.

"This is a beautiful place," Johnson said.

"But you haven't seen everything," Thomas said.

"What else is there?"

Thomas thought about all the dreams that were murdered here, and the bones buried quickly just inches below the surface, all waiting to break through the foundations of those government houses built by the Department of Housing and Urban Development. Thomas still lived in the government HUD house where he had grown up. It was a huge house by reservation standards, with two bedrooms, a kitchen, a bathroom, and living room and two more bedrooms and a bathroom in the basement. However, the house had never really been finished because the Bureau of Indian Affairs cut off the building money halfway through construction. The water pipes froze every winter, and windows warped in the hot summer heat. During his childhood, Thomas had slept in the half-finished basement, with two blankets for walls and one blanket for his bed.

"There's a whole lot you haven't seen," Thomas said.

"Things you don't want to see, you know? Big Mom could tell you all about it. She's been around a long time."

"Take me to Big Mom," Robert Johnson said. "Maybe she's the woman I been dreamin' about."

"Ain't nobody goes up the mountain to see her," Thomas said. "We always wait for her to come down. Only special visitors get to go up the mountain. Nobody has ever seen one of them. We just hear them late at night, sneaking through town. We don't ever get to see them."

"She has to be the one," Johnson said. "She has to be. Don't you see? I'm one of those special visitors. I'm supposed to see her. I just come too early."

Robert Johnson climbed into the driver's seat of the blue van. Thomas pushed him out of the way and shut the door. A few dozen members of the Spokane Tribe had gathered at the crossroads. Some trembled with fear, most laughed. Only Thomas Builds-the-Fire would let this stranger any further into his van and his life.

"Take me there," Johnson said. "Take me to Big Mom."

"Tell me everything," Thomas said, "and I'll take you."

"Mr. Builds-the-Fire, I sold my soul to the Gentleman so I could play this damn guitar better than anybody ever played guitar. I'm hopin' Big Mom can get it back."

Thomas put the van in gear and drove Robert Johnson to the base of Wellpinit Mountain. He wanted to go farther, to deliver Johnson to the front door of Big Mom's house, but the van shuddered and died in the middle of the road.

"This is as far as I can go," Thomas said. "You have to walk from here."

Johnson stepped out of the van, looked toward the summit.

"It's a long walk, ain't it?" Johnson asked.

Thomas watched Johnson walk up the mountain until he

was out of vision and beyond any story. Then Thomas saw the guitar, Robert Johnson's guitar, lying on the floor of the van. Thomas picked it up, strummed the strings, felt a small pain in the palms of his hands, and heard the first sad note of the reservation blues.

† † †

One hundred and thirty-four years before Robert Johnson walked onto the Spokane Reservation, the Indian horses screamed. At first, Big Mom thought the horses were singing a familiar song. She had taught all of her horses to sing many generations before, but she soon realized this was not a song of her teaching. The song sounded so pained and tortured that Big Mom could never have imagined it before the white men came, and never understood it later, even at the edge of the twenty-first century. She listened carefully to the horses' song, until she had memorized it, and harmonized. She wanted to ask many questions about the new song when she visited the horses next.

Finally, the horses stopped screaming their song, and Big Mom listened to the silence that followed. Then she went back to her work, to her buckskin and beads, to CNN. The horses' silence lasted for minutes, maybe centuries, and made her curious. She understood that silence created its own music but never knew the horses to remain that quiet. After a while, she stood and started the walk down her mountain to the clearing where the horses gathered. Of course, she wanted to ask about the silence that followed their new song.

As she stepped out of her front door, Big Mom heard the first gunshot, which reverberated in her DNA. She pulled her dress up around her waist and ran for the clearing, heard a gunshot with each of her footfalls. All she heard were the gunshots, singular at first, and then in rapid plural bursts that she could not count.

Big Mom ran to the rise above the clearing where the

horses gathered. There, she saw the future and the past, the white soldiers in blue uniforms with black rifles and pistols. She saw the Indian horses shot and fallen like tattered sheets. Big Mom stood on the rise and watched the horses fall, until only one remained.

Big Mom watched the Indian colt circled by soldiers. The colt darted from side to side, looked for escape. One soldier, an officer, stepped down from his pony, walked over to the colt, gently touched its face, and whispered in its ear. The colt shivered as the officer put his pistol between its eyes and pulled the trigger. That colt fell to the grass of the clearing, to the sidewalk outside a reservation tavern, to the cold, hard coroner's table in a Veterans Hospital.

Big Mom wept as the soldiers rode away on their own pale ponies and heard their trumpets long after. She walked to the clearing where the horses had fallen, walked from corpse to corpse, and searched for any sign of life. After she counted the dead, she sang a mourning song for forty days and nights, then wiped the tears away, and buried the bodies. But she saved the bones of the most beautiful horse she found and built a flute from its ribs. Big Mom played a new flute song every morning to remind everybody that music created and recreated the world daily.

In 1992, Big Mom still watched for the return of those slaughtered horses and listened to their songs. With each successive generation, the horses arrived in different forms and with different songs, called themselves Janis Joplin, Jimi Hendrix, Marvin Gaye, and so many other names. Those horses rose from everywhere and turned to Big Mom for rescue, but they all fell back into the earth again.

For seven generations, Big Mom had received those horses and held them in her arms. Now on a bright summer day, she watched a black man walk onto the Spokane Indian Reservation. She heard that black man talk to Thomas Builds-the-Fire. She watched Thomas give that black man a ride to the base of her mountain and smiled as the blue van shuddered to a stop. Big Mom sat in her rocking chair and waited to greet her latest visitor.

† † †

"The end of the world is near!" shouted the crazy old Indian man in front of the Spokane Tribal Trading Post. He wasn't a Spokane Indian, but nobody knew what tribe he was. Some said Lakota Sioux because he had cheekbones so big that he knocked people over when he moved his head from side to side. The old man was tall, taller than any of the Spokanes, even though age had shrunk him a bit. People figured he was close to seven feet tall in his youth. He'd come to play in an all-Indian basketball tournament in Wellpinit thirty years ago and had never left. None of the Spokanes paid him much mind because they already knew the end was just around the corner, a few miles west, down by Turtle Lake.

Thomas was the only Spokane who talked much to the-man-who-was-probably-Lakota. But then, most of the Spokanes thought Thomas was pretty goofy, especially after he gave Robert Johnson that ride up to Big Mom's place. Thomas had carried Johnson's guitar around with him ever since then. He so strongly identified with that guitar that he wrapped it in a beautiful quilt and gave it a place of honor in his living room. When he went out for his daily walks, Thomas cradled the guitar like a baby, oblivious to the laughter all around him. But the-man-who-was-probably-Lakota didn't laugh at Thomas.

"Ya-hey," Thomas called out.

"Ya-hey, Thomas," the-man-who-was-probably-Lakota said. "The end of the world is near."

"I know it is," Thomas said and dropped a few coins into the old man's hat, which already contained some change and a check from Father Arnold, priest of the Catholic Church. Although the Spokanes ignored the-man-who-was-probably-Lakota, they weren't going to let him starve, and Father Arnold constantly recruited lost souls.

"That's a good-looking guitar," the-man-who-was-probably-Lakota said. "I hear you got it from the black man."

"That I did," Thomas said.

"You be careful with that music, enit? Music is a dangerous thing."

Thomas smiled and walked into the Trading Post, one of the few lucrative businesses on the reservation. Its shelves were stocked with reservation staples: Diet Pepsi, Spam, Wonder bread, and a cornucopia of various carbohydrates, none of them complex. One corner of the Trading Post was devoted to the gambling machines that had become mandatory on every reservation. The Tribe had installed a few new slot machines earlier that day, and the Spokanes lined up to play. Dreams of the jackpot. Some Indian won a few hundred dollars every afternoon and fell down broke by the next morning. Thomas didn't gamble with his money, but he did gamble with his stomach when he heated up a microwave burrito. He paid for the burrito and a Pepsi and, carrying his food and guitar, walked back outside to eat.

He sat on a curb outside the Trading Post, hungry and ready to eat, just as Victor Joseph and Junior Polatkin walked up. Victor was the reservation John Travolta because he still wore clothes from the disco era. He had won a few thousand dollars in Reno way back in 1979, just after he graduated from high school. He bought a closet full of silk shirts and polyester pants and had never had any money since then to buy anything new. He hadn't gained any weight in thirteen years, but the clothes were tattered and barely held to his body. His wardrobe made him an angry man.

"Ya-hey, Builds-the-Shithouse," Victor said.

"Ya-hey," Thomas said.

"Is that your guitar?" Junior Polatkin asked.

"That's his woman," Victor said.

Junior Polatkin was Victor's sidekick, but nobody could figure out why, since Junior was supposed to be smart. A tall, good-looking buck with hair like Indians in the movies, long, purple-black, and straight, Junior was president of the Native American Hair Club. If there had been a hair bank, like a blood bank or sperm bank, Junior could have donated yards of the stuff and made a fortune. He drove a water truck for the Bureau of Indian Affairs and had even attended college for a semester or two. There were rumors he had fathered a white baby or two at school.

A job was hard to come by on the reservation, even harder to keep, and most figured that Victor used Junior for his regular income, but nobody ever knew what Junior saw in Victor. Still, Junior could be an asshole, too, because Victor was extremely contagious.

"This isn't my guitar," Thomas said. "But I'm going to change the world with it."

Victor and Junior sat beside Thomas, one on either side. The three Spokane Indians sat together on the sidewalk in front of the Trading Post. Everybody likes to have a place to think, to meditate, to eat a burrito, and that particular piece of accidental sidewalk mostly belonged to Thomas. He usually sat there alone but now shared it with Victor and Junior, two of the most accomplished bullies of recent Native American history.

A few years earlier, after the parking lot for the Trading Post was built, the BIA contractor had a little bit of cement left over. So he decided to build a sidewalk rather than lug the cement all the way back to the warehouse and fill out complicated, unnecessary, and official government papers. Thomas was watching the BIA workers pour the cement and never saw Victor and Junior sneak up on him. Victor and Junior knocked Thomas over, pressed his face into the wet cement, and left a permanent impression in the sidewalk. The doctors at Sacred Heart Hospital in Spokane removed the cement from his skin, but the scars remained on his face. The sidewalk belonged to Thomas because of that pain.

"You named that guitar?" Junior asked.

"It's a secret name," Thomas said. "I ain't ever going to tell anybody."

Victor pulled Thomas into a quick headlock.

"Tell me," Victor said and cut off Thomas's air for a second.

"Come on," Junior said. "Take it easy."

"I ain't letting you go until you tell me," Victor said.

Thomas was not surprised by Victor's sudden violence. These little wars were intimate affairs for those who dreamed in childhood of fishing for salmon but woke up as adults to shop at the Trading Post and stand in line for U.S.D.A. commodity food instead. They savagely, repeatedly, opened up cans of commodities and wept over the rancid meat, forced to eat what stray dogs ignored. Indian men like Victor roared from place to place, set fires, broke windows, and picked on the weaker members of the Tribe. Thomas had been the weakest Indian boy on the whole reservation, so small and skinny, with bigger wrists than arms, a head too large for its body, and ugly government glasses. When he grew older and stronger, grew into an Indian man, he was the smallest Indian man on the reservation.

"Tell me the name of your goddamned guitar," Victor said and squeezed Thomas a little harder.

Thomas didn't say a word, didn't struggle, but thought *It's a good day to die. It's a good day to get my ass kicked.*

"Come on, Victor," Junior said. "Let him go. He ain't going to tell us nothing."

"I ain't leaving until he tells us," Victor said, but then had a brainstorm. "Or until he plays us a song."

"No way," Junior said. "I don't want to hear that."

"I'll make you a deal," Thomas said. "If I can play your favorite Patsy Cline song, will you leave me alone?"

"What happens if you can't play the song?" Victor asked.

"Then you can kick my ass some more."

"We'll kick your ass anyway," Victor said. "If you can't play the song, we get the guitar."

"That's a pretty good deal, enit?" Junior asked.

"Enit," Victor said. "It's better than hearing another one of his goddamn stories."

Thomas repeated stories constantly. All the other Indians on the reservation heard those stories so often that the words crept into dreams. An Indian telling his friends about a dream he had was halfway through the telling before everyone realized it was actually one of Thomas's stealth stories. Even the white people on the reservation grew tired of Thomas's stories, but they were more polite when they ran away.

Thomas Builds-the-Fire's stories climbed into your clothes like sand, gave you itches that could not be scratched. If you repeated even a sentence from one of those stories, your throat was never the same again. Those stories hung in your clothes and hair like smoke, and no amount of laundry soap or shampoo washed them out. Victor and Junior often tried to beat those stories out of Thomas, tied him down and taped his mouth shut. They pretended to be friendly and tried to sweet-talk Thomas into temporary silences, made promises about beautiful Indian women and cases of Diet Pepsi. But none of that stopped Thomas, who talked and talked.

"I got a better idea," Victor added. "If you can't play the song, then you have to stop telling all your fucking stories."

"Okay," Thomas said, "but you have to let me go first."

Victor released Thomas from the headlock but picked up the guitar and smashed it against the sidewalk. Then he handed it to Junior, who shrugged his shoulders and gave it back to Thomas. Indians around the Trading Post watched this with indifference or ignored it altogether.

"There," Victor said. "Now you can play the song."

"Oh, yeah, enit," Junior said. "Play it now."

Thomas looked around at the little country he was trying to save, this reservation hidden away in the corner of the world. He knew that Victor and Junior were fragile as eggs, despite their warrior disguises. He held that cracked guitar tenderly, strummed the first chord, and sang that Patsy Cline song about falling to pieces.

Victor looked at Thomas, looked at Junior, sat on the sidewalk again. Thomas managed to sing that song pretty well, but Victor had been looking forward to the silence. He might have to kick Thomas's ass anyway. Victor, fresh from thirty-two years of fried chicken lunches, ran his hands along his greasy silk shirt and tried to think.

"Jeez," Junior said, "that was pretty good, Thomas. Where'd you learn to sing?"

"Shut the fuck up," Victor said. "I'm thinking."

The-man-who-was-probably-Lakota watched these events unfold. He walked over to the trio of Spokane Indians on the sidewalk.

"The end of the world is near!"

"When is that going to happen?" Junior asked. "I need to set my alarm clock."

"Don't mock me," the-man-who-was-probably-Lakota said. "The end of the world is near!"

"Why don't all of you shut up?" Victor said.

Junior pretended his feelings were hurt so he could storm off. He needed to drive the water truck down to the West End of the reservation anyway but didn't want Victor to know how much he cared about his job. The West End ran out of water every summer. Indians and pine trees competed for water down there, and the trees usually won.

"Where you going?" Victor asked Junior.

"To the West End."

"Wait up, I'll ride with you," Victor said and ran after Junior.

Thomas had received a pardon because of Victor's short attention span. Still, Victor never actually hurt him too seriously. Victor's natural father had liked Thomas for some reason. Victor remembered that and seemed to pull back at the last second, left bruises and cuts but didn't break bones. After Victor's father died, Thomas had flown with Victor to Phoenix to help pick up the ashes. Some people said that Thomas even paid for Victor's airplane tickets. Thomas just did things that made no sense at all.

"I'll be back for you!" Victor yelled and climbed into the water truck with Junior.

"The end of the world is near!"

"My ass is near your face!" Victor yelled out the window as the truck pulled away.

The-man-who-was-probably-Lakota helped Thomas to his feet. Thomas started to cry. That was the worst thing an Indian man could do if he were sober. A drunk Indian can cry and sing into his beer all night long, and the rest of the drunk Indians will sing backup.

"Listen," the-man-who-was-probably-Lakota said as he put his arm around Thomas's shoulders. "Go on home. Glue the guitar back together. Maybe things will be better in the morning."

"You think so?" Thomas asked.

"Yeah, but don't tell anybody I said so. It would ruin my reputation."

"Okay. I'll see you tomorrow."

Thomas climbed into his blue van with that broken guitar, wondered if he could fix it, and noticed his fingers were cut shallowly, as if the first layers of skin had been delicately sliced by a razor. The-man-who-was-probably-Lakota picked up a hand drum and pounded it in rhythm with his words as Thomas drove away.

"The end of the world is near! It's near! It's near! The end is near!"

† † †

Junior was a good driver. He kept that water truck firmly on the road, negotiating the reservation obstacle course of potholes and free-range livestock, as he made his way to the West End. He had been driving truck since a few days after he had returned from college. Victor had been riding with him all that time, falling asleep as soon as his head fell back against the vinyl seat. On that particular day, as the-man-who-was-probably-Lakota comforted Thomas, Victor fell asleep before they passed the city limits. At least, his eyes were closed when the nightmare came to him.

Victor fought against his nightmare, twisted and moaned in his seat, as Junior drove the water truck. Junior, who had always paid close attention to dreams, wondered which particular nightmare was filling Victor's sleep. He had majored in psychology during his brief time in college and learned a lot about dreams. In Psychology 101, Junior had learned from Freud and Jung that dreams decided everything. He figured that Freud and Jung must have been reservation Indians, because dreams decided everything for Indians, too. Junior based all of his decisions on his dreams and visions, which created a lot of problems. When awake, he could never stomach the peanut butter and onion sandwiches that tasted so great in his dreams, but Junior always expected his visions to come true. Indians were *supposed* to have visions and receive messages from their dreams. All the Indians on television had visions that told them exactly what to do.

Junior knew how to wake up in the morning, eat breakfast, and go to work. He knew how to drive his water truck, but he didn't know much beyond that, beyond that and the wanting. He wanted a bigger house, clothes, shoes, and something more. Junior didn't know what Victor wanted, except money. Victor wanted money so bad that he always spent it too quick, as if the few dollars in his wallet somehow prevented him from getting more. Money. That's all Victor talked about. Money. Junior didn't know if Victor wanted anything more, but he knew that Victor was dreaming.

Victor tossed and turned in his sleep, pushed against the door, kicked the dashboard. He spouted random words and phrases that Junior could not understand. Junior glanced over at his best friend, touched his leg, and Victor quieted a little.

Victor slept until Junior pulled up at Simon's house on the West End. Simon stood on his front porch. His pickup, which he only drove in reverse, was parked on the remains of the lawn.

"Ya-hey, Simon," Junior called out as he stepped down from his truck.

"Ya-hey," Simon said. "Bringing me some water?"

"Yeah."

"Good. I need water. My lawn."

Junior looked at the dusty ground and the few struggling grass shoots.

"Jeez," Simon said, "I really need some water."

Junior nodded his head.

"Where are we?" Victor asked from inside the truck.

"At Simon's."

"That crazy backward driving old man?" Victor said. "What are we doing here?"

"Water," Junior said. "Can you help me?"

Victor climbed out of the truck and helped Junior insert the hose into Simon's well. They pumped water for a few minutes, then removed the hose and made as if to leave.

"Wait," Simon said. "Aren't you thirsty? Don't you want something to drink?"

He was a good host.

"Yeah," Victor said. "Do you got a beer?"

"He don't drink like that," Junior said.

"I don't drink like that," Simon said.

"All he has is Pepsi and coffee," Junior said.

"All I have is Pepsi and coffee," Simon said.

"Enit?" Victor asked.

"Enit."

"Well," Victor said, "I'm feeling like a beer. What do you think, Junior? Let's knock off early and head for the tavern."

Junior ignored him.

"Come on," Victor said. "Let's go."

"I've got work to do," Junior said. "I need to finish. It's my job."

Junior climbed into the water truck. Victor sighed deeply and climbed in, too. They'd had this same conversation for years. Simon waved from the front porch and then ran over to the truck. He stood on the running board and leaned into the truck.

"Hey," Simon said, "did you see that black man the other day?"

Junior nodded.

"What do you think?"

"I think it's bullshit," Victor said.

"What do you think?" Simon asked Junior, who just shrugged his shoulders and cleared his throat.

"Yeah," Simon said, shrugging his shoulders and clearing his throat. "It's just like that, enit? That's what I've been thinking, too. Just like that. You know, the whole reservation's been talking. People think that Thomas is goofy."

"He is goofy," Victor said. "Now, get down. We're heading out. Got work to do."

Simon stepped off the running board.

"See you," Junior said.

Simon waved again.

"Hey," Victor said, "how come you don't walk backwards like you drive?"

"Because I'd bump into things."

"Oh," Victor said, "that makes a whole lot of sense. You keep in touch, okay? We'll do lunch."

"Can't," Simon said. "I'm going out of town. Headed to the coast to visit my relatives. Won't be back for a while."

Junior smiled at the thought of Simon hurtling backwards down Interstate 90, passing hundreds of cars, and pulling gracefully into rest stops.

"Send us a postcard," Victor said.

"You take care," Junior said.

"Jeez," Victor said as they pulled away, "that man is crazy."

"He's fine. He's fine."

"Whatever you say. Aren't you thirsty?"

Junior looked at his best friend.

"We've got five more houses to do. Then we can go to the tavern."

"Cool. You're buying, enit?"

"Yeah, I'm buying."

† † †

While Junior and Victor got drunk in the tavern and Thomas slept, Robert Johnson's guitar fixed itself. He had left it outside by the smokehouse because he planned to burn it as firewood. It had held together long enough for the Patsy Cline song but completely fell apart before he got it home. He planned on smoking some salmon anyway and figured the smoke from the burning guitar would make salmon taste like the blues. But the guitar came together overnight and waited for Thomas, who walked outside with salmon in his hands.

"Thomas," the guitar said. It sounded almost like Robert Johnson but resonated with a deeper tone, some other kind of music. Thomas wasn't surprised that the guitar sounded almost like Robert Johnson.

"Good morning," Thomas said. "How you feeling this morning?"

"Little sore, little tired."

"I know what you mean, enit?"

Thomas tried to hide the salmon behind his back, but the guitar saw it.

"We're plannin' on burnin' me up?" the guitar asked.

"Yeah," Thomas said. He could not lie.

The guitar laughed.

"That's all right," the guitar said. "You eat your fish. I'll just play some blues right here."

The guitar played itself while Thomas smoked the salmon. Before she died, Thomas's mother, Susan, had draped the salmon across a bare mattress frame, threw the frame over the fire, and smoked it that way. Thomas didn't have the courage to do that, so he cooked salmon in the old smokehouse that Samuel, his father, had built years ago. Susan died of cancer when Thomas was ten years old; Samuel had been drunk since the day after his wife's wake.

"The blues always make us remember," the guitar said.

"They do, enit?" Thomas said.

"What do the blues make you remember?"

"My mom used to sing," Thomas said. "Her voice sounded like a flute when she was happy, but more like glass breaking when she was in pain."

Thomas remembered how she used to hold him late at night, rocking him into sleep with stories and songs. Sometimes she sang traditional Spokane Indian songs. Other times, she sang Broadway show tunes or Catholic hymns, which quite similar.

"Was she pretty?" the guitar asked.

"Beautiful, I guess."

Thomas and the guitar sat in silence for a long time, re-mained quiet until the salmon was cooked. King salmon. Thomas ate it quickly, barely stopping to wipe his face and fingers clean.

"Can you play me a sad song?" Thomas asked.

The guitar played the same song for hours while Thomas sat by the fire. That guitar sounded like Robert Johnson, like a cedar flute, like glass breaking in the distance. Thomas closed his eyes, listened closely, and wondered if Victor and Junior heard the song.

"They hear me," the guitar said. "Those two hear me good."

Victor and Junior were passed out in the water truck on an old logging road. After they'd delivered water to the West End, they spent a long night in the Powwow Tavern and ended up here. The guitar's song drifted through the truck's open windows, fell down on the two Indians, and worked its way into their skins. They both tried to push the music away from their hangover dreams.

"They be comin' soon," the guitar said.

"Why?" Thomas asked.

"Y'all need to play songs for your people. They need you. Those two boys need you."

"What you talking about?" Thomas asked.

"The music. Y'all need the music."

Thomas thought he needed more money than music. Music seemed to be a luxury most days. He'd received some life insur-ance money when his mom died, but that was almost gone, and nobody on the reservation ever hired him to work. Still, Thomas heard music in everything, even in money.

"Maybe you and me should go on the road," Thomas said.

"On the road, on the road," the guitar said. "We takin' those two with us. We startin' up a band."

"Those guys ain't going to play with me," Thomas said. "They don't even like me."

The guitar played on and ignored Thomas's doubts. Music rose above the reservation, made its way into the clouds, and rained down. The reservation arched its back, opened its mouth, and drank deep because the music tasted so familiar. Thomas felt the movement, the shudder that passed through tree and stone, asphalt and aluminum. The music kept falling down, falling down.

† † †

After the tavern had closed, Junior and Victor climbed into the water truck and passed out. They spent many nights asleep in parking lots. During this night, they dreamed of their families.

Junior dreamed of his two brothers, two sisters, mother and father. They all stood at a bus stop in Spokane, the white city just a few miles from the reservation, waiting to go downtown. Pawn shops and secondhand stores. The world was beautiful sometimes.

Junior's father had owned a couple hundred acres of wheat that he rented out to a white farmer. Every harvest, Junior's father made enough money for a family vacation in Spokane. They stayed at the Park Lane Motel, ate Kmart submarine sandwiches, and watched bad karate movies at the Trent Drive-In.

Junior dreamed of his parents' funeral in the Spokane Indian Longhouse. His siblings, who had long since dispersed to other reservations and cities, couldn't afford to come back for the funeral. None of his siblings had enough money to mourn properly.

Victor dreamed of his stepfather, a short, stocky white man, red-headed and so pale that veins flowed through his skin like rivers on a map. Victor's mother and stepfather had met in a cowboy bar in Spokane when Victor was nine years old, a few weeks after his real father had moved to Phoenix, Arizona. His mother and stepfather had two-stepped to Hank Williams all night long and fell in love.

"It was the cowboy hat," Victor's mother had said more than once.

In Victor's dream, he could smell the dead body, his real father's. His real father had died of a heart attack during a heat wave in Phoenix and lay on a couch for a week before a neighbor discovered him. Victor hadn't seen his real father for years before his death. Victor could still smell that dead body smell. That smell never fully dissipated, had always remained on the edges of Victor's senses.

In that way, both dreamed of their families.

Then the morning came and brought Robert Johnson's guitar with it. In Thomas's yard, the guitar played itself and the music did rise into the clouds. It did rain down on the reservation, which arched its back and drank deeply. It did fall on the roof of the water truck, disturbing Junior's and Victor's sleep. The music talked to them in their dreams, talking so loudly that neither could sleep.

"Shit," Victor said, "what the hell is that noise?"

"It's music," Junior said. "I think."

"Man, I got a hangover."

"Me, too."

The music played on, and gradually changed.

"Jeez," Victor said, "now it sounds like Thomas singing out there. I'm going to kick his ass. As soon as I can lift my head."

"Thomas," Junior said, "will you keep it down? I got a headache."

The music kept playing.

"That's it," Victor said. "I'm kicking his ass good this time."

Victor and Junior staggered out of the truck, but Thomas was nowhere to be found. The music continued.

"What the hell is that?" Victor asked.

"I don't know."

"That fucking Thomas has to be doing this. It's his voice. He's doing this. I say we go find him and kick his ass."

"It's getting louder."

"That's it," Victor said as he slowly climbed back into the truck. "Let's go get him."

Junior found his way into the driver's seat, started the truck, and made his way toward Thomas's house. He was a good driver.

† † †

"I smell water," the guitar said.

"It's the pond," Thomas said and pointed. "Down there."

Benjamin Pond used to be called Benjamin Lake, but then a white man named Benjamin Lake moved to the reservation to teach biology at the Tribal High School. All the Indians liked the teacher so much that they turned the lake into a pond to avoid confusion.

"They're comin' now," the guitar said. "I feel 'em."

Thomas walked into the house to get some food ready. He had to offer food to his guest, no matter how little he had, even if Junior and Victor were the guests. The cupboards were nearly bare, but Thomas managed to find a jar of peanut butter and some saltine crackers.

"Tell me a story 'fore they get here," the guitar said when Thomas came back outside with a plate of reservation appetizers.

Thomas sat, closed his eyes, and told this story:

"Benjamin Pond has been on the reservation longer than anything. Jesus sipped water from the pond. But Turtle Lake, on the other side of the reservation, has been here a long time, too.

Genghis Khan swam there and was nearly eaten by the giant tur-tles. He decided not to conquer the Americas because even its tur-tles were dangerous.

"The tribal elders say that Benjamin Pond and Turtle Lake are connected by a tunnel. Those turtles swim from pond to lake; they live in great caverns beneath the reservation and feed on failed dreams.

"The elders tell the story of the horse that fell into Benja-min Pond, drowned in those waters, but washed up on the shore of Turtle Lake. Children swim in both places, but their grandmothers burn sage and pray for their safety.

sweet smoke, save us, bless us now

"Indian teenagers build fires and camp at the water. They sometimes hear a woman crying but can never find the source of the sound. Victor, Junior, and I saw Big Mom, the old woman who lives on the hill, walk across Benjamin Pond. Victor and Junior pretend they don't know about Big Mom, but we heard her sing all the way.

sweet smoke, save us, bless us now

"I am in love with water; I am frightened by water. I never learned to swim. Indians have drowned in both Benjamin Pond and Turtle Lake, and I wonder if we can taste them when we drink the water.

sweet smoke, save us, bless us now

"I watched Victor learn to swim when he was ten years old. His stepfather threw him in Turtle Lake, which doesn't have a bottom, which used to be a volcano. Victor's screams rose like ash, drifted on the wind, and blanketed the reservation. Junior watched his oldest brother James slip on the dock at Benjamin Pond. James fractured his skull and woke up as somebody different."

Thomas opened his eyes. The guitar was silent.

"Ya-hey," Thomas whispered, but the guitar didn't respond. The sun was almost directly overhead when Junior and Victor pulled up in the water truck. They stepped out of the rig at the same time and walked toward Thomas.

"They're here," Thomas whispered to the guitar, which remained silent. He picked it up and strummed a few chords, thinking how nobody believed in anything on this reservation. All the Indians just dropped their quarters into the jukebox, punched the same old buttons, and called that music. Thomas shared his stories with pine trees because people didn't listen. He was grateful for the trees when the guitar left him.

"I don't know what the fuck is going on," Victor said to Thomas. "But I can't get your voice out of my head."

"What's he saying to you?" Junior asked Victor.

"Something about being on the cover of *Rolling Stone*."

"Yeah," Junior said. "Me, too."

"I was wondering if you guys wanted to be in my band," Thomas said. "I need a lead guitarist and drummer."

"I'll do it," Junior said, already convinced. Two peanut butter and onion sandwiches waited in his lunch box.

"What's in it for me?" Victor asked.

"This," Thomas said and handed Robert Johnson's guitar to him. Victor picked at the strings and flinched.

"Damn," Victor said. "This thing is hot. How long it been in the sun?"

"I thought we broke that thing," Junior said.

"Nothing's broken yet," Thomas said.

"Why the hell you want us in your band anyway?" Victor asked. "Who's to say I won't break this guitar over your head every damn day?"

"Nothing I can say about that," Thomas said.

But Victor held on to that guitar too tenderly to ever break it again. He already gave it a name and heard it whisper. Thomas couldn't hear the guitar at all anymore but saw it snuggle closer to Victor's body.

"Play that thing a little," Thomas said. "Then tell me you don't want to be in my band."

"No problem," Victor said.

"He don't even play the guitar," Junior said.

"He does now," Thomas said.

Victor's fingers moved toward the chord: index finger on first two strings, first fret; middle finger on third string, second fret; ring finger on fourth string, third fret. He strummed the strings, hit the chord, and smiled.

"I'll be your lead guitarist," Victor said. "But what are you going to do?"

"I'm the bass player," Thomas said. "And the lead singer."

2

Treaties

Listen to me, listen to me, listen to me

Somebody breaks a hard promise
Somebody breaks your tired heart
The moon tears the sun in half
Love can tear you apart

chorus:
What do you want from your father?
What do you want from your brother?
What do you want from your sister?
What do you want from your mother?

Treaties never remember
They give and take 'til they fall apart

Treaties never surrender
I'm sure treaties we made are gonna break this Indian's heart

I don't know what I want from love
I just know it ain't easy
I just know how it all feels
It's just like signing a treaty

(repeat chorus)

I just know it ain't easy
It's just like signing a treaty

Thomas, Victor, and Junior rehearsed in Irene's Grocery Store. Even though the building had been condemned for years, boarded up and dangerous, everybody still called it Irene's. The band crawled through a hole in the back wall and practiced for hours at a time. Thomas had spent most of his savings on a bass guitar and an amplifier for himself and a drum set for Junior. Victor wore gloves when he played Robert Johnson's guitar but still suffered little burns and scratches. At first, Thomas had worried that his amplified bass and Junior's drums would overwhelm the acoustic lead guitar, but Victor could have kicked the guitar around the floor and it would have sounded good enough. Even without an amplifier or microphones, Robert Johnson's guitar filled the room.

Pretty soon, the band's practice sessions started to draw a crowd. In the beginning, only Lester FallsApart materialized, like a reservation magician, and usually knocked somebody or something over, like a reservation clown. After a few days, however, a dozen Spokanes showed up and started to dance, even in the heat. Undercover CIA and FBI agents dressed up like Indians and infiltrated the band practices but didn't fool anybody because they danced like shit. The crowds kept growing and converted the rehearsal into a semi-religious ceremony that made the Assemblies of God, Catholics, and Presbyterians very nervous. United in their outrage, a few of those reservation Indian Christians showed up at rehearsals just to protest the band.

"You're damned!" shouted an old Catholic Indian woman. "You're sinners! Rock 'n' roll is the devil's music!"

"Damn right it is!" Victor shouted back and hit an open

chord that shook the protestors' fillings out of their teeth. The Indian Health Service dentist spent the next two weeks with his hands deep in Christian mouths.

"No," the dentist had to say more than once to Catholic patients, "I don't think there is a saint of orthodontics."

† † †

Father Arnold, priest of the reservation Catholic Church, didn't care much about the band one way or the other. He thought the whole thing was sort of amusing and nostalgic. He'd been a little boy, maybe five years old, when Elvis appeared on "The Ed Sullivan Show" and threw the entire country into a righteous panic. Arnold would never have thought that Indians would be as judgmental as those white people way back when, but he was discovering exactly how Catholic Spokanes could become.

"Listen," he said to one of his more rabid parishioners, "I really don't think God is too concerned about this band. I think hunger and world peace are at the top of His list of things to worry about, and rock music is somewhere down near the bottom."

Father Arnold had waited tables in a restaurant and sung in a rock band for a few years after he graduated college, before he received his calling into the priesthood. They'd played mostly fifties songs, like "Teen Angel" and "Rock Around the Clock" with Father Arnold on lead vocals. He'd had a good voice, still had a good voice, but now the music he sang was in church and was much more important than the stuff he used to sing at American Legion dances and high school proms.

Arnold was twenty-eight, buying a Big Mac at a McDonald's, when the call came to him. He'd always been a Catholic, alternating between devotion and laziness, but had never thought of himself as a priest. He had always believed, had always been taught, that priests were extraordinary men, nearly heroic. He had never been anything but ordinary. An ordinarily handsome man, with ordinary intelligence and an ordinary car, he'd graduated college with a 3.1 G.P.A. in English. Surely not the makings of a Catholic priest. Even now, when he talked about his calling in that McDonald's, he was embarrassed by how ordinary it all seemed.

He had just picked up his order when he heard the voice. At first, he thought the cashier was talking to him, but the cashier was busy with another customer. The voice didn't say anything exactly. It was just a voice, a series of words, or sounds. He was never quite sure about the voice, but he knew there was no music, no harps, no sudden shaft of light, no shift of the earth.

He found a table, ate his Big Mac, and then walked across the street to the Catholic church.

"Hello," he had said to the priest there. "My name is Robert Arnold. I want to be a priest. But I'm not a virgin. Can you help me?"

"You don't have to be a virgin," the priest had said. "You just have to be celibate from now on."

"Well, okay," Arnold said. "But I really hope you're right about this celibacy thing, you know?"

He had quickly gone through seminary, assisted at a few churches, and then was shipped to the Spokane Indian Reservation when the residing priest died.

"Father," the bishop had said to him just before he left for the reservation. "We need you out there. You have youth, a robust faith that is needed to reach these Indians. We have tried discipline. We have tried strength. But they need something different. Someone like you."

Father Arnold had never been too concerned about the vagueness of his assignment. He was never sure how faith could be robust and often worried that his prayers were too thin, stretched to the point of breaking. Still, he knew he was a good priest and could deliver a homily with the best of them. Sometimes it was almost like being a lead singer again, onstage, with the audience hanging on his every word. As a lead singer, as a priest, he could change the shape of the world just by changing the shape of a phrase.

"A-men," Father Arnold often whispered to himself, practicing different pronunciations of the word. "Ah-men. Ay-yyyy-men. Uh-man."

Arnold came to the reservation in his yellow VW van, expecting tipis and buffalo, since he had never been told otherwise. He was genuinely shocked when the Indians in his congregation spoke English.

"Buffalo?" asked Bessie, the oldest Catholic on the reservation. "What do you mean, buffalo? You really thought there were going to be buffalo here?"

"Yes," he said, "I was looking forward to it."

"Oh, Father," Bessie said and laughed. "There weren't any buffalo here to begin with. We're a salmon tribe. At least, we were a salmon tribe before they put those dams on the river."

"What about the buffalo? I mean, Indians were always hunting buffalo on television."

"It was those dang Sioux Indians. Those Sioux always get to be on television. They get everything."

Arnold's Indian education was quick and brutal. He heard much laughter.

"Father Arnold, we're not laughing *with* you, we're laughing *at* you."

He was impressed by the Spokanes' ability to laugh. He'd never thought of Indians as being funny. What did they have to laugh about? Poverty, suicide, alcoholism? Father Arnold learned to laugh at most everything, which strangely made him feel closer to God.

However, he was most impressed by the Spokanes' physical beauty. Perhaps it was because he had spent most of his life surrounded by white people and had grown used to their features. The Spokanes were exotic. Perhaps it was because of the Indians' tremendous faith. But Father Arnold thought the Spokanes were uniformly beautiful. When members of other Indian tribes visited the Spokane Reservation, he began to believe that every Indian in the country was beautiful.

It's their eyes, he finally decided. *Those Indians have the most amazing eyes. Truly amazing.*

† † †

David WalksAlong, the Spokane Tribal Council Chairman, showed up at the band's rehearsal a few times. He was a tall, light-skinned Indian with brown eyes and a round face. He'd been a great basketball player in his youth, a slashing, brutal point guard who looked almost like an old-time Indian warrior. But he spent most of his time playing golf now and had grown fat in the belly and thighs. WalksAlong had long, dark, beautiful hair twenty years ago but had cut it shorter and shorter as it grew more gray.

"Kind of loud, enit?" WalksAlong asked Thomas after a particularly intense set.

"What'd you say?" asked Thomas. His ears were ringing.

"I said you're disturbing the peace!"

"Yeah," Thomas shouted. "We're a three-piece band!"

"No, I said you're too loud!"

"Yeah," Thomas agreed. "It is a pretty good crowd!"

WalksAlong was visibly angry.

"Listen," the Chairman said, "you better quit fucking with me! You're just like your asshole father!"

"Really?" Thomas asked. "You really think we're rock-ing? You think my father will like us, too?"

WalksAlong jabbed Thomas's chest with a thick finger.

"You might think you're funny!" he shouted loud enough

for Thomas to understand him, "but I can shut you down anytime I want to! I just have to give the word!" He stormed off, but Thomas just shrugged his shoulders. David WalksAlong had never cared much about the Builds-the-Fire family. He always thought the Builds-the-Fires talked too much. And Thomas's father, Samuel, had been a better basketball player than WalksAlong. Not a lot better but enough to make all the Indian women chase him after the games, while WalksAlong walked home alone.

"What was that all about?" Junior asked Thomas.

"I don't know," Thomas shouted. "I don't think he likes us."

"Bullshit," Victor shouted. "He just doesn't like you. He ain't never liked you."

WalksAlong walked back to the Spokane Tribal Headquarters, cussing to himself all the way. He stormed through the front door, ignored his secretary's attempts at conversation, and used his whole body to push open his office door. The contractor had used cheap, warped wood for the door, and it was nearly impassable on warm days.

"H'llo, Uncle," said Michael White Hawk.

"Shit," WalksAlong said, surprised. "What the hell are you doing here? Why didn't you call me?"

"Jus' got out," White Hawk said. "Walked here."

Michael White Hawk had been in Walla Walla State Penitentiary for two years. He was a huge man before he went to jail, but hours of weightlifting had turned him into a monster.

"Jeez, Nephew," WalksAlong said. "You been shooting up steroids or what?"

"Pumped iron, you know?"

White Hawk had been in the same class as Victor and Junior but didn't graduate from high school. He dropped out in eighth grade, unable to read and write. He could sign his name, but he did that purely by rote.

"Man," WalksAlong said and hugged his nephew. "It's good to have you back. It's really good."

WalksAlong had raised his nephew since he was a toddler. Michael's mother had died of cirrhosis when he was just two years old, and he'd never even known his father. Michael was conceived during some anonymous three-in-the-morning pow-wow encounter in South Dakota. His mother's drinking had done obvious damage to Michael in the womb. He had those vaguely Asian eyes and the flat face that alcohol babies always had on reservations. But he'd grown large and muscular despite the alcohol's effects. Even in grade school, he'd been as big as most men and terrorized his classmates. He bullied even older kids past the point of reason. He once shoved a pencil up a seventh grader's nose. That kid was in the hospital for a month and then moved to another reservation to live with some cousins. They'd sent White Hawk to a boys' school near Spokane. But he beat the crap out of a few delinquent white boys, so they sent him back to the reservation.

"Uncle," White Hawk said and hugged WalksAlong too hard.

"Oh," WalksAlong said. "Take it easy. You're going to bust my ribs."

White Hawk did not ease up, however, hugging his uncle with all he had. WalksAlong was about to pass out when White Hawk finally let him go.

"Uncle, Uncle! Look what I fuckin' got in prison!"

White Hawk took off his t-shirt to show his uncle the dozen tattoos he had received in prison. There were dragons, bears, feathers, and naked women. There was a naked Indian woman with braids on his back and a naked Indian woman with un-braided hair on his stomach. The tattoos were incredibly crude, little more than scars with ink imbedded in them. WalksAlong was amazed by how much pain his nephew must have gone through.

"How was it in there?" WalksAlong asked.

"Okay," White Hawk said. "How come you di'nt come 'n see me?"

WalksAlong had driven to Walla Walla many times in the two years his nephew had been in prison, but he never once went inside. He sat in his car in the prison parking lot and smoked cigarettes.

"I didn't want to see you in there," WalksAlong said. "You didn't belong in there."

"Uncle, it hurt in here."

White Hawk pointed to his chest, pressed his finger against a horse tattoo. WalksAlong had not seen his nephew cry in years, although White Hawk had screamed his way through childhood. But White Hawk didn't cry. He just pointed to his chest.

"Jeez," WalksAlong said, "we have to celebrate. Let me call the other Councilmen."

Old Jerry, Buck, and Paula, the other Councilmen, hastily declined the offer when they heard that Michael White Hawk was home. David WalksAlong's secretary, Kim, had already been on the phone with her sister, Arlene, and the gossip soon spread all over the reservation. Michael White Hawk was home. The news made it to Irene's Grocery.

"White Hawk is home," whispered one Indian to another. "No shit? White Hawk is home?"

Lester FallsApart staggered up to Thomas after a song.

"Thomas!" Lester shouted. "White Hawk is home!"

Thomas looked back at Junior and Victor. Junior cleared his throat loudly. Victor shrugged his shoulders but felt something drop in his stomach. They barely made it through the next song and then went home, disappointing the crowd.

† † †

White strangers had begun to arrive on the Spokane Indian Reservation to listen to this all-Indian rock and blues band. A lot of those

New Agers showed up with their crystals, expecting to hear some ancient Indian wisdom and got a good dose of Sex Pistols covers instead. In emulation of all their rock heroes, who destroyed hotel rooms with style and wit, Victor and Junior trashed their own HUD house. Both lived together in a tiny HUD house with faulty wiring and no indoor plumbing. They slept in the house only when there was no other alternative.

One evening, after a long rehearsal, Victor decided he was the Beatles.

"I'm McCartney and Lennon all rolled up into one," Victor said. "Thomas is George. And Junior, you get to be Ringo."

"Shit," Junior said, "how come I have to be Ringo?"

"If the Ringo fits," Victor said, "then wear it."

Thomas knew it was just the beginning but was already frightened by how much Victor and Junior had improved. Victor, especially. He played that guitar like a crazy man, and chords and riffs and notes jumped out of that thing like fancydancers. If you looked close enough, you *saw* the music rising off the strings and frets.

Two white women, Betty and Veronica, had somehow found their way to the reservation and showed up at every rehearsal. They even parked their car outside Irene's Grocery and set up camp. Betty slept in the front seat and Veronica slept in the back. Both had long blonde hair and wore too much Indian jewelry. Turquoise rings, silver feather earrings, beaded necklaces. They always appeared in sundresses with matching Birkenstocks.

"Jeez," said one Spokane woman to another, "those New Age princesses like Indian men, enit?"

"Enit, but they don't know what they're getting into, do they?"

Betty and Veronica always stood in the front row and sang along with the band. They had great voices, which could be heard even through the noise that the band created. After the band had

quit for the night, Betty and Veronica often entertained the stragglers by playing a few songs themselves. Both played guitar, and
they sang duet on their own songs:

> *Indian boy, don't go away*
> *Indian boy, what did you say?*
> *Indian boy, I'll turn on the light*
> *Indian boy, come home tonight*

Most of the Spokane Indian women wanted to kick Betty
and Veronica off the reservation, but the Indian men lined up every
night to listen to the white women's songs. David WalksAlong had
even invited them to his home for dinner. WalksAlong was nearly
a gourmet cook and could do wondrous things with commodity
food. But Betty and Veronica were scared of Michael White Hawk.

They did go home with Junior and Victor one night, and
everybody on the reservation knew about it. Little Indian boys
crept around the house and tried to peek in the windows. All of
them swore they saw the white women naked, then bragged it
wasn't the first time they'd seen a naked white woman. None of
them had seen a naked Indian woman, let alone a white woman.
But the numbers of naked white women who had visited the Spokane Indian Reservation rapidly grew in the boys' imaginations, as
if the size of their lies proved they were warriors.

Betty and Veronica did not take off their clothes that night,
although Betty shared a bed with Junior and Veronica with Victor.

"Am I your first Indian man?" Junior asked Betty.

"No."

"How many?"

"A few."

"How many is a few?"

"About five or six, I guess."

"You guess?"

"Well, some were only part Indian," Betty said.

"Jeez, which part?" asked Junior. Betty kissed him then to shut him up. Both fell asleep with their shoes on.

In the other bedroom, Victor had his hand down Veronica's pants within a few seconds. She kept pushing it away, but Victor was persistent.

"Stop," Veronica said. "I don't want you to do that."

"Why you come in here, then?" Victor asked.

"Because I like you."

"How much do you like me?"

"You're the best. I mean, you're an Indian and a guitar player. How much better could you be?"

Victor pushed his hand down her pants again.

"Please stop," she said. "I just want to kiss. I'm not ready to do that."

Victor removed his hand but pushed Veronica's head down near his crotch.

"Do that," he said.

"No, I don't do that. I don't like it."

"Come on."

"No. But I'll do it with my hand."

Victor unbuttoned his pants and closed his eyes. Afterwards, Veronica curled up next to him as he snored. She was cold and wanted to get under the blankets but didn't want to wake him up.

Betty and Veronica left the next morning, before Junior and Victor even woke, but they left a note. Junior read it to Victor.

"Shit," Victor said. "They live where?"

"Seattle," Junior said. "They have to go back to work."

"Work? Where do they work?"

"At some bookstore, I guess. But it says here they own the bookstore."

"Own the bookstore? Man, they must be rich, enit?"

"I guess."

Betty and Veronica were co-owners of a New Age book-store in the Capitol Hill section of Seattle. They had temporarily closed it down when rumors of the all-Indian rock band hit the store. They had driven to Wellpinit, three hundred and six miles away, in six hours.

"What's the name of the bookstore?" Victor asked.

"I don't know. They left a bookmark though. It says 'Dop-pelgangers.' "

"What the hell is a doppelganger?"

"I think it means twins or something. Like a shadow of you."

"White shadows, enit?" Victor asked.

"I guess," Junior said.

"Do you think they'll be back?"

"I hope so."

† † †

The gossip about the band spread from reservation to reservation. All kinds of Indians showed up: Yakama, Lummi, Makah, Snohom-ish, Coeur d'Alene. Thomas and his band had developed a small following before they ever played a gig. If they'd had a phone, it would have been ringing. If they'd had a post office box, it would have been stuffed. Indians talked about the band at powwows and feasts, at softball tournaments and education conferences. But the band still didn't have a name.

"We need a name for this band," Thomas said after an-other well-attended rehearsal.

"How about Bloodthirsty Savages?" Victor asked.

"That's a cool name, enit?" Junior asked.

"I was thinking about Coyote Springs," Thomas said.

"That's too damn Indian," Junior said. "It's always Coyote this, Coyote that. I'm sick of Coyote."

"Fuck Coyote," Victor said.

Lightning fell on the reservation right then, and a small fire started down near the Midnight Uranium Mine. Coyote stole Junior's water truck and hid it in the abandoned dance hall at the pow-wow grounds. The truck was too big for the doors, so nobody was sure how that truck fit in there. Junior lost his job, but he had to take that truck apart piece by piece and reassemble it outside first.

The entire band was unemployed now, and Coyote had proven his strength, so the band accepted the name and became Coyote Springs. But it wasn't a happy marriage. Coyote Springs argued back and forth all the time. Victor and Junior threatened to quit the band every day, and Thomas brought them back with promises of money and magazine covers. Victor and Junior liked to sit outside the Trading Post in Thomas's blue van and pose for all the women who happened to walk by.

"Ya-hey," Victor called out to the full-blood Indian women. He also called out to the white women who worked for the Tribe, especially those nurses from the IHS Clinic. Victor had a thing for white nylons, but the nurses ignored him.

"Ya-hey," the Indian women shouted back, which was the extent of conversation. Most Indians never needed to say much to each other. Entire reservation romances began, flourished, and died during the hour-long wait to receive commodity food on the first of each month.

At first, Coyote Springs just played covers of other people's songs. They already knew every Hank Williams song intimately because that's all their fathers sang when drunk. They learned the entire Buddy Holly catalogue, picked up a few Aerosmith songs, and sang Spokane Indian words in place of the Spanish in Ritchie Valens's version of "La Bamba."

"You know," Thomas said, "I'm going to start writing our own songs."

"Why?" Junior asked.

"Well," Thomas said, "because Buddy Holly wasn't a Spokane Indian."

"Wait," Junior said. "Buddy was my cousin."

"That's true," Victor said. "He was quarter-blood, enit?"

"Besides," Victor said, "how come you get to write the songs?"

"Yeah," Junior said.

"Because I have the money," Thomas said. He had forty-two dollars in his pocket and another fifty hidden at home, much more than Junior and Victor had together. Victor understood the economics of the deal, how money equals power, especially on a reservation so poor that a dollar bill once changed the outcome of tribal elections. David WalksAlong was elected Councilman by a single vote because he'd paid Lester FallsApart a dollar to punch the ballot for him.

"Okay, then, asshole," Victor said, "write the songs. But I'm still the Guitar God."

So Thomas went home and tried to write their first song. He sat alone in his house with his bass guitar and waited for the song. He waited and waited. It's nearly impossible to write a song with a bass guitar, but Thomas didn't know that. He'd never written a song before.

"Please," Thomas prayed.

But the song would not come, so Thomas closed his eyes, tried to find a story with a soundtrack. He turned on the television and watched *The Sound of Music* on channel four. Julie Andrews put him to sleep for the seventy-sixth time, and neither story nor song came in his dreams. After he woke up, he paced around the room, stood on his porch, and listened to those faint voices that echoed all over the reservation. Everybody heard those voices, but nobody liked to talk about them. They were loudest at night, when Thomas tried to sleep, and he always thought they sounded like horses.

For hours, Thomas waited for the song. Then, hungry and tired, he opened his refrigerator for something to eat and discovered that he didn't have any food. So he closed the fridge and opened it again, but it was still empty. In a ceremony that he had practiced since his youth, he opened, closed, and opened the fridge again, expecting an immaculate conception of a jar of pickles. Thomas was hungry on a reservation where there are ninety-seven different ways to say *fry bread*.

Fry bread. Water, flour, salt, rolled and molded into shape, dropped into hot oil. A traditional food. A simple recipe. But Indians could spend their whole lives looking for the perfect piece of fry bread. The tribe held a fry bread cooking contest every year, and most Spokanes had their own recipe. Contestants gossiped about the latest secret ingredient. Even the little kids dropped their basketballs long enough to roll up their own bread, while Lester FallsApart mixed his flour with Thunderbird Wine. Big Mom came down from her mountain annually and won the contest for thirty-seven straight years. The-man-who-was-probably-Lakota had taken second place for the last twenty years.

"Fry bread," Jana Wind had whispered into the ear of Bobby Running-Jones as they lay down together.

"Well, fry bread to you, too," Bobby had said to Jana after he came home late from the bar.

"Do you want to do the fry bread?" Indian boys often asked Indian girls at their very first reservation high school dance.

"Shit," Victor had said once. "I ain't got much fry bread left. How long before we get to play some real music?"

As his growling stomach provided the rhythm, Thomas sat again with his bass guitar, wrote the first song, and called it "Reservation Blues." Soon after that, the Federal Express showed up at his door with an overnight package.

"This is for Thomas Builds-the-Fire," the FedEx guy said. He was nervous and kept scanning the tree line.

"I'm him," Thomas said.

"Sign here," the FedEx guy said. "Did you know I was in the war?"

"Which war?"

"All of them," the FedEx guy said, handed the package over, and ran for his van. Thomas waved. The FedEx guy smiled, saluted, and drove away. Thomas figured that Federal Express sent its bravest and craziest couriers out to the reservation, but that made sense. Thomas opened the package. It was a letter from some Flathead Indian in Arlee, Montana. He said he was the owner of the Tipi Pole Tavern and wanted Coyote Springs to come play that weekend. He would pay.

"He'll pay," Thomas whispered, then chanted, then sang.

† † †

From Thomas Builds-the-Fire's journal:

Coyote: A small canid *(Canis latrans)* native to western North America that is closely related to the American wolf and whose cry has often been compared to that of Sippie Wallace and Janis Joplin, among others.

Coyote: A traditional figure in Native American mythology, alternately responsible for the creation of the earth and for some of the more ignorant acts after the fact.

Coyote: A trickster whose bag of tricks contains permutations of love, hate, weather, chance, laughter, and tears, e.g., Lucille Ball.

Spring: An ultimate source of supply, especially a source of water issuing from the ground.

Spring: To issue with speed and force, as in a raging guitar solo.

Spring: To make a leap or series of leaps, e.g., from stage to waiting arms of Indian and non-Indian fans.

† † †

The blue van, tattered and bruised, cruised down an anonymous highway on the Flathead Indian Reservation and searched for the dirt road that led to the Tipi Pole Tavern. Actually, Thomas, Junior, and Victor attempted to drive and navigate. As a result of this partnership, the blue van and its three occupants, along with their musical equipment, were lost.

"Shit, Junior," Victor said, "there ain't but two or three roads on this whole reservation, and you're telling me we're lost."

"This goddamn map is useless," Junior said. "There are all sorts of roads ain't even on it. This road we're on now ain't on the map."

"Listen," Thomas said, "maps just give advice anyway."

The blue van suddenly stopped at a crossroads.

"Which way?" Thomas asked because he was driving.

"I don't know," Victor and Junior said because they weren't driving.

"Let's decide it the old Indian way," Thomas said because he tried to be as traditional as the twentieth century allowed.

"What's that?" Victor and Junior asked because they were as contemporary as cable television.

"We'll drive straight," Thomas said and pointed with his lips. "Then we find a house and ask somebody for directions."

The blue van started again, shuddered a little bit, then traveled down the highway for nearly a mile before it came upon a HUD house. Those government houses looked the same from reservation to reservation. The house on the Flathead Reservation looked like Simon's house on the Spokane Reservation. A Flathead woman and her granddaughter stood outside in their near-yard, hands on hips, waiting.

"We heard you coming from a long ways off," the Flathead woman said as the blue van pulled into her almost-driveway and stopped.

"Where's the Tipi Pole Tavern?" Junior asked.

"Over there," the woman answered and waved her arm in a random sort of way.

"Can you be more specific?" Victor asked, irritated.

The woman looked at her granddaughter, who was about five years old with her hair already gray in places. Wise old kid. The grandmother and granddaughter actually looked like sisters, except the granddaughter was forty years younger and two feet shorter.

"It's over there, not too far," the granddaughter answered and waved her arm in a general sort of direction.

"Jeez," Victor said. "How do we get there?"

"Why you want to know?" the woman and granddaughter asked.

"Because we're playing over there tonight," Junior said.

"Playing what?" the granddaughter asked.

"Music," Victor said. "We're a band."

"What's your name?" the grandmother asked.

"Coyote Springs," Thomas said.

The grandmother walked close to the blue van, picked up her granddaughter so she could see inside, and looked the band over closely.

"Who's the lead singer?" the granddaughter asked.

"I am," Thomas said.

"Well, then," the granddaughter said directly to Thomas. "Just go back down the way you came, take a left at the first intersection after a big tree stump painted red. Drive down that road for a while and then take the first right you see. About three mailboxes down that way is the Tipi Pole Tavern."

"Thanks, cousin," Thomas said, and the blue van pulled back onto the highway and made its way to the tavern.

"Jesus," Junior said. "Ain't that the way it always is? They only want to talk to the lead singer. All they want to know is the lead singer. Lead singer this. Lead singer that."

"Enit," Victor said. "Where the fuck would Mick Jagger be without Keith Richards?"

"He'd be at the Tipi Pole Tavern," Thomas said, "already done with the sound check."

The blue van pulled up to the tavern only two hours later than scheduled. A little old Flathead man sat alone by the front door. The tavern was closed, but that old man wanted to be the first customer when it opened.

"Ya-hey," the old Indian man called out.

"Ya-hey," the blue van called back.

"Are you the band?"

"Yeah, we're Coyote Springs."

"Little bit early, enit?"

"We thought we was two hours late by real time. At least an hour late by Indian time."

"Shit, people out here work on double Indian time. You could've showed up tomorrow and been okay. What kind of music you play, anyway?"

"Little bit of everything. Whole bunch of the blues."

"Reservation blues, huh?"

"That's it, uncle."

Coyote Springs climbed out of the blue van and sat with the old man. They offered him cigarettes, candy, dirty jokes. Then it was dark.

"About time," the Flathead said.

"Time for what?"

The old man pointed down the road and smiled as dozens of headlights appeared.

"Shit," Victor said. "It's either your whole damn tribe or the cavalry."

"Well," the old man said, "we heard you was an all-Indian band, and we wanted to hear you play. I guess even some of the sober ones are coming. Hope the bar has enough Diet Pepsi.''

The owner of the bar pulled up. He took a minute getting out of his pickup because of his enormous cowboy hat and dinner-plate belt buckle engraved with the name JIMMY. The cowboy hat and belt buckle walked up to Coyote Springs and the old man.

"You must be Coyote Springs," he said.

"Yeah, we are. You must be Jimmy."

"Nah," the man said and looked down at his belt buckle. "I ain't Jimmy. Not really."

"Well," Thomas said, confused. "We really are Coyote Springs."

"The one and only," Victor said.

"So," the bar owner asked, "who's the lead singer?"

Thomas raised his hand.

"Let's go, then."

The tavern soon filled with Indians of all sizes, shapes, and colors. They all waited to hear Coyote Springs for the first time.

"Look at all those Skins," Victor said. "They must think it's Bingo night."

"Are you ready?" Thomas asked.

"Ready to be fucking immortal," Victor said. His fifteen-year-old green silk shirt and matching polyester pants glowed in the spotlight.

Coyote Springs counted one, two, three, then fell into their first paid chord together, off rhythm. They stopped, counted again, rose into that first chord again, then the second, third, and in a move that stunned the crowd and instantly propelled them past nearly every rock band in history, played a fourth chord and nearly a fifth. Four and a half chords, and then Thomas Builds-the-Fire stepped up to the microphone to sing.

3

Indian Boy Love Song

I saw you walking with those dark legs of yours
I felt you walking through my sweatlodge doors
And don't you wonder when you're there in the dark
Just hear the drummer beating time with your heart

I hear you talking about your Trail of Tears
If you feel the need I can help calm all your fears
I'll be here watching and I'll wait for your call
I'll catch you sweetheart when you feel you may fall

chorus:
And I want to say hey, ya-hey, ya-hey, ya-hey
I want to say hey, ya-hey, ya-hey
And I want to say hey, ya-hey, ya-hey, ya-hey
I want to say hey, ya-hey, ya-hey, ya-hey

I can see you playing stickgame all night long
I can see you smiling when you're singing the song
I'll be here guessing which hand holds the bone
I hope I choose right so I won't be alone

(repeat chorus until end)

Chess and Checkers Warm Water, Flathead Indian sisters, pushed their way to the front of the crowd in the Tipi Pole Tavern. Both wanted to get a closer look at Coyote Springs. The audience cheered like it was a real concert rather than a low-paying gig in a reservation bar. A few Flatheads even raised lighters, flicked their Bics, and singed the braids of their friends. For safety, Chess and Checkers tucked their braids under cowboy hats. Chess wore glasses.

"They're not too good," Checkers said. A few inches taller than her older sister, Checkers was the most beautiful Indian woman on the Flathead Reservation, and quite possibly in all of Indian country. All the young Flathead men called her Little Miss Native American, but she still refused to listen to their courting songs. She liked the old Indian men and their traditional songs. All the other Flathead women respected Checkers's selective ear, even as they chased the young Indian boys themselves.

"Yeah, they ain't too good at all," Chess said of Coyote Springs. "But that lead singer is kind of cute, enit?"

"Cute enough."

Chess and Checkers danced in front of the stage. Chess had fancydanced when she was a teenager and shook to Three Dog Night on her childhood radio. She danced well in both the Indian and white ways. Not as obviously pretty as her sister, Chess, living up to her nickname, planned all of her moves in advance.

"God," Chess said, "that drummer is awful."

Junior and Victor started the evening sober but drank all the free booze offered. Thomas stayed sober but could not stop his bandmates, so they all sounded worse with each beer. Junior nearly fell off his stool when he swung and missed the snare drum completely. Victor strummed an open chord continually because he forgot how to play any other. Still, it was only the sisters who noticed that the band fell apart, because most of the audience drank more than Coyote Springs. All the other sober Flatheads had already left.

"Let's go home," Checkers said.

"No," Chess said. "That lead singer is staring at me."

"Thank you, thank you," Thomas said after a particularly sloppy number. "We're going to take a short break now. We'll be back in a few."

Coyote Springs staggered off the stage. Thomas left his guitar onstage, but Victor always carried Robert Johnson's guitar with him.

"Did you see that woman in the front row?" Thomas asked.

"Yeah, the one with black hair and brown skin?" Victor asked.

"No, really," Thomas said. "Did you see her?"

"Yeah," Victor said. "The one with the cowboy hat and big tits."

"Don't be an asshole," Thomas said. "I mean the one with glasses."

"Yeah," Junior said, "I saw her."

"She's pretty, enit?" Thomas asked.

"She's all right," Junior said.

"Shit," Victor said. "I'd take the one with big tits."

"She wouldn't have nothing to do with your drunk ass," Thomas said.

"So what?" Victor said. "Who says I want an Indian woman anyway? I see some good-looking white women here."

Surprised, Thomas and Junior looked around the room,

because they hadn't noticed any white women and wondered what Victor saw.

"You must be having a vision," Junior said. "I'm jealous."

"Listen," Thomas said, "I want to play her a song."

"Who?" Junior and Victor asked.

"The woman in the front row."

"That white woman?" Victor asked. Junior, completely confused, scanned the room again for any evidence of white women.

"No," Thomas said, "the Indian woman. The one with glasses."

"Why?" Victor asked. "Is Thomas trying to get laid?"

"I want to play 'Indian Boy Love Song,' " Thomas said.

"Shit no," Victor said. "We ain't even practiced that one."

"I don't think so," Junior said. "Ain't no Indian wants to hear a slow song anyway."

"Well, I'll just go out there and do it myself."

"Jesus Christ," Victor said as Thomas walked back onstage. "The little asshole's already thinking about a solo career."

"Well, let's go," Junior said. "We're a band."

Junior followed Thomas, but Victor stayed behind and made goofy eyes at a blond mirage near the back of the bar.

Victor had started to drink early in life, just after his real father moved to Phoenix, and he drank even harder after his stepfather moved into the house. Junior never drank until the night of his high school graduation. He'd sworn never to drink because of his parents' boozing. Victor placed a beer gently in his hand, and Junior drained it without hesitation or question, crashing loudly, like a pumpkin that dropped off the World Trade Center and landed on the head of a stockbroker. Thomas's father still drank quietly, never raising his voice once in all his life, just staggering around the reservation, usually covered in piss and shit.

"Come on, Victor," Junior yelled from the stage. "Get up here."

"Fuck you," Victor said, but the guitar throbbed in his hands and pulled him to the stage.

"Thank you, thank you," Thomas said as Coyote Springs reclaimed the stage amid a drunken ovation. "We're going to slow things down a little now. I want to play this song for that Indian woman standing right here in front of me."

Thomas pointed at Chess. The whole crowd, because they had known the Warm Water sisters all their lives, chanted her name.

"Well, Chess," Thomas said, "this one is for you."

Nerves and bar smoke cracked his voice, but Thomas sang loudly, shut the whole bar up, and even sobered up a few drunks. Thomas stunned all the Flatheads when he dared to serenade an Indian woman with his ragged voice. They figured he must be in love.

"You're not going to fall for this?" Checkers asked her sister.

"Not completely," Chess said. "Maybe just a little."

Thomas got carried away, though, and warbled his song for Chess a few more times. He sang blues, country, and punk versions, even recited it like a poem. Once, he closed his eyes and told it like a story. The crowd went crazy and pushed Chess onstage in their frenzy.

"Can you sing?" Thomas asked her.

"Yeah," she said.

"Let's do it, then," Thomas said.

The two launched into a duet. Chess felt like a Flathead Reservation Cher next to the Spokane Indian version of Sonny, but the music happened, clumsy and terrifying.

† † †

From *The Western Montana Alternative Bi-Weekly*:

Coyote Springs on Tipi, Crushes It Flat

A new band, dubbed Coyote Springs and hailing from the Spokane Indian Reservation in Washington State, took its first step toward musical oblivion the other night at the Tipi Pole Tavern on the Flathead Reservation.

Playing a mix of blues, rock, pop, gospel, rap, and a few unidentifiable musical forms, the band made up in pure volume what it lacked in talent. In fact, Coyote Springs seemed to take the term *rock* literally and landed hard on all of our eardrums before *rolling* out the door to their ugly blue tour van, all headed for destinations unknown. It didn't help anything that two of the band members were drunk as skunks.

The highlight of the evening came when Chess Warm Water, a local Flathead Indian, was pushed onto the stage for a few duets with Coyote Springs's lead singer, Thomas Builds-the-Fire. Warm Water has a voice exactly like her surname, which provided an interesting, if not altogether beautiful, contrast with Builds-the-Fire's sparkless vocals.

The dictionary defines unforgettable as "incapable of being forgotten," and Coyote Springs, all considerations aside, was certainly that. Unforgettable and maybe even a little forgivable.

† † †

After the show at the Tipi Pole, Chess and Checkers helped Coyote Springs pack away all their gear. Actually, Junior and Victor passed out in the back of the van, so Chess and Checkers did most of the work.

"So," Thomas said, "how long you two lived out here?"

"Long enough," Checkers said angrily, because she wanted to go home.

"Don't pay her no mind," Chess said. "We've lived here our whole lives."

"You're Flatheads, enit?" Thomas asked.

"Yeah," Chess said. "And you guys are all Spokanes?"

"Yeah," Thomas said and struggled to say more.

Montana filled Thomas's mind. He used to think every Indian in the world lived in Montana. Now he had played guitar in Montana and sang duet with a beautiful Indian woman. Chess had never considered herself beautiful, but she liked her face well enough. She had broken her nose in a softball game in high school, which gave her face strange angles, and it had never looked quite right since. She didn't believe that shit about a broken nose adding character to a face. Instead, her broken nose made her feel like her whole life tilted a few degrees from center. She never minded all that much, except that her glasses were continually slipping down her nose. She spent half of her time readjusting them. Still, she had dark, dark eyes that seemed even darker behind her glasses. They were Indian grandmother eyes that stayed clear and focused for generations.

"So," Thomas said again, "is Chess your real name?"

"No."

"What's your real name?"

"I ain't going to tell you," Chess said. "You'd run off if you knew."

"It can't be that bad," Thomas said.

Checkers watched, surprised that Thomas chose her sister. Checkers usually received all the attention, but she didn't miss it this time. Thomas Builds-the-Fire looked especially goofy as he stumbled his way through the first stages of courtship.

They finished all the packing, even pretended to pack Junior and Victor into suitcases. The sisters stood with Thomas in the parking lot of the Tipi Pole Tavern. A few stragglers shouted lewd suggestions at Thomas, but he mostly ignored them.

"Well," Thomas said, "I hope to see you again."

"Maybe you'll play here again," Chess said.

"Maybe," Thomas said.

Checkers sent a telepathic message to her sister: *Invite him back to the house, you fool. You've got him snagged.*

"Listen," Chess said, "you want to come back to our house? I've got you snagged, fool."

"You've got me what?" Thomas asked. He didn't know what *snag* meant, although every other Indian on the planet understood that particular piece of reservation vocabulary: *snag* was noun and verb. A *snag* was a potential lover or the pursuit of a lover. *Snagged* meant you'd caught your new lover.

"I meant," Chess corrected herself, "that you must be all dragged out. Why don't you come back to the house?"

"What about them?" Thomas asked of Junior and Victor.

"They can sleep in the van," Checkers said.

Thomas thought about the offer, but he felt a little shy and knew that Victor and Junior might be pissed if they woke up in the sisters' yard. Though they always pretended to be the toughest Indian men in the world, they suffered terrible bouts of homesickness as soon as they crossed the Spokane Indian Reservation border.

"I don't know," Thomas said. "We should probably head back."

"Kind of crazy, enit?" Chess asked. "What if you fall asleep driving?"

"Well," Thomas said. "I'll stay for a little while. Maybe drink some coffee. How does that sound?"

"Sounds good enough."

Chess and Checkers jumped into the van with Thomas and

directed him to their little HUD house on the reservation. All the lights burned brightly.

"You live with your parents?" Thomas asked.

"No," Chess and Checkers said.

"Oh. I was just wondering about the lights."

"We leave them on," Chess said. "Just in case."

In case of what? Thomas asked in his mind but remained silent.

"Our parents are gone," Checkers said.

The trio walked into the house, left Victor and Junior in the car, and sat down to coffee at the kitchen table. Checkers emptied her cup quickly and said good night but left her bedroom door open a little.

"Your sister is nice," Thomas said.

"She's always crabby," Chess said, because she knew that Checkers was eavesdropping.

"Oh, I didn't notice," Thomas lied.

"Tell me about yourself," Chess said, because she couldn't think of anything else to say, because she wanted to know.

"Not much to say," Thomas replied, feeling shy. "What about you?"

"Well, we grew up on the reservation," Chess said. "Way up in the hills in this little shack with our mom and dad. Luke and Linda Warm Water."

"Do you have any brothers or sisters?" Thomas asked.

"Yeah, we had a baby brother, Bobby. We called him Backgammon."

"What happened to him?" Thomas asked.

"You know," Chess said, "those winters were always awful back then. Ain't no IHS doctor going to come driving through the snowdrifts and ice to save some Indian kid who was half dead anyway. I don't know. We feel less pain when we're little, enit? Bobby was always a sick baby, born coughing in the middle of a bad winter and died coughing in the middle of a worse winter."

"I'm an only kid," Thomas said.

"Did you ever get lonely?" Chess asked.

"All the time."

"Yeah, you must have," Chess said. "I get lonely when I think about the winters. I mean, it got so cold sometimes that trees popped like gunshots. Really. All night long. Pop, pop, pop. Kept us awake sometimes so we'd all play rummy by candlelight. Mom, Dad, Checkers, me. Those were some good times. But it makes me lonely to think about them."

Thomas and Chess sipped at their coffee.

"How about your parents?" Chess asked.

"My dad's still on our reservation, drinking and staggering around," Thomas said. "But my mom died when I was ten."

"Yeah, my mom is dead, too."

"What about your dad?" Thomas asked.

"He went to Catholic boarding school when he was little," Chess said. "Those nuns taught him to play piano. Ain't that funny? They'd teach him scales between beatings. But he still loved to play and saved up enough money to buy a secondhand piano in Missoula. Man, that thing was always out of tune.

"He used to play when it was too cold and noisy to sleep. He'd play and Mom would sing. Old gospel hymns, mostly. Mom had a beautiful voice, like a reservation diva or something. Mom taught Checkers and me to sing before we could hardly talk. Bobby slept in his crib by the stove. Those really were good times."

"What happened after Bobby died?" Thomas asked, although he wanted to know more about her mother's death, too.

"You know, my dad never drank much before Backgammon died. I mean, he always brought home some food, and Mom always managed to make stews from whatever we had in the cupboards and icebox. We didn't starve. No way. Checkers and I were just elbows and collarbones, but we didn't starve.

"It was dark, really dark, when Backgammon died. I don't know what time it was exactly. But all of us were awake and pretending to be asleep. We just laid there and listened to Backgammon struggle to breathe. His lungs were all filled up with stuff. No. That's not true. It was just Mom, Checkers, and me who listened. Dad had tied on his snowshoes a few hours earlier.

" 'I'm going for help,' he said, and none of us said a word to him. Mom helped him put his coat on and then she kissed his fingers before he put on his gloves. Really. It's still so vivid in my head. Mom kissed his fingertips, ten kisses, before he tramped out the door into the dark.

"I don't know for sure how long we waited for him. We weren't even sure he could make it back. He walked out in a Montana snowstorm to find help. He wasn't even sure what kind of help he was looking for. There weren't no white doctors around. There weren't no Indian doctors at all yet. The traditional medicine women all died years before. Dad just walked into the storm like he was praying or something. I mean, even if he made it to other Indians' houses, like the Abrahamson family or the Huberts, they couldn't have done much anyway. The Abrahamson family had their own sick kids, and the Huberts were an old Indian couple who didn't speak English and only stayed alive to spite the BIA."

"Your father must have been scared," Thomas said. He didn't know what to say to Chess.

"Yeah, he must have been really scared," Chess said. "But I don't know how far he walked or when he decided to turn back. I always imagined he pounded on some stranger's door, but there was no answer.

"As he was walking back home, my mother held onto Backgammon and sang to him. Checkers and I lay quietly in the bed we shared. We heard Mom singing and the baby struggling to breathe. I reached across the bed and set my hand on Checkers's chest to make sure she was breathing. She reached across and did the same on my chest. We felt the rise and fall, the rise and fall. We did that until we heard Mom stop singing and the baby stop breathing.''

Tears welled in Chess's eyes. She breathed deep and looked at Thomas, who kept silent and waited for the rest of the story. Then Chess excused herself and went to the bathroom, so Thomas just sat at the table and looked around the small, clean house. The kitchen sat in the center, while the living room, two bedrooms, and bathroom surrounded it. Nothing spectacular, but spotless by reservation standards. A clean, clean house.

''Your sister left her light on,'' Thomas said to Chess as she came back to the kitchen. ''Is she still awake?''

''She might be,'' Chess said. ''But she does sleep with her light on.''

Just in case, Thomas thought.

''Jeez,'' Chess said as she sat down at the table. ''You're probably tired of me babbling, enit? You want some more coffee?''

''No, thanks. I'll be awake for weeks.''

In her bed, Checkers listened to the conversation and cried a little. She remembered Backgammon. After he died, their mom held him against her chest and cried and cried. Checkers and Chess refused to move from their bed. They knew nothing touched them when they stayed still. Their mom cried even louder after their father stormed back into the room, shouted and cursed like a defeated warrior. He shouted until his wife raised Backgammon up to him like an offering.

Luke Warm Water started to scream then, a high-pitched wail that sounded less than human. Maybe it sounded *too* human. Colors poured out of him. Red flowed out of his mouth, and black seeped from his pores. Those colors mixed together and filled the room. Chess grabbed Checkers's hand and squeezed it until both cried out in pain.

"Don't look," Chess said to her sister. "Don't even move."

The sisters kept their eyes closed for minutes, hours, days. When Chess and Checkers opened them again, they buried Backgammon in a grave Luke Warm Water dug for three days because the ground was frozen solid. When the sisters opened their eyes, Linda Warm Water took a knife to her skin and made three hundred tiny cuts on her body. In mourning, in mourning. When the Warm Waters opened their eyes, Luke traded his snowshoes for a good coat, a case of whiskey, and stayed warm and drunk for weeks. Checkers remembered so much about her father. She was sure she remembered more than her sister ever did and wondered if Chess would tell Thomas any secrets.

"You know," Chess said to Thomas in the kitchen, just as Checkers fell into the sleep and familiar nightmares of her uncomfortable bed, "I still miss Backgammon. I didn't know him very long. But I miss him."

"What did you do after he died?" Thomas asked.

"We mostly kept to ourselves," Chess said. "We'd wake up before our parents and be out the door into the trees and hills. We'd play outside all day, eat berries and roots, and only come back home when it got too cold and dark.

"Sometimes we'd climb tall trees and watch the house. We'd watch our father storm out the door and down the road to town. He'd stay away for days at a time, drinking, drunk, passed out on the muddy streets in Arlee. Mom played the piano when Dad was gone, and we could hear it. We'd stay close enough to hear it.

"I used to think her songs drifted across the entire reservation. I imagined they knocked deer over and shook the antlers of moose and elk. Can you believe that? The music crept into the dreams of hibernating bears and turned them into nightmares. Those bears wouldn't ever leave their dens and starved to death as spring grew warmer. Those songs floated up to the clouds, fell back to the earth as rain, and changed the shape of plants and trees. I once bit into a huckleberry, and it tasted like my brother's tears. I used to believe all of that.''

Thomas smiled at her. He had just met the only Indian who told stories like his. He took a sip of his coffee and never even noticed it was cold. How do you fall in love with a woman who grew up without electricity and running water, who grew up in such poverty that other poor Indians called her family poor?

''Jeez,'' Chess said, ''there I go again, running at the mouth. You must be tired. Why don't you sleep on the couch?''

Thomas stretched in his chair, rubbed his eyes.

''I am tired,'' he said. ''Do you think it's okay?''

''Yeah,'' she said. ''Why don't you go lay down and I'll bring you a blanket.''

''Okay. But can I use the bathroom?''

''Sure,'' Chess said and went to look for bedding.

Thomas used the bathroom and marveled at the order. The fancy soaps waited perfectly and patiently in their dishes, but Thomas used a little sliver of Ivory soap to wash his hands and face.

''Are you okay in there?'' Chess asked through the door.

''Oh, yeah,'' Thomas said, unaware of the time he'd spent in the bathroom. ''Do you have a toothbrush I can borrow?''

''Yeah, use mine. It's the red one.''

Thomas picked up Chess's toothbrush, unsure if she meant it. *She brushed her teeth with this toothbrush,* he thought. *She had this in her mouth.* He hurriedly squeezed Crest onto the bristles and brushed slowly.

''Jeez,'' Chess said after he came out, ''I thought you fell in.''

"I had a life preserver," Thomas said, embarrassed.

"You can sleep here," Chess said and motioned toward the couch. He lay down and pulled the quilt over himself. She sat beside him and touched his face.

"You know," she said, "my mom made this quilt."

Thomas studied the patterns.

"You think Junior and Victor are okay outside?" he asked.

"They're fine," she said. "It's warm."

"How did your mom die?" he asked.

"Of cancer," she lied.

"Mine, too."

"You go to sleep now. I'll see you in the morning."

She leaned over quickly and kissed him on the cheek. A powerful kiss, more magical than any kiss on the mouth. She kissed him like he was a warrior; she kissed him like she was a warrior.

"Good night," he said.

"Good night," she said and walked to her bedroom.

Chess tried to sleep, but the memories crowded and haunted her. The sisters grew strong in those Montana summer days but felt weak when they crawled into their shared bed. Before Backgammon died, they had often listened carefully to their parents' lovemaking. The hurried breathing and those wet, mysterious noises shook the sisters' bodies. It was good.

After the baby died, those good sounds stopped. The sisters heard their father push at their mom, wanting it, but Linda rolled over and pretended to sleep. She slapped his hands. Luke fought and fought, but eventually he gave up if sober. If drunk, however, he forced himself on his wife. Sometimes, he came home from drinking and woke everybody with his needs. He fell on their mother while Chess and Checkers listened and waited for it to end. Sometimes their mother fought their father off, punched and kicked until he left her alone. Other times he passed out before he did anything.

The winters and summers arrived and left, as did the family's seasons. Luke and Linda Warm Water raged like storms, lightning in the summer, blizzards in the winter. But sometimes both sat in the house, placid as a lake during spring or an autumn evening. The sisters never knew what to expect, but Checkers grew taller and more frightened with each day. Chess just wanted to be older, to run away from home. She wanted to bury her parents beside Backgammon, find a way to love them in death, because she forgot how to love them in life.

Then it was winter again, and Linda Warm Water walked into the woods like an old dog and found a hiding place to die. Checkers and Chess nearly fell back in love with their father that winter. He quit drinking after his wife disappeared and spent most of his time searching for her. He refused to believe she had dug a hole and buried herself, or climbed into a den and lay down in the bones of a long dead bear. Because he'd convinced himself that Linda ran away with another man, Luke wandered all over Montana in search of his unfaithful wife.

Whenever he returned from his endless searches, Luke brought his daughters little gifts: ribbons, scraps of material, buttons, pages torn from magazines, even food, candy bars, and bottles of Pepsi. One time, he brought the sisters each a Pepsi from Missoula. Chess and Checkers buried those soft drinks in a snowbank so they would be cold, cold. Luke sat at his piano then and played for the first time since the baby died. The sisters ran inside and sang with him. They sang for a long time.

"Where are those Pepsis?" Luke asked his daughters.

"Outside," Chess said and knew they were in trouble. The three rushed outside to the snowbank and discovered the Pepsis had exploded from the cold. The snow was stained brown with Pepsi. Luke grabbed Checkers by the arm and shook her violently.

"Goddamn it," he shouted, "you've wasted it all!"

He shook her harder, then let her go and ran away. The sisters fell to their knees in the snow and wept.

"I'm sorry," Checkers said. "The Pepsi's gone. It's all my fault."

"No, it's not," Chess said, scooped up a handful of Pepsi-stained snow, and held it in front of her sister. "Not everything's your fault."

"What?" Checkers asked.

"Look," Chess said. The snow was saturated with Pepsi. Chess bit off a mouthful, tasted the cold, sweet, and dark. Checkers buried both hands in the snowbank, away from the broken glass, and shoved handful after handful of snow into her mouth. The sisters drank that snow and Pepsi until their hands and mouths were sticky and frozen. Soon, they went into the house to build a fire and wait for their father's return. Checkers and Chess lay down together by the stove and held onto each other. They held on.

† † †

As he slept in the Warm Waters' house, Thomas dreamed about television and hunger. In his dream, he sat, all hungry and lonely, in his house and wanted more. He turned on his little black-and-white television to watch white people live. White people owned everything: food, houses, clothes, children. Television constantly reminded Thomas of all he never owned.

For hours, Thomas searched the television for evidence of Indians, clicked the remote control until his hands ached. Once on channel four, he watched three cowboys string telegraph wire across the Great Plains until confronted by the entire Sioux Nation, all on horseback.

We come in friendship, the cowboys said to the Indians.

In Thomas's dream, the Indians argued among themselves, whooped like Indians always do in movies and dreams, waved their bows and arrows wildly. Three Indian warriors dismounted and grabbed hold of the telegraph wire.

We come in friendship, the cowboys said, cranked the genera-
tor, and electrocuted the three Indians. Those three Indians danced
crazily, unable to release the wire, and the rest of the Sioux Nation
rode off in a superstitious panic.

In his dream, Thomas watched it all happen on his television until he suddenly returned to the summer when Victor and
Junior killed snakes by draping them over an electric fence.

Watch this, Victor said as he dropped a foot-long water
snake onto the fence. Thomas nearly choked on the smell.

The electric fence belonged to a white family that had
homesteaded on the reservation a hundred years ago and never
left. All the Spokanes liked them because the white family owned
a huge herd of cattle and gave away free beef. The homesteaders
built the fence to keep the cows away from the forests, but the
cows ignored the pine trees anyway. The fence burned on and
on.

Victor and Junior draped a hundred snakes over the fence
that summer and dragged Thomas there once or twice a week.

Come on, Victor said to Thomas and put him in yet another
headlock. *You're coming with us.*

Ya-hey, Junior said. *Don't you think he's had enough?*

I'll tell you when he's had enough, Victor said.

Victor and Junior carried Thomas to the fence, where they
kept a rattlesnake in a plastic barrel.

Look, Victor said, and Thomas saw the snake.

Where'd you get that? he asked, frightened.

From your momma's panties, Victor said.

Thomas strained against Victor and Junior, but they pushed
him down and held his face close to the barrel.

Grab the fence, Victor said. *Or grab the snake.*

No, Thomas said.

Wait a second, Junior said, scared as Thomas.

Fence or snake, Victor said.

Thomas looked down at the rattler, which remained still.

No sound, no rattles shaking. Then he reached out as if to grab the
fence but grabbed the rattlesnake instead and threw it at Victor.

Oh, shit, shit, shit, Victor said and jumped away from the
dead snake.

Junior and Thomas laughed.

You think that's funny? Victor asked as he picked up the rattler. *You think that's funny?*

Yeah, Junior and Thomas said.

Victor shoved the snake in Thomas's face while Junior
jumped back.

Eat this, Victor said and pushed the snake against Thomas's
mouth. Thomas tripped, fell to the ground, and Victor shoved that
snake at him until the game grew old.

Jesus, Junior said. *He's had enough.*

Victor draped the dead snake across the electric fence. It
danced and danced, fell off the wire, squirmed its way back to life,
and started to rattle.

Oh, shit, Victor said and ran away. Junior and Thomas ran
after him, kept running. Soon, in his dream, Victor and Junior ran
into a large empty room. Thomas followed them. The three picked
up musical instruments and started to practice.

You know, Thomas said between songs. *I hope we don't
make it.*

Make what? Junior asked.

Make it big. Have a hit song and all that, Thomas said.

Why the hell not? Victor asked.

*I don't know. Maybe we don't deserve it. Maybe we should have
something better in mind. Maybe something bad is going to happen to us if
we don't have something better on our minds.*

Like what? Victor asked.

Well, Thomas said, *what if we get rich and eat too much? We'll
all get fat and disgusting.*

Shit, Victor said. *I'm not Elvis.*

Ya-hey, Junior said, *did you know Elvis was a cavalry scout in a previous life?*

In his dream, Thomas strummed the guitar and pleaded with Victor.

Really, Thomas said. *I'm scared to be famous.*

Well, Junior said, *I think we should worry about learning to play our instruments better first.*

Yeah, Victor said. *And we don't have nothing to worry about if we keep you as the lead singer anyway.*

Yeah, Junior said. *And besides, the only famous Indians are dead chiefs and long-distance runners.*

In his dream, Thomas looked at his bandmates. He wondered what they really felt. He wondered what those snakes felt on the electric fence. Thomas held his guitar closely and felt its power, then noticed that he was holding Robert Johnson's guitar. In the dream, he hit a chord, felt a sharp pain in his wrists, but the music tasted like good food.

"What you doing with my guitar?" Victor shouted and ripped Thomas from his dream. Thomas lay on the couch in the Warm Waters' house with Robert Johnson's guitar beside him. *It's Victor's guitar now,* Thomas corrected himself.

"I didn't want it to get cold," Thomas mumbled, although he had no idea how the guitar ended up in the house, and handed it over to Victor.

"Well, thanks for nothing," Victor said. "It was hotter than hell outside."

"Oh, man," Junior said as he stumbled into the house. "I got a hangover."

"There's coffee in the kitchen," Thomas said.

Junior made his way to the kitchen just as Chess and Checkers emerged from their rooms.

"What's going on?" Checkers asked.

"What's for breakfast?" Victor asked.

"Your ass on a plate," Chess said. "Fix it yourself."

"Oh, a rowdy one," Victor said. "I like them rowdy."

Victor opened the refrigerator, pulled out the ingredients for a cheese and vegetable omelet, and cooked up enough for everybody. They were all shocked by Victor's culinary skills.

"Where'd you learn to cook?" Chess asked. "Prison?"

"My father used to cook," Victor said.

"Your stepfather?" Junior asked.

"Yeah, only thing he was good for."

Coyote Springs sat down to breakfast with Chess and Checkers. The omelets tasted great. Victor wanted to say something profound and humorous about eggs but couldn't think of anything, so he farted instead.

"You're disgusting," Chess said, picked up her plate, and walked outside to eat. Thomas gave Victor the old Spokane Indian evil eye and followed her.

Checkers finished her breakfast, washed her plate and fork in the sink, and then returned to her bedroom. Junior and Victor watched her the entire time.

"She's real pretty, enit?" Junior asked after Checkers closed her bedroom door.

"A great ass," Victor said.

"You don't have a chance!" Checkers shouted from her room. Victor and Junior ate the rest of their omelets in silence.

Outside, Chess and Thomas talked between bites.

"You know," Thomas said, "Coyote Springs is better than we sounded last night."

"I hope so," Chess said.

"No, really. Victor and Junior were all drunk."

"Do you drink?"

"No," Thomas said, "I don't drink."

Chess smiled. When Indian women begin the search for an

Indian man, they carry a huge list of qualifications. *He has to have a job. He has to be kind, intelligent, and funny. He has to dance and sing. He should know how to iron his own clothes. Braids would be nice.* But as the screwed-up Indian men stagger through their lives, Indian women are forced to amend their list of qualifications. Eventually, Indian men need only to have their own teeth to get snagged.

Chess suffered through an entire tribe of Indian boyfriends. Roscoe, the champion fancydancer, who passed out in full regalia during the Arlee Powwow and was stripped naked during the night. Bobby, the beautiful urban Indian, transferred to the reservation to work for the BIA, who then left Chess for a white third-grade teacher at the Tribal School. Joseph, the journalist, who wrote a powerful story on the white-owned liquor stores camped on reservation borders and then drank himself into cirrhosis. Carl, the buck from Browning, who stashed away a kid or two on every reservation in the state, until his friends called him The Father of Our Country.

"Really?" Chess asked Thomas again to make sure. Maybe she had snagged the only sober storyteller in the world. "You mean, you've *never* drank. Not even when you were little?"

"No," Thomas said. "I read books."

"Do you have any kids?" Chess asked.

Thomas hid his face.

"Oh," Chess said, disappointed. "You do have kids. How many?"

She loved kids but placed a limit on the number of children and ex-wives she allowed her potential snags to claim.

"No, no," Thomas said. "I don't have any kids. You just surprised me. I'm not used to personal questions. Nobody ever asked me any personal questions before."

"You ever been married?"

"No, have you?"

"No. Any girlfriends?"

"Not really," Thomas said.

"Ya-hey!" Victor shouted from the kitchen. "I think Junior is going to throw up."

"You know," Chess said, "that Victor is a jerk. And his clothes. He looks like he got in a fight with the seventies and got his ass kicked."

"Well," Thomas said, "he doesn't have any money. That's why he's in the band. That's why we're all in the band, you know?"

"I was wondering why you put up with him," Chess said. She and Checkers fought fires for the BIA during the summers, traveling all over the country, and struggled to make the money last through winter.

"Only problem is we're not making any money."

"Really? Even a bad band can make money, enit?"

"I hope so. But we're pretty good, really."

"I believe you, really," Chess said. "That Junior is nice, enit? He's good-looking, but sort of goofy, though. He sure lets Victor boss him around, enit?"

"Yeah, it's always been that way."

"Too bad," Chess said. "Junior could be a major snag."

"You mean," Thomas said, "that he's in the way?"

"No," Chess said. "I mean he could be a good catch for an Indian woman. A snag, you know?"

"Oh," Thomas said, still clueless, so he changed the subject. "I really liked singing with you last night. You're really good."

"Yeah, I had a good time, too."

"You know," Thomas said, "I have an idea. How would you and Checkers like to join the band?"

"I don't know," Chess said. "Do we have to dress like Victor?"

"Not at all."

"I don't know," she said again. "We have to hang around here during the summer. In case we get called to fight a fire."

"Listen. You can sing great, and I'm sure Checkers can sing, too. We need you. Something tells me we need you."

"I don't think so, Thomas. I mean, I like you a lot, but Checkers and I live here. We're from here. We shouldn't leave."

"You have to think about it," Thomas said. "Give us a chance."

Chess shook her head.

"Wait!" Thomas shouted. "Victor. Junior. Get out here. Let's practice some."

Victor and Junior strolled outside, followed by Checkers.

"What's all the shouting about?" Checkers asked.

"Thomas wants us to join Coyote Springs," Chess said to her sister.

"No fucking way," Victor said. "We're a warrior band."

"Well," Thomas said. "We're a democracy. How about we vote on it?"

"Okay, go for it," Victor said, confident that Junior hated the idea, too.

"All those in favor, raise your hand," Thomas said and held his right hand up. Junior raised his hand and smiled weakly at Victor.

"That does it," Thomas said. "The women are in."

"No way," Victor said again.

"You agreed to vote," Thomas said.

"Hey," Chess said. "I said we don't want to be in the band."

Checkers never liked her sister to speak for her, but she agreed with Chess. Forest fires paid the bills.

"Wait," Thomas pleaded with everybody. "How about we play some? Then you can decide if you want to join."

Junior ran to the van, pulled out a hand drum, and beat out

a rhythm. He surprised the sisters with his sudden talent. Thomas sang the first bar of a jazzed-up Carpenters song, while Victor stood sullenly with his guitar at his side. He wanted to resist all of it, but the guitar moved in his hands, whispered his name. Victor closed his eyes and found himself in a dark place.

Don't play for them. Play for me, said a strange voice.

Victor opened his eyes and hit the first chord hard. Junior and Thomas let him play alone; Chess and Checkers stepped back. Victor grew extra fingers that roared up and down the fingerboard. He bent strings at impossible angles and hit a note so pure that the guitar sparked. The sparks jumped from the guitar to a sapling and started a fire. It was a good thing that Chess and Checkers had extensive firefighting experience, and they hurriedly doused the flames, but Victor continued to toss sparks. His hair stood on end, his shirt pitted with burn holes, and his hands blistered.

Victor raised his right arm high above the reservation and windmilled the last chord, which echoed for hours. He dropped the guitar, staggered back a few steps, then bowed.

"Jeez," Chess and Checkers said after a long while. "Where do we sign up?"

† † †

Thomas, Junior, and Victor camped on the Flathead Reservation for a week after the Warm Waters joined the band, living meagerly on their shared money. The boys stayed at the sisters' house, although Chess and Checkers objected to the smell, but all agreed the band needed to practice with its new members. Thomas even drove down into Missoula to buy a thirdhand synthesizer for Chess and Checkers to share.

"How much that cost you?" Victor asked him.

"Five bucks and a funny story," Thomas told him.

Coyote Springs rehearsed for hours in the Warm Waters'

backyard. At first, they sounded awful, dissonant, discordant. Victor only occasionally replicated the stunning performance that convinced the sisters to join the band. Junior broke so many drumsticks that he switched to pine branches instead. Chess and Checkers sang better than Thomas, which made the distinction between backup and lead singers less sure. Thomas decided to share the lead. Still, Coyote Springs melded faster than any garage band in history.

"We should call that Tipi Pole Tavern guy," Victor said. "I think we're ready to rock."

The owner of the Tipi Pole Tavern listened to the newest incarnation of Coyote Springs and agreed to hire them again. Coyote Springs packed their gear into the blue van and headed for the tavern.

"Ladies and braves," the bartender announced. "It's a great honor to welcome back that rocking band from the Spokane Indian Reservation, Coyote Springs."

The crowd cheered.

"And it's a special honor to introduce the two newest members of the band," the bartender continued. "Two of our own Flathead Indians, Chess and Checkers Warm Water."

Coyote Springs walked on stage with confidence. Thomas smiled as he stepped to the microphone.

"Hello, Arlee," Thomas shouted, and the place went crazy. Victor counted off, and the band launched into its first song, a cover of an old KISS tune.

The sisters joined in on the vocals after a bit; Chess pounded the keyboard hard, like her fingers were tiny hammers. She wanted to play it right but loved the noise of it all. Checkers pulled the ties from her hair and sang unbraided. Chess picked the ties up from the floor and somehow braided her hair with one hand. Both threw a *way ya hi yo* into the chorus of the song.

Coyote Springs created a tribal music that scared and excited the white people in the audience. That music might have chased away the pilgrims five hundred years ago. But if they were forced, Indians would have adopted the ancestors of a few whites, like Janis Joplin's great-great-great-great-grandparents, and let them stay in the Americas.

The audience reached for Coyote Springs with brown and white hands that begged for more music, hope, and joy. Coyote Springs felt powerful, fell in love with the power, and courted it. Victor stood on the edge of the stage to play his guitar. Despite his clothes, the Indian and white women in the crowd screamed for him and waited outside after the show.

After the Tipi Pole Tavern finally closed at 4 A.M., Chess, Checkers, and Thomas sat inside and drank Pepsi, while Junior and Victor grabbed a few beers and disappeared.

"You sounded great tonight," Thomas said to the sisters.

"We all sounded great," Chess said.

"Jeez," Checkers said. "Even Victor and Junior, enit?"

"We just got to keep them sober," Chess said. "Victor's the best guitar player I ever heard, when he's sober."

"I'm tired," Thomas said.

"Where'd Victor and Junior go anyway?" Chess asked.

"Outside," Checkers said. "Probably getting drunk in the van."

"Well," Chess said, "I'm tired, too. Let's get them and go home."

Thomas and the sisters walked outside to the van. He opened the sliding door of the van and surprised Victor and Junior, who were literally buck naked and drunk. The two naked white women in the van were even drunker and scrambled for their clothes. Thomas just stood there and stared. It was Betty and Veronica.

"Shut the goddamn door!" Victor shouted.

"Jeez," Junior said, reached out, and slid the door shut.

"Oh, man," Checkers said. "That's the last thing I wanted to see."

"I think I'm going to get sick," Chess said.

Thomas just walked away. Checkers looked at Chess, who shrugged her shoulders. Who knew why Thomas did anything? Chess followed him to a picnic bench behind the tavern. Checkers threw her arms up, walked back into the bar, and fell asleep on the pool table.

"I can't believe they did that," Chess said to Thomas. "We have to ride in that van."

"Yeah, I know," Thomas said.

Chess sat beside Thomas at the picnic table, took his hand, studied it for a minute. Beautiful hands, beautiful hands.

"Where's Checkers?" Thomas asked.

"I don't know. She's probably beating the crap out of Junior and Victor."

Chess and Thomas sat there quietly. Thomas thought about stories and songs, but Chess only thought about those white women in the van. She hated Indian men who chased after white women; she hated white women who chased after Indian men.

"You know," she said. "I really don't like that. I don't like Junior and Victor hanging out with white women."

"Why?" Thomas asked.

"I don't know. I guess it's about preservation, enit? Ain't very many Indian men to go around. Even fewer good ones."

Thomas nodded his head.

"And you know," Chess said, "as traditional as it sounds, I think Indian men need Indian women. I think only Indian women can take care of Indian men. Jeez, we give birth to Indian men. We feed them. We hold them when they cry. Then they run off with white women. I'm sick of it."

"Yeah," Thomas said. "I never dated no white woman."

"Thomas, you never dated nobody."

They laughed.

"Seriously, I think Junior and Victor are traitors," Chess said. "I really do. They keep running off with white women and pretty soon, ain't no Indian women going to touch them. We Indian women talk to each other, you know? We have a network. They're two of the last full-blood Indians on your reservation, enit? Jeez, Junior and Victor are betraying their DNA."

"Well," Thomas, a full-blood Spokane himself, said, "do you like me or my DNA?"

"I like you and your DNA."

Thomas agreed with Chess, but he also knew about the shortage of love in the world. He wondered if people should celebrate love wherever it's found, since it is so rare. He worried about the children of mixed-blood marriages. The half-breed kids at the reservation school suffered through worse beatings than Thomas ever did.

"I wonder what it's like," he said.

"Wonder about what?" Chess asked.

"What's it like to be a half-breed kid? How do you think it feels to have a white mom or dad? It must be weird."

"My grandmother was a little bit white," Chess said.

"Really?" Thomas said. "What kind?"

"German, I guess. *Achtung.*"

"What was she like?"

"She hated to be Indian," Chess said. "She didn't look very Indian. That white blood really showed through. She left my grandfather, moved to Butte, and never told anybody she was Indian. She left her son on the reservation, too. Just left him, and they hardly ever heard from her again."

Thomas shook his head, closed his eyes, and told a story:

"A long time ago, two boys lived on a reservation. One was an Indian named Beaver, and the other was a white boy named Wally. Both loved to fancydance, but the white boy danced a step fancier. When the white boy won contests, all the Indian boys beat him up. But Beaver never beat up on the white boy. No matter how many times he got beat up, that white boy kept dancing.''

Thomas opened his eyes, smiled, and shrugged his shoulders.

"Wally and Beaver were half-brothers, enit?" Chess asked.

"You got it."

"What's that mean?"

"Don't know. Maybe it means drums make everyone feel like an Indian."

† † †

From *The Wellpinit Rawhide Press*:

Coyote Springs Home

Coyote Springs, our own little rock band, returned to the reservation late last night, with the addition of two Flathead Indians, Chess and Checkers Warm Water. The two sisters reportedly sing vocals and play piano.

Lester FallsApart saw the familiar blue van pull in about 3 A.M., Standard Indian Time.

"They was going the speed limit," said FallsApart.

Father Arnold of the Catholic Church called early this morning to offer a prayer of thanks that the band returned safely.

According to an anonymous source, Michael White Hawk, recently released from Walla Walla State Penitentiary, is unhappy with Coyote Springs.

"They think they're hot [manure]," White Hawk was rumored to have said. "They play a few shows and they think they're [gosh darn] stars. [Forget] them."

Coyote Springs could not be reached for comment.

† † †

After they arrived back at the Spokane Indian Reservation, Chess fell into an uneasy sleep in Thomas's bed with Checkers, while he lay on the floor. Junior and Victor slept in the blue van even though there was plenty of room in the house. Chess dreamed of a small Indian man on a pale horse. With an unpainted body and unbraided brown hair, the small Indian looked unimposing. Even as she dreamed, Chess knew the unpainted Indian in her dream was not Spokane or Flathead, but she had no idea what kind of Indian he was. The unpainted one was unhappy as he rode into a cavalry fort. Many other Indians greeted him. Some with pride, others with anger.

Come along, an angry Indian shouted loudly at the unpainted one, who dismounted, and walked to an office. A dozen Indians stood in the office while hundreds of other Indians gathered outside. The white soldiers kept rifles at the ready, while the Indians and white civilians gossiped nervously. The unpainted one waited. Soon, a white officer appeared and told the unpainted one it was too late for talk. They all needed to rest.

Ho, the Indians called out and left the office. The unpainted one left last with the white officer in front of him, the angry Indian behind him, and two soldiers on either side. The unpainted one followed the officer without question. They led him to a small building, and the unpainted one quickly pulled a knife when he saw the barred windows and chains. The angry Indian grabbed the unpainted one from behind. In that way, both staggered into the open.

He's got a knife!

In Chess's dream, the soldiers trained their rifles on the Indians who might help the unpainted one. The angry Indian knocked the knife away from the unpainted one and pinned his arms behind his back.

Kill the Indian!

A soldier lunged forward with his bayonet and speared the unpainted one once, twice, three times. The Indians gasped as the unpainted one fell to the ground, critically wounded. The angry Indian trilled. Nobody stepped forward to help the unpainted one; he lay alone in the dust.

He's dying!

Then a very tall Indian man stepped through the crowd and kneeled down beside the unpainted one.

My friend, the tall Indian said, picked up the unpainted one, and carried him to a lodge. Other Indians sang mourning songs; the soldiers shook their heads. Dogs yipped and chased each other.

In Chess's dream, the tall Indian sat beside the unpainted one as he bled profusely. The white doctor came and left without song, as did the medicine woman. The unpainted one tried to sing but coughed blood instead.

My father? the unpainted one asked.

He's coming, the tall one said.

The tall one greeted the father when he arrived, and both watched the unpainted one die.

Chess woke from her dream with a snap. Unsure of her surroundings, she called out her father's name. Checkers stirred in her sleep. Chess held her breath until she remembered where she was.

''Thomas?'' she asked but received no response. *He's dead,* Chess thought but was not sure whom she meant. Then she heard music, so she crawled from bed and made her way to the kitchen.

Thomas sat at the kitchen table and wrote songs. He hummed to himself and scribbled in his little notebook.

"Thomas?" Chess said and startled him.

"Jeez," he said. "You about gave me a heart attack."

Chess sat beside him.

"When you coming back to sleep?" Chess asked.

"Pretty soon," he said. "I'm sorry if I woke you up."

"You didn't wake me up. I had a bad dream."

"It's okay. You're awake now."

"Is it okay? Really?"

Chess smiled at Thomas, reached over and mussed his already messy hair. She took the guitar out of his hands and set it aside, then kissed him full and hard on the mouth.

"What was that for?" he asked.

She kissed him again. Harder. Put her hand on his crotch.

"Jeez," he said and nearly fell over in his chair.

Their lovemaking was tender and awkward. Afterwards, in the dark, they held each other.

"We should've used some protection," Chess said.

"Yeah. It was kind of stupid, enit?" Thomas asked. "Are you sure it's okay?"

"I'm sure."

"Next time."

They lay there quietly for a long time. Chess thought Thomas fell asleep.

"Listen," he said suddenly and surprised her.

"To what?" she asked.

"What do you hear?"

"The wind."

"No," Thomas said. "Beyond that."

Chess listened. She heard the Spokane Reservation breathe. An owl hooted in a tree. Some animal scratched its way across the roof. A car drove by. A dog barked. Another dog barked its answer. She heard something else, too. Some faint something.

"Do you hear that?" Thomas asked.

"I hear something," she said.

"Yeah," Thomas said. "That's what I mean. Do you hear it?"

"Sort of."

Chess listened some more and wondered if it was her imagination. Did she hear something just because Thomas wanted her to hear something? She listened until she fell asleep.

† † †

Coyote Springs scheduled their first nonreservation gig in a cowboy bar in Ellensburg, Washington, of all places, and drove down I-90 to get there. The old blue van rapidly collected the miles.

"Thomas," Victor yelled from the back. "I think it's about time we picked up a new rig."

Coyote Springs agreed with Victor, but Thomas wanted no part of it.

"This van is older than any of us," Thomas said. "It has seen more than any of us. This van is our elder, and we should respect it. Besides, we have no money."

Coyote Springs laughed, even Thomas, and kept laughing until something popped under the hood. The van shuddered and stopped in the middle of the freeway.

"Shit," said Coyote Springs in unison.

A few cars honked at the five Indians pushing an old blue van down the road.

"Thomas," Victor said. "We need a new rig."

Coyote Springs pushed that blue van twenty miles down the road, across a bridge over the Columbia River, into a little town called Vantage. The band sprawled around the van in various positions and barely moved when the cop pulled up. That cop climbed out of his cruiser, pulled on a pair of those mirrored sunglasses that cops always wear.

"What seems to be the problem?" he asked.

"Our van broke down," Thomas said.

The cop walked close to the van and looked inside.

"Is all of this your equipment?" the cop asked.

"Yes, sir," Thomas said.

"Are you in a band or what?"

"Yeah," Thomas said. "We're Coyote Springs."

The officer studied the band, tapped his foot a little, and took off his sunglasses.

"Where you guys from?" he asked.

"From Wellpinit. Up on the Spokane Indian Reservation."

"How about you girls?"

"We're Flathead Indians," Chess said. "From Arlee, Montana."

"Where you headed to?"

"Ellensburg," Thomas answered. "We're playing a bar called Toadstools."

"I know that place. You sure you're playing there?"

The cop waited briefly for an answer, then asked the band for identification. Thomas and the women pulled out their driver's licenses. Junior offered his Spokane Tribal Driver's License, and Victor lifted his shirt and revealed his own name tattooed on his chest.

"Are you serious about this tattoo?" the cop asked.

"Yeah," Victor said.

"You all just wait here a second," the cop said and walked back to his cruiser. He talked on his radio, while Coyote Springs counted the money for bail.

"We can take him," Victor said. "He's only one guy."

"But he's a big guy," Junior said.

"Shut up," Thomas said. "Here he comes."

"Okay," the cop said when he came back. "I called my

cousin over in Ellensburg. He's got a tow truck. He's going to come over here and haul your butts to Toadstools.''

"Really?" Coyote Springs asked.

"Yeah, but it'll cost you a hundred bucks. You got that?"

"Sure."

"Well, you can pay my cousin directly, but you're on your own after that."

"Thanks, officer."

"You're welcome. By the way, what kind of music you play?"

"All kinds. The blues, mostly."

"Well, good luck."

The cop started to walk away, but stopped, turned back.

"Hey," he said, "who's the lead singer?"

Thomas raised his hand and smiled. The cop smiled back, put his sunglasses on, climbed into his cruiser, and left with a wave.

"Who the hell was that masked man?" Chess asked.

"I don't know," Junior said. "But if I find any silver bullets laying around here, I'm going to pass out."

† † †

From *The Ellensburg Tri-Weekly*:

Indian Musicians Play More Than Drums

An all-Indian rock band from the Spokane Indian Reservation played for the cowboys in Toadstools Tavern last Saturday night, and nobody was injured.

Seriously, the band named Coyote Springs was very professional and played their music with passion and pride.

"They knew what they was doing," said Toadstools owner Ernie Lively.

"I was kind of nervous about hiring Indians and all," Lively added. "Worried they might not show up or maybe they'd stir up trouble."

On the contrary, Coyote Springs served up a healthy dish of country music, spiced it with a little bit of rock, and even threw in a few old blues tunes for dessert.

"I think the highlight of the night was when those Indians sang 'Mommas, Don't Let Your Babies Grow Up to Be Cowboys.' Everybody sang along with that one," Lively said.

† † †

The blue van, repaired by an honest mechanic in Ellensburg and a few stories that Thomas whispered into the engine, traveled down the mostly empty freeway toward home. Coyote Springs rode in a silence interrupted only by the sudden rush of a passing truck or a name whispered by one of those sleeping. Thomas drove the van, and Chess kept him awake. Checkers, Junior, and Victor slept.

"Why you like freeway driving so much?" Chess asked. "But don't close your eyes to tell me some story."

"I don't know."

"What do you think?"

"There's a lot of songs out here, I guess. I can hear them."

"You want me to turn on the radio?" Chess asked.

"Yeah, but keep it low. We don't want to wake the van up."

"They all need a lot of beauty sleep, enit?"

Chess turned on the radio. The Black Lodge Singers still drummed away in the cassette player, but she popped that tape out and searched for a radio station. She twisted the tuner back and forth through a short history of American music until she happened upon Hank Williams.

Hank Williams is a goddamned Spokane Indian! Samuel Builds-the-Fire shouted in Thomas's memory. Thomas smiled because so many people visited him in memories.

"Ya-hey," Thomas said. "Leave it there."

Chess played with the radio until Hank sang true and clear. Coyote Springs and Hank Williams continued down the freeway, past a lonely hitchhiker who heard the music through the open windows. The blue van swept by so quickly all he heard were a few isolated notes. But he heard enough to make everything weigh a little more, his shoes, his backpack, his dreams.

The music rose past the hitchhiker up into the sky, banged into the Big Dipper, and bounced off the bright moon. That's exactly what happened. The music howled back into the blue van, kept howling until Coyote Springs became echoes. That's exactly what happened.

"Thomas," Chess said and wanted to explain what she heard.

"I know," he said, wide awake, and slowly drove them all the way back home.

4

Father and Farther

Sometimes, father, you and I
Are like a three-legged horse
Who can't get across the finish line
No matter how hard he tries and tries and tries

And sometimes, father, you and I
Are like a warrior
Who can only paint half of his face
While the other half cries and cries and cries

chorus:
Now can I ask you, father
If you know how much farther we need to go?
And can I ask you, father
If you know how much farther we have to go?

Father and farther, father and farther, 'til we know
Father and farther, father and farther, 'til we know

Sometimes, father, you and I
Are like two old drunks
Who spend their whole lives in the bars
Swallowing down all those lies and lies and lies

Sometimes, father, you and I
Are like dirty ghosts
Who wear the same sheets every day
As one more piece of us just dies and dies and dies

(repeat chorus)

Sometimes, father, you and I
Are like a three-legged horse
Who can't get across the finish line
No matter how hard he tries and tries and tries

Coyote Springs returned to the Spokane Indian Reservation without much fanfare. Thomas drove through the late night quiet, the kind of quiet that frightened visitors from the city. As he pulled up in his driveway, the rest of the band members woke up, and the van's headlights illuminated the old Indian man passed out on the lawn.

"Who is that?" Victor asked. "Is it my dad or your dad?"

"It's not your dad," Junior said. "Your dad is dead."

"Oh, yeah, enit?" Victor asked. "Well, whose dad is it?"

"It ain't my dad," Junior said. "He's dead, too."

Coyote Springs climbed out of the van, walked up to the man passed out on the lawn, and rolled him over.

"That's your dad, enit?" Junior asked Thomas.

Thomas leaned down for a closer look.

"Yeah, that's him," Victor said. "That's old Samuel."

"Is he breathing?" Junior said.

"Yeah."

"Well, then leave him there," Victor said.

Thomas shook his father a little and said his name a few times. He had lost count of the number of times he'd saved his father, how many times he'd driven to some reservation tavern to pick up his dad, passed out in a back booth. Once a month, he bailed his father out of jail for drunk and disorderly behavior. That had become his father's Indian name: Drunk and Disorderly.

"He's way out of it," Victor said.

"He's out for the night," Junior said.

Junior and Victor shrugged their shoulders, walked into

Thomas's house, and looked for somewhere to sleep. Decorated veterans of that war between fathers and sons, Junior and Victor knew the best defense was sleep. They saw too many drunks littering the grass of the reservation; they rolled the drunks over and stole their money. When they were under age, they slapped those drunks awake and pushed them into the Trading Post to buy beer. Now, when they saw Samuel Builds-the-Fire passed out on the lawn, they crawled into different corners of Thomas's house and fell right to sleep.

"Ain't they going to help?" Chess asked.

"It's my father," Thomas said. "I have to handle this myself."

But Chess and Checkers helped Thomas carry his father into the house and lay him down on the kitchen table. The three sat in chairs around the table and stared at Samuel Builds-the-Fire, who breathed deep in his alcoholic stupor.

"I'm sorry, Thomas," Chess and Checkers said.

"Yeah, me, too."

Chess and Checkers were uncomfortable. They hated to see that old Indian man so helpless and hopeless; they hated to see the father's features in his son's face. It's hard not to see a father's life as prediction for his son's.

"Our father was like this, too," Chess said. "Just like this."

"But he never drank at all until Backgammon died," Checkers said.

"Where's your dad now?" Thomas asked.

"He's gone."

The word *gone* echoed all over the reservation. The reservation was gone itself, just a shell of its former self, just a fragment of the whole. But the reservation still possessed power and rage, magic and loss, joys and jealousy. The reservation tugged at the lives of its Indians, stole from them in the middle of the night, watched impassively as the horses and salmon disappeared. But the reservation forgave, too. Sam Bone vanished between foot falls on the way to the Trading Post one summer day and reappeared years later to finish his walk. Thomas, Chess, and Checkers heard the word *gone* shake the foundation of the house.

"Where's he gone to?" Thomas asked.

"He's just gone," Checkers said. "He's AWOL. He's MIA."

The secondhand furniture in Thomas's house moved an inch to the west.

"It wasn't always this way," Thomas said and touched his father's hand. "It wasn't always this way."

Samuel slept on the table while Thomas closed his eyes and told the story:

"Way back when, my father was an active alcoholic only about three months of every year. He was a binge drinker, you know? Completely drunk for three days straight, a week, a month, then he jumped back on the wagon again. Sober, he was a good man, a good father, so all the drinking had to be forgiven, enit?

"My father was Washington State High School Basketball Player of the Year in 1956. Even the white people knew how good that Indian boy played. He was just a little guy too, about five-foot-six and a hundred and fifty pounds, hair in a crewcut, and big old Indian ears sticking out. Walter Cronkite came out to the reservation and interviewed him. Cronkite stood on the free-throw line and shouted questions at my father, who dribbled from corner to corner and hit jumpshots.

"He was such a good basketball player that all the Spokanes wanted him to be more. When any Indian shows the slightest hint of talent in any direction, the rest of the tribe starts expecting Jesus. Sometimes they'll stop a reservation hero in the middle of the street, look into his eyes, and ask him to change a can of sardines into a river of salmon.

"But my father lived up to those expectations, you know? Game after game, he defined himself. He wasn't like some tired old sports hero, some little white kid, some Wonder-bread boy. Think about it. Take the basketball in your hands, fake left, fake right, look your defender in the eyes to let him know he won't be stopping you. Take the ball to the rim, the hoop, the goal, the basket, that circle that meant everything in an Indian boy's life.

"My father wasn't any different. After his basketball days were over, he didn't have much else. If he could've held a basketball in his arms when he cut down trees for the BIA, maybe my father would've kept that job. If he could have drank his own sweat after a basketball game and got drunk off the effort, maybe he would've stayed away from the real booze."

Thomas opened his eyes and looked at his father, lying still on the kitchen table. A wake for a live man. Thomas tried to smile for the sisters. Checkers looked at the overweight Indian man on the table, saw the dirt under his fingernails, the clogged pores, the darkness around his eyes and at the elbows and knees.

"I would've never thought he played basketball," Chess said.

"Me, neither," Checkers said.

Thomas looked at his father again, studied him, and touched Samuel's big belly.

"Did you ever play?" Chess asked.

"No," Thomas said.

"Why not?"

"Well, even Moses only parted the Red Sea once. There are things you just can't do twice."

"Sometimes," Checkers said, "I hate being Indian."

"Ain't that the true test?" Chess asked. "You ain't really Indian unless there was some point in your life that you didn't want to be."

"Enit," Thomas said.

"You know," Chess said, "like when you're walking downtown or something, and you see some drunk Indian passed out on the sidewalk."

Thomas looked at his father.

"Oh," Chess said. "I didn't mean your father."

"That's okay," Thomas said. "I *have* been walking in downtown Spokane and stumbled over my father passed out on the sidewalk."

"Yeah," Checkers said. "And I hate it when some Indian comes begging for money. Calling me sister or cousin. What am I supposed to do? I ain't got much money myself. So I give it to them anyway. Then I feel bad for doing it, because I know they're going to drink it all up."

Checkers was always afraid of those Indian men who wandered the streets. She always thought they looked like brown-skinned zombies. Samuel Builds-the-Fire looked like a zombie on the kitchen table. Those Indian zombies lived in Missoula when she was little. Once a month, the whole Warm Water family traveled from their little shack on the reservation to pick up supplies in Missoula. Those drunk zombies always followed the family from store to store.

Still, Checkers remembered how quiet and polite some of those zombies were, just as quiet as Samuel passed out on the table. In Missoula they stood on street corners, wrapped in old quilts, and held their hands out without saying a word. Just stood there and waited.

Once, Checkers watched a white man spit into a zombie's open hand. Just spit in his palm. The zombie wiped his hand clean on his pants and offered it again. Then the white man spit again. Checkers saw all that happen. After the white man walked away, she ran up to the zombie and gave him a piece of candy, her last piece of candy.

Thank you, the zombie said. He unwrapped the candy, popped it in his mouth, and smiled.

"What are we supposed to do?" Chess asked Thomas, as Checkers remembered her zombies. "What should we do for your father?"

"I don't know."

Samuel groaned in his sleep, raised his hands in a defensive position.

"Listen," Thomas said, "do you want something to drink?"

Thomas gave them all a glass of commodity grape juice. It was very sweet, almost too sweet. Thomas loved sugar.

"Our cousins are drinking this stuff mixed with rubbing alcohol at home," Chess said.

"Really?" Thomas said. The creativity of alcoholics constantly surprised him.

"Yeah, they call it a Rubbie Dubbie."

"Drinking that will kill them."

"I think that's the idea."

Thomas, Chess, and Checkers stayed quiet for a long time. After a while, Chess and Checkers started to sing a Flathead song of mourning. For a wake, for a wake. Samuel was still alive, but Thomas sang along without hesitation. That mourning song was B-7 on every reservation jukebox.

After the song, Thomas stood and walked away from the table where his father lay flat as a paper plate. He walked outside while the women stayed inside. They understood. Once outside, Thomas cried. Not because he needed to be alone; not because he was afraid to cry in front of women. He just wanted his tears to be individual, not tribal. Those tribal tears collected and fermented in huge BIA barrels. Then the BIA poured those tears into beer and Pepsi cans and distributed them back onto the reservation. Thomas wanted his tears to be selfish and fresh.

"Hello," he said to the night sky. He wanted to say the first word of a prayer or a joke. A prayer and a joke often sound alike on the reservation.

"Help," he said to the ground. He knew the words to a million songs: Indian, European, African, Mexican, Asian. He sang "Stairway to Heaven" in four different languages but never knew where that staircase stood. He sang the same Indian songs continually but never sang them correctly. He wanted to make his guitar sound like a waterfall, like a spear striking salmon, but his guitar only sounded like a guitar. He wanted the songs, the stories, to save everybody.

"Father," he said to the crickets, who carried their own songs to worry about.

† † †

Just minutes, days, years, maybe a generation out of high school, Samuel Builds-the-Fire, Jr., raced down the reservation road in his Chevy. He stopped to pick up Lester FallsApart, who hitchhiked with no particular destination in mind.

"Ya-hey," Samuel said. "Where you going, Lester?"

"Same place you are. Now."

"Good enough."

Samuel dropped the car into gear and roared down the highway.

"I hear you're getting married to that Susan," Lester said.

"Enit."

"You want to have kids."

"There's already one on the way."

"Congratulations," Lester said and slapped Samuel hard on the back. Surprised, Samuel swerved across the center line, which caused Spokane Tribal Police Officer Wilson to suddenly appear. Officer Wilson was a white man who hated to live on the reservation. He claimed a little bit of Indian blood and had used it to get the job but seemed to forget that whenever he handcuffed another Indian. He read Tom Clancy novels, drank hot tea year round, and always fell asleep in his chair. At one A.M. every morning, he woke up from the chair, brushed his teeth, and then fell into bed. The years rushed by him.

"Shit," Lester said. "It's the cops."

"Shit. You're right."

Samuel pulled over. Wilson stepped out of his car, walked up to the driver's window, and shone his flashlight inside the Chevy.

"You two been drinking?"

"I've been drinking since I was five," Lester said. "Kindergarten is hard on a man."

"I'll pretend you didn't say that," Wilson said.

"And we'll pretend you're a real Indian," Samuel said.

Wilson reached inside the Chevy, grabbed Samuel by the collar, and grinned hard into his face. Officer Wilson was a big man.

"Better watch your mouth," Wilson said. "Or I'll have to hurt those precious hands of yours. I wonder how you'd play ball after that."

"He'd still kick your ass," Lester said.

"Shit," Wilson said. "Let's go for it right now. Let's go over to the courts and go one on one. Hell, I'll call up Officer William and we'll play two on two."

"Two of you ain't going to be near enough," Samuel said. "Lester and me will take on all six of you fake bastards. Full court to ten by ones. Make it. Take it."

"No shit, enit?" Lester asked. "How's that fucking treaty for you, officer?"

"You're on," Wilson said, and got on his radio to round up his teammates.

"Shit," said Lester, who never played basketball on purpose. "What are you doing?"

"Don't worry about it," Samuel said. "Just give me the ball and get out of the way."

Samuel and Lester arrived at the basketball courts behind the Tribal School a few moments after the entire Spokane Tribal Police Department. Wilson and William were the big white men. Certifiably one-quarter Spokane Indian, William had made the varsity basketball team in junior college. The brothers Plato, Socrates, and Aristotle Heavy Burden were the forwards. Everybody on the reservation called them Phil, Scott, and Art. The Tribal Police Chief, David WalksAlong, tied up his shoes and stretched his back. He would later be elected Tribal Chairman, but on that night, he played point guard.

"You take it out first," WalksAlong said and threw the ball hard at Samuel's chest.

"You better take it out," Samuel said and threw the ball back. "It's the only time you'll touch it."

The Chief faked a pass to his right and passed left, but Samuel stole the ball and dribbled downcourt for the slam.

SAMUEL & LESTER—1
TRIBAL COPS—0

† † †

Thomas stood outside while Chess and Checkers jealously watched Samuel Builds-the-Fire sleep. The sisters really needed to sleep but knew those Stick Indians might haunt Thomas if he stayed up alone.

"What should we do?" Chess asked.
"I don't know."
"I don't know, either."
"I know you're falling in love, enit?"
"With Samuel?" Chess asked. "No way."
"You know who I'm talking about."

"Maybe I am. Maybe I ain't. I mean, he's got a lot going for him. He's got a job, he's sober, he's got his own teeth."

"Yeah," Checkers said. "Remember the one I dated? Barney?"

Chess remembered that Checkers always chased the older Indian men and never even looked at the young bucks. Checkers dated Indian men old enough to be her father. Once she went after Barney Pipe, a Blood Indian old enough to be her grandfather. "Jeez," Chess had said after she first met the old man, "I know we're supposed to respect our elders, but this is getting carried away." Barney liked to take out his false teeth while dancing and usually dropped them in the front pocket of his shirt. One night, old Barney pulled Checkers really close during a slow dance, and his false teeth bit her.

"Do you remember Barney's false teeth?" Chess asked.

"Damn right, I remember. I still have a scar. Biggest hickey I ever got," Checkers said. "Samuel's about the same age as Barney, enit?"

"Enit."

"Man, Barney had a house, a car, and three pairs of cowboy boots."

Samuel Builds-the-Fire wore a ragged pair of Kmart tennis shoes. The laces had been broken and retied a few times over.

"Indians would be a lot better off," Chess said, "if we took care of our feet."

"Yeah," Checkers said. "And those cavalry soldiers would've been much nicer if the government had given them boots that fit. Ain't nothing worse than a soldier with an ingrown toenail."

"Samuel would be all right if he'd gotten a good pair of hiking boots when he was little."

Chess tried to fix Samuel's hair with her fingers. Then she took out her brush and went to work. Samuel breathed deeply in his sleep. Chess hummed a song as she brushed; Checkers pulled out her brush and sang along. The song, an old gospel hymn, reminded the sisters of the Catholic Church on the Flathead Reservation. Their hands stayed in Samuel's hair, but their minds traveled back over twenty years.

"Hurry up!" Chess, age twelve, shouted at Checkers, who had just turned eleven. "We're going to be late for church."

The Warm Water sisters struggled into their best dresses, dingy from too many washes but still the best they owned, and hurried to Flathead Reservation Catholic Church.

"Father James says I get to sing the lead today," Checkers said.

"Not if I get there first."

Chess and Checkers pulled on their shoes and tiptoed into their dad's room, which stank of whiskey and body odor. Luke Warm Water slept alone and dreamed of his missing wife.

"Hey, Dad," Chess whispered. "We're going to church. Is that okay?"

Luke snored.

"Good. I'm glad you agree. Do you want to come this time?"

Luke snored.

"I don't think it's a good idea, either. Maybe next time?"

Luke snored.

"Don't get mad at me. Jeez. If you walked into church, everybody might die of shock."

"Yeah," Checkers said. "The whole roof might fall down."

The sisters walked to the church, which was one of those simple buildings, four walls, a door, a crucifix, and twenty folding chairs. Those folding chairs were multidimensional. Set them up facing the front, and they served as pews. Circle them around a teacher in the middle, and you had Sunday School. Push them up to card tables, and you feasted on donated food. Fold those chairs, stack them in a corner, and you cleared a dance space. Folding chairs proved the existence of God.

Chess and Checkers helped with communion and sang in the church choir. The sisters were the choir, but they sang loud enough to shake the walls.

"The louder we get," Father James preached, "the better God can hear us."

Chess and Checkers believed Father James. They sang until their lungs ached. Chess opened her arms wide and looked toward heaven; Checkers opened her arms wide and looked at Father James. Both sisters were in love.

"Do you remember all those gospel songs we used to sing?" Chess asked her sister as they continued to brush Samuel Builds-the-Fire's hair.

"I remember."

Chess and Checkers kept singing as they brushed, while Samuel dreamed of beautiful Indian nuns.

† † †

"Lucky fuckers," Chief WalksAlong said and threw the ball back to Lester. Samuel cut behind Lester, took a handoff, shrugged off Wilson and William, and launched a thirty-foot jumper.

"For Crazy Horse," Samuel said as he released the ball.

SAMUEL & LESTER—2
TRIBAL COPS—0

"That's traveling," WalksAlong said.

"No way," Samuel said. "You can't make that call."

"I can make any call I want. I'm Chief."

"Yeah, that's the only way you're going to stop me. With a pistol."

Lester squared off with the other five cops, danced like a boxer, flicked a few harmless jabs at the Heavy Burden brothers, and sprained his wrist.

"Our ball," Samuel said.

† † †

As Thomas stood outside and the Warm Waters brushed Samuel's hair, Victor dreamed. In his dream, his stepfather was packing the car. Victor had sworn never to say his parents' names again. But his stepfather, **Harold**, roared to life and threw Victor's mother, **Matilda**, into the trunk beside the dead body of Victor's real father, **Emery**. Victor struggled to leave the nightmare, the naming, but his mother's cries pulled him back. **Matilda** held tightly to **Emery**'s body in the trunk.

Where you going? Victor asked **Harold**.

Away.

Let me get my stuff.

I've already packed your stuff. Your suitcase is in the house.

Where we going?

You ain't going anywhere with us. You can go any damn place you please, but I don't want no Indian kid hanging around us no more.

Harold slammed the trunk shut, and the force knocked Victor to the ground. By the time he had gotten to his feet, **Harold** was sitting in the driver's seat, turning the ignition. The car whined and whined but would not start.

Wait for me, Victor called and ran to the driver's window. He pounded on the glass while **Harold** turned the key again. Victor ran into the house to find his suitcase. He ran from room to room. When he finally found it stuffed under a bed, he heard the car start outside.

Wait for me, Victor shouted and ran outside, dropping his suitcase. He ran after his stepfather's car, followed him down the road as far as he could. He galloped down the pavement, his suddenly long hair trailing in the wind. He ran until his body lathered with sweat. He ran until he fell on all fours.

When he stood again, his head was shaved bald. Huge white men in black robes milled around.

What happened to your hair? a black robe asked.

It's gone.

No, it's not, the black robe said. He took Victor's hand and led him through all the other black robes. The black robe and Victor walked down flights of stairs.

Are you tired? the black robe asked.

Yes.

Do you want me to carry you?

No.

The black robe lifted him anyway and carried him on his shoulders. Victor felt the hard muscles through the black robe. He knew that man could crush him. But the black robe carried him to the bottom of the stairs and into a large room. Paintings adorned every wall.

Look here, the black robe said. *This is my favorite one.*

Victor looked at the painting. A battle scene. Two armies fighting. Guns, horses, men, flags, horses, smoke, blood, horses. Victor stared at the painting until he smelled blood and smoke.

Please, Victor said, *let me down.*

The black robe set him down. Victor rubbed his head, scratched his head, and looked at his hand. Blood.

I'm bleeding.

So you are, the black robe said, pulled out a handkerchief, and dabbed at Victor's wounds. When the cloth was saturated, the black robe rolled it up into a little ball and swallowed it.

Here, the black robe said, *I want to show you something.*

The black robe held Victor's hand and led him through a series of doors. Victor lost track of place and time. He closed his eyes and followed the black robe. He heard the black robe sing.

Here, the black robe said. *We're here.*

Victor opened his eyes in a room filled with the stink of burning hair. Other black robes shoveled hair into burning barrels, furnaces, and open fires. Long, black hair.

Here we are, the black robe said. *We made it.*

Victor ran from the room. He ran past doors into strange rooms. He ran until he lost his breath and collapsed on the cold, hard floor of a barren room. He lay there for hours, until the floor grew warm, then grew grass. He dug his fingers and toes into the grass, the dirt. He dug until his fingers and toes bled with the effort. He dug because he had forgotten how to stand. He dug because his father, **Emery**, and mother, **Matilda**, waited on a better reservation at the center of the world.

† † †

Samuel dribbled the ball between his legs, between William and Wilson, who crashed into each other in their defensive effort, then breezed past Phil, Art, and Scott Heavy Burden, and jumped over WalksAlong for the bucket.

SAMUEL & LESTER—3

TRIBAL COPS—0

"That shot was for every time one of you assholes wrote somebody a traffic ticket on this reservation," Samuel said. "I mean, how could you find some Indian who doesn't have enough money to feed his kids?"

"Yeah," Lester said. "They wrote old Moses a ticket for failure to stop when there wasn't another car on the reservation even working at the time. Moses had to pawn one of his eagle feathers to pay that fine. Never got it back either.''

"Fuck both of you,'' the Chief said. "Quit talking smack and play ball.''

"Shit,'' Samuel said. "I should be writing you all tickets for failing to stop me.''

Samuel gave the ball to Lester, who dribbled it to his left, off his feet, and into the hands of Officer Wilson. Enraged by his turnover, Lester played tough defense by breathing on the officer with Thunderbird Wine breath. Wilson nearly threw up but recovered well enough to break Lester's nose with an elbow and throw a nice pass to the Chief for an easy basket.

SAMUEL & LESTER——3

TRIBAL COPS——1

Lester kicked and screamed on the ground. The Tribal Police celebrated their first basket, while Samuel stood with hands on hips and knew it was the same old story.

"That was a foul,'' Samuel said.

"We didn't see nothing.''

† † †

As Victor, in one corner of the house, dreamed of black robes, Junior fell into his own dream in another corner. In his dream, Junior was in the back seat of his parents' car outside the Powwow Tavern. Below freezing, so he shared a sleeping bag with his two brothers and two sisters. Junior struggled to remember his siblings' names.

Run the heat for a little while, his siblings pleaded, because he had the car keys.

No, Junior said. *Mom and Dad said I have to save gas. We just got enough to get home.*

In his dream, Junior tried to remember his parents' names, but they eluded him. Those names always eluded him, even in waking. In his dream, Junior's siblings tried to wrestle the keys away, but he fought them off. They wrestled and argued until their parents staggered out of the bar.

Oh, good, his siblings said. *We're going home.*

Junior's parents knocked on the window; he rolled it down.

You warm? they asked.

Warm enough, Junior said and silenced his siblings with a mean look.

Here's some food, mother-and-father said, and shoved potato chips and Pepsi through the open window into the arms of their children.

We'll be out soon, okay? mother-and-father said.

Junior and his siblings watched their parents stagger back toward the bar. Mother-and-father turned and waved. Then they danced a clumsy two-step.

Jeez, Junior said in his dream. *They love each other.*

Mother-and-father wove their way back inside the bar, and Junior turned back to his siblings.

Make sure everybody gets enough, Junior said.

They ate their potato chips and Pepsi.

I'm bored, his siblings said after dinner, so Junior sang to them.

I'm bored, his siblings said again, and Junior started to cry. He cried as each of his siblings climbed out of the car and ran away on all fours. They ran into the darkness; hands and feet sparked on the pavement. They ran to other reservations and never returned. They ran to crack houses and lay down in the debris. They ran to tall buildings and jumped off. They joined the army and disappeared in the desert. Junior cried until his parents came out of the bar at closing time.

Where is everybody? mother-and-father asked.

Gone, gone, gone, gone.

Mother-and-father cried. Then they drove down the highway and looked for their children.

I don't mean to say it's all your fault, mother-and-father said. *But it is all your fault.*

They drove and drove. Mother-and-father sat behind the wheel and drank beer. When finished, they rolled down the window and threw the empty bottles into the dark. Junior heard them shatter against road signs. He saw the little explosions they made at impact. Impossible reds, impossible reds. He lost count of the bottles.

Ya-hey, Junior called out, but his parents pushed him back.

I don't want to hurt you, mother-and-father said. *But I might hurt you.*

Junior leaned back, curled into a ball in the back seat. He heard the road sing under the wheels of the car. He heard his parents' soft tears and quiet whispers. Then he noticed the car moving faster and faster, his parents' tears and whispers growing into sobs and shouts.

Wait, Junior said, but the car suddenly rolled. Junior counted the revolutions: one, two, three, four, all the way to twenty. The car came to rest on its wheels, with Junior still tucked into a ball in the back seat. He listened to a faint song in the distance. He heard something dripping in the engine. He heard coughing.

Ya-hey, Junior said as he climbed out of the car and saw his mother-and-father completely still on the grass. He grabbed his parents by the arms and dragged them across the grass. It took hours. He dragged his parents up stairs and into a strange house. It took days. He dragged his parents into a bedroom and laid them down on the bed. It took years. He kneeled at the foot of the bed. He folded his hands to pray.

He opened his mouth, but nothing came out. He strained and strained, his vocal cords ached with the effort, but nothing came out. Then he heard music from the radio beside the bed. He turned up the volume until the walls and bed shook. His parents stared with fixed pupils. They danced on the bed. Their arms and legs kicked wildly, until their fingers locked, and they pulled each other back and forth, back and forth.

† † †

Chief WalksAlong hit two quick jumpshots over a seriously handicapped Lester FallsApart, who protected his broken nose with one hand. Officers William and Wilson made baskets, and Samuel ran ragged trying to defend himself against the entire world.

TRIBAL COPS——5
SAMUEL & LESTER——3

"Samuel," the Chief asked, "don't you sing pretty good? I might want to hear a few verses of 'I Fought the Law and the Law Won' after this game."

"I don't know that one. But I know how to sing 'I Shot the Sheriff.' "

The Chief threw the ball to Art Heavy Burden, who missed a jumper, but the Chief followed the shot and put the rebound back in.

TRIBAL COPS——6
SAMUEL & LESTER——3

"That shot was for every time one of you drunk ass Indians told me I wasn't real," the Chief said. "That was for every time you little fuckers think pissing your pants is a ceremonial act."

† † †

"Did you ever drink?" Thomas asked Chess after he came back inside the house. His father still snored on the table.

"No."

"Not ever?"

"Neither of us ever drank," Chess said.

"We were afraid of it," Checkers said. "Even when we wanted to drink, we were too scared, enit?"

Thomas looked at his father on the table.

"Look what it did to my father," he said.

Chess looked at Thomas, at his father, at both. She saw her father, Luke, in their faces. She missed her father, even after all he had done.

Checkers also saw her father in Samuel's face, in Thomas's eyes. She saw that warrior desperation and the need to be superhuman in the poverty of a reservation. She hated all of it.

I'm Super Indian Man, those pseudo-warriors always shouted on the reservation. *Able to leap tall HUD houses in a single bound. Faster than a BIA pickup. Stronger than a block of commodity cheese.* Checkers tried to ignore them, but the Indian men visited her dreams. *Look at my big cowboy hat. Look at my big boots. Look at my big, big belt buckle.* Those men, those ghosts, crawled into her bed at night, lifted her nightgown, and forced her legs apart. After they finished with her, those Indian men sat on the edge of the bed and cried. *Ha-oh, ha-oh, ha-oh. I lost my cowboy hat. Somebody stole my boots. I pawned my belt buckle.* No matter how bad she felt, those tears always moved her heart. She reached for the Indian men in her dreams and held them tightly. Her stomach turned, and she swallowed bile, but she held on.

"I hate this," Thomas said. "I hate my father."

"You don't hate him," Chess said. "You're just upset."

"I hate him," Thomas said again and squeezed his hands into fists.

A few days earlier, Chess and Thomas had driven to Spokane for a cheap hamburger. They walked in downtown Spokane and stumbled onto a drunk couple arguing.

"Get the fuck away from me!" the drunk woman yelled at her drunk husband, who squeezed his hand into a fist like he meant to hit her.

Thomas and Chess flinched, then froze, transported back to all of those drunken arguments they'd witnessed and survived.

The drunk couple in downtown Spokane pulled at each other's clothes and hearts, but they were white people. Chess and Thomas knew that white people hurt each other, too. Chess knew that white people felt pain just like Indians. Nerve endings, messages to the brain, reflexes. The doctor swung hammer against knee, and the world collapsed.

"You fucker!" the white woman yelled at her husband, who opened his hands and held them out to his wife. An offering. That hand would not strike her. He pleaded with his wife until she fell back into his arms. That white woman and man held each other while Chess and Thomas watched. A hundred strangers walked by and never noticed any of it.

After that, Chess and Thomas had sat in the van in a downtown parking lot. Thomas began to weep, deep ragged tears that rose along his rib cage, filled his mouth and nose, and exploded out.

"You don't hate him," Chess said to Thomas as Samuel Builds-the-Fire inhaled sharply and held his breath too long. They all waited for the next breath. When he finally exhaled loudly, it surprised him to be alive, and he smiled in his sleep.

Chess looked across Samuel's body lying on that table,

looked at Samuel's son, and wanted a mirror. *Here,* she wanted to say to Thomas. *You don't look anything like your father. You're much more handsome. Your hair is longer, and your hands are beautiful.* But Thomas needed more than that. His father lay on the table, but it could have been any Indian man. It could have been a white man on the table.

"What's going to happen to him?" Checkers asked.

"What's going to happen to who?" Chess and Thomas asked her back.

† † †

Samuel made two beautiful moves and scored twice, but the Tribal Cops answered with two buckets of their own. The game broke down into a real war after that. Hard fouls on drives to the hoop, moving screens, kidney punches. The cops targeted Lester's broken nose and drove Samuel into a basket support pole. Fresh wounds.

"That's a foul!" Samuel yelled as he made a move on the Chief.

"You goddamn pussy."

Samuel held the ball in his arms like a fullback and ran the Chief over.

"First down!" Lester yelled.

"Now," Samuel said, "that's a foul."

The Chief stood, touched his head where it hit the court, and found blood.

"That's assaulting an officer," he said. "Good for a year in Tribal Jail."

"This is a game," Samuel said. "It don't count."

"Everything counts."

The Chief took the ball from Samuel, passed it to Phil Heavy Burden, took a pass right back, and popped a jumper.

TRIBAL COPS—9
SAMUEL & LESTER—5

"Game point, shitheads," the Chief said. "You two best be getting ready for jail."

"Fuck you," Samuel said as he stole the ball, drove down the court, and went in for a two-handed, rattle-the-foundations, ratify-a-treaty, abolish-income-tax, close-the-uranium-mines monster dunk.

"That was for every one of you Indians like you Tribal Cops," Samuel said. "That was for all those Indian scouts who helped the U.S. Cavalry. That was for Wounded Knee I and II. For Sand Creek. Hell, that was for both the Kennedys, Martin Luther King, and Malcolm X."

"Yeah," Lester said. "That was for Leonard Peltier, too."

"And for Marilyn Monroe."

"And for Jimi Hendrix."

"Yeah, for Jimi."

"What about Jim Morrison," Wilson and William asked. White guys obsessed on Jim Morrison.

"You can have Jim Morrison," Samuel said. "We'll take the ball."

Lester took the pass from Samuel, faked a pass back, dribbled once, and threw up a prayer that banked in. It was the first and last basket of Lester FallsApart's basketball career.

TRIBAL COPS—9
SAMUEL & LESTER—7

† † †

Thomas, Chess, and Checkers never slept that night. They talked stories around the table where Samuel Builds-the-Fire snored.

"Your mom died of cancer, enit?" Chess asked.

"Yeah, stomach cancer," Thomas said.

"I'm sorry."

"It ain't your fault. She died a long time ago."

Checkers shivered at the thought of cancer. Cancer rose from the bodies of dead Indians and walked down the hallways of hospitals.

"Did she drink?" Chess asked.

"She did. But she quit. She was sober when she died."

"Really? Quit just like that?"

"Cold as a turkey," Thomas said. "She quit the morning after this really bad New Year's Eve party at our house. This house."

"What happened?"

"Dad got real drunk, kicked everybody out, and then took all the furniture out on the front lawn, and burned it."

"Shit, you must have been scared."

"Not too scared. It wasn't that big a fire. I mean, we barely had any furniture. But then he threatened to burn down the house with all of us in it. So Mom threw me into the car, and we drove to her sister's up in Colville. Her sister wasn't home, so we sat in this all-night diner and waited. The sun came up, and we drove back here. Mom never drank again."

"What happened then?"

"She kicked Dad out. Divorced him Indian style, enit? Then went to work for the Tribe as a driver. She drove the Senior Citizens' van all over the countryside. Took the elders to every powwow. She got all traditional. Started dancing, singing, playing stickgame again."

"Jeez," Checkers said. "That must have been some party, enit?"

"Yeah," Thomas said. "Dad even hired a band."

"A real band?"

"Kind of. It was just a couple of guys from the reservation.

Louie and Merle. They played the blues. They were pretty good when they weren't drunk.''

"Sounds like a couple guys we know.''

"What else happened at the party?''

"Same old things,'' Thomas said. "People got drunk. People fought. People got pregnant in the back rooms. A couple went to jail. One got his stomach pumped. Two died in a car wreck on the way home. And there was a partridge in a pear tree.''

"Who died?''

"Junior's parents.''

"Jeez,'' Chess said. "He must have been really young.''

"Yeah,'' Thomas said. "He was the oldest, too. Had a bunch of brothers and sisters. Their auntie took them in and raised them. She died a few years ago.''

"What about Victor's parents?''

"They're all gone.''

"Jeez,'' Checkers said. "Samuel is the only one who made it.''

Samuel rolled over on the table and coughed. He curled into a fetal position and mumbled something.

"Hard to believe, enit?''

"Yeah,'' Thomas said. "The only things that will survive a nuclear war are cockroaches and my father.''

"Our father was crazy, too,'' Chess said. "He'd come home all drunk and screaming. Be talking about how he was a radio man during World War II.''

"I thought all those radio men were Navajo,'' Thomas said.

"They all were Navajo. And my dad was too young for the war anyway, but he kept saying it.''

"Man, you never hear about those Navajo radio guys, do you? They won the war. Those Germans and Japanese couldn't figure that code out.''

"Yeah, just like that. Mom would tell him about all that, too. But my dad kept going on and on. He was a war hero, jumped out of airplanes. He killed Hitler."

"Enit?" Thomas asked.

"Yeah," Chess said. "Old Luke Warm Water told us he was the one who killed Hitler. Caught up to him in that bunker and made him drink poison."

Thomas laughed.

"What's so funny?"

"My dad always told me *he* was the one who killed Hitler. They must have been on that mission together."

"Our fathers, the war heroes."

Thomas thought about all the imagined and real wars their fathers fought. He thought about that New Year's Eve party, all those parties that seemed to celebrate nothing at all. He remembered the two Indians who played the blues at that party, where Samuel burned the furniture on the front lawn. Two old Indian men played blues. In sunglasses. Big bellies. Big knuckles. Thomas tried to remember if they were any good. He searched his mind for some melody they played but heard nothing.

"You know," Chess said. "I heard beer bottles breaking so much that I got used to it. I kind of miss them sometimes."

† † †

Exhausted, Samuel took the ball out. His body ached. Once, pain had been a drug to him. He needed pain, but then it had just become pain. Just more weight on his body.

"It's over," the Chief said. "You don't have nothing left."

Art, Scott, and Phil Heavy Burden surrounded Lester and prevented him from moving. The Chief and the two white officers guarded Samuel.

"Fuck you twice," Samuel said.

Samuel looked at Chief WalksAlong, at all the Tribal Cops, at Lester. He shifted the ball from his left hip to his right. He spun the ball in his hands, felt the leather against his fingertips, and closed his eyes.

"What the hell you doing?" the Chief asked.

With his eyes still closed, Samuel drove to the basket, around his defenders, and pulled up for a short jumper. The ball rotated beautifully. Years later, Lester still swore that ball stopped in midair, just spun there like it was on a stick, like the ball wanted to make sure everyone noticed its beauty.

"That shot was vain," Lester said.

"That shot was the best story I ever told," Samuel said.

TRIBAL COPS—9

SAMUEL & LESTER—8

† † †

The man-who-was-probably-Lakota stood in front of the Trading Post every morning. He studied his watch, waited for the top of the hour, and then started his ceremony at the same exact time every morning.

"The end of the world is near!" he chanted. "The end of the world is near!"

"Jeez," Thomas said as he heard the chant. "It can't be six already. We stayed up all night."

Victor and Junior stumbled into the room.

"Shit," Victor said. "Does that crazy Lakota have to do that every morning?"

"Enit?" Junior said. "He must think he's one of those Plains Indian roosters."

"Jeez," Victor said and looked at Samuel. "How's your old man?"

"He's all right."

"I'm hungry," Junior said.

"There's some applesauce in the fridge."

"Commodity applesauce or real applesauce?"

"Commodity."

"Shit, we'll eat it anyway."

"Ya-hey," Victor said. "Maybe we should stick an apple in Samuel's mouth and roast him up."

Checkers rose in anger and slapped Victor.

"What the fuck's wrong with you?" Victor asked as he grabbed her wrists.

"That ain't funny. That ain't funny."

Victor held Checkers until she stopped struggling. He let her go, and Checkers slapped him again. She wailed on Victor. The rest of Coyote Springs remained silent, too sleepy and stunned to move. Checkers slapped and kicked the Indian man in front of her. That Indian man, those Indian men.

"Stop it!" Chess shouted as she came back to life. She tried to separate Checkers and Victor, but her sister pushed her away. Checkers balled her hands into fists and started to punch Victor.

"That's it," Victor said, picked Checkers up, and threw her down. Checkers bounced back up and threw a few more wild punches.

Thomas jumped Victor then, and the two wrestled around the room, bumped into walls and the other band members. Checkers crawled under the kitchen table for cover, while Samuel Builds-the-Fire slept on. Chess screamed at Thomas and Victor.

"Knock this shit off!"

Victor pulled away from Thomas. They stood face to face like boxers before a bout. Breathing hard, they stared each other down.

"You assholes," Chess said. "Quit this macho bullshit."

"Ya-hey," Junior said. "I've got applesauce."

Junior stepped between Thomas and Victor.

"I've got enough spoons for all of us, too."

"I don't want any," Thomas said and walked out the door. Chess followed him. Victor took the applesauce and spoons from Junior. Checkers stayed beneath the table, while Samuel sat up, looked around, then fell back to sleep.

"Hey," Chess said as she caught up to Thomas outside. "What the hell you think you're doing? You think you're some kind of tough guy, enit?"

"He can't do that to people no more," Thomas said. "I won't let him. I don't give a shit what that guitar said. I don't care."

"Well, call it off," Chess said. "Let's kick them out of the band. We don't need them. We can be a trio. Me, you, and Checkers. We'll get a new name. We'll move to a new place. Get the hell away from this reservation. Any reservation."

The horses screamed.

"What do you think?" Thomas asked. "Should we do that?"

"Yeah, we should."

Victor swallowed the last bite of applesauce just as Thomas and Chess returned to the house. Junior had crawled beneath the table with Checkers. She pushed and kicked at him, but he still sat under there. He wanted some applesauce.

"I think she's hurt," Junior said to Chess, who crawled beneath the table, too.

"Is she okay?" Thomas asked.

"My ass hurts," Checkers said. She shook as Chess held her.

"She's completely fucking nuts is what she is," Victor said.

"Listen," Thomas said, and the rest of Coyote Springs looked at him. He wanted to tell them about the new plan to kick Junior and Victor out of the band, but he heard a knock on the door.

"Who the hell is that?" Victor asked.

Thomas opened the door to nothing. He looked around. Nobody. He was about to shut the door when he heard a voice.

"Hey," the voice whispered from inside a bush on the front lawn. "You're Builds-the-Fire, right?"

"Yeah."

"The lead singer, right?"

"Yeah."

"Okay," the voice said. "I have a letter for you."

The Federal Express guy jumped out of the bush and handed the letter to Thomas. Then he saluted him, jumped off the porch, and ran for his truck. Thomas watched the FedEx truck kick up dust and smoke as it peeled out of the driveway.

"What was that?" Chess asked.

"This," Thomas said and opened the letter. He read it slowly.

"Well," Chess said, "what is it?"

"We got an offer to play at this place in Seattle. The Backboard. I guess they saw us play in Ellensburg. They'll pay us a thousand dollars."

"No shit!" Victor yelled and started to dance with Junior. They tangoed up and down the floor. Junior picked up a stray feather and stuck it in his teeth.

"It's our chance," Thomas said.

"Chance for what?" Chess asked.

"The money. We need the money. Don't we?"

Chess knew that Coyote Springs needed the money. She needed the money. The forest fire season was nearly over. Nobody hired Flathead Indians on the Spokane Indian Reservation. Two hundred dollars a head. Checkers and Chess would have four hundred together. With Thomas and his share, they would have enough money to dump Victor and Junior.

"What do you think?" Chess asked her sister.

"I ain't going anywhere with that asshole," Checkers said.

"Besides, how the hell do these people know who we are? They couldn't have seen us in Ellensburg. That was just last night. I don't trust them. I don't trust any of this."

"We don't need you," Victor said. "You can't sing anyway."

Checkers, Chess, and Junior climbed out from under the table. Victor stepped behind Thomas because Checkers knew how to punch.

"I think we all need to sleep on this," Chess said. "Jeez, Checkers and I ain't got any sleep at all. You neither, Thomas."

"We ain't got time to sleep on it," Thomas said. "They want us to be there tomorrow night for sound check."

"Are you serious?"

"Serious enough."

"Jeez," Chess asked her sister again, "what do you want to do?"

"I told you. I ain't going anywhere with that caveman."

"I'm going," Victor said.

"Me, too," Junior said.

"This ain't enough time to decide anything," Chess said. "That's not fair. How could they do that to us?"

"Strangers ask us to sing for them, and they'll pay us a thousand bucks," Victor said. "And you think they're being assholes. We should be grateful."

"Will you shut up? I'm trying to think."

"I'm going," Thomas said. "I have to go."

Victor whooped. Junior hugged Thomas.

"Checkers," Chess said, "are you sure you don't want to go?"

"I'm sure."

"Okay, she's not going. But she still gets her share of the money."

"No fucking way," Victor said.

"Okay," Thomas said, "we're a democracy. We'll take a vote."

"Not this voting shit again," Victor said. "Who pays attention to voting in this goddamn country anyway?"

"All those in favor of Checkers getting a full share if she stays home, raise your hand."

Thomas, Chess, and Checkers voted for full share. Junior abstained. Victor was pissed.

"She stays home," Thomas said, "and she gets full share."

Lord, I'm sorry, Chess said to herself. *We need the money.*

"Well, Jesus," Victor said, more worried about his share. "So she gets the money. But we got to get packed. We got to get going. Seattle, Seattle."

The city waited.

† † †

Samuel flew. He had dreamed of flying before. But there he was, flying for real. Flying true. Flying four feet above the basketball court. He flew over the Tribal Cops. Over Chief WalksAlong. He switched the ball from left to right hand and back again. He closed his eyes, opened them, shuttered them like a camera taking photos of a historic moment. Samuel laid the ball gently over the rim. Samuel missed the shot.

"Shit," Samuel yelled as Officer Wilson grabbed the rebound. He was still cussing as WalksAlong received a pass and drove the baseline. Samuel stopped the drive, forced the Chief toward the middle of the court.

"This is game point!" the Chief yelled. "We make it, we win."

The Chief dribbled once, twice, three times and lifted off the ground. Samuel leapt with him, arms outstretched, watched the ball float just above his fingertips, and still watched as the ball made its lazy way toward the hoop.

† † †

Checkers waved goodbye as the blue van pulled onto the reservation highway. She waved at Chess with most of her hand, saved a little for Thomas, and maybe a bit for Junior. She excluded Victor from her wave.

"What are you going to do this weekend?" Chess had asked her sister before she climbed into the van.

"I think I'll go to church. It's been a while."

"Yeah, the Catholic Church is down by the crossroads, enit?"

"Yeah, I've walked by it a couple times," Checkers had said.

Checkers continued to wave goodbye as the blue van rolled out of sight. She walked back into the house, nervous, unsure what to do with her time. Maybe she should sing scales, ready her voice for the Sunday hymns. Father Arnold was the priest down there. She had read his name on the greeting board when she walked by the church. Father Arnold. She wondered about Father Arnold's favorite song.

"You think Checkers will be all right?" Thomas asked as he drove the van off the reservation.

"She's a grown woman," Chess said.

"She makes me groan," Victor said.

Everybody ignored Victor. In a unanimous vote taken just before they left, Coyote Springs had decided that was the best policy. Even Victor raised his hand for that one.

"What's Seattle like?" Junior asked.

"It rains there," Chess said. "It rains a lot."

The blue van rolled through the wheat fields of eastern Washington, across the central desert, and into the foothills of the Cascades. They climbed Snoqualmie Pass and stopped at the Indian John Rest Area.

"Who is this Indian John?" Victor asked as they parked the van.

"I'm Indian John," Junior said.

Chess and Thomas sat on the grass and shared a warm Pepsi. Victor and Junior walked to the bathroom. Inside, a little white boy stared at them.

"Hello there," Junior said.

"Hello," the boy said.

"What's your name?"

"Jason. Are you an Indian?"

"Yes, I am."

"Hey, Daddy, there's a real Indian out here."

A huge white man stepped out of a stall.

"Who you talking to?" the white man asked his son.

"This Indian. He's real."

Junior waved weakly to the man. Victor turned away and pretended not to know Junior. But they were the only two Indians in the bathroom. Both wore white t-shirts that had COYOTE SPRINGS scribbled across the front, although Junior had on jeans and Victor had on his purple bell bottoms.

"You're an Indian, huh?" the white man asked.

"Yeah," Junior said and prepared to run. On a reservation, this white man would have been all alone. In America, this white man was legion.

"That's cool," the white man said. "Did you know this rest area was named after an Indian?"

"Yeah," Victor said and put his arm around Junior. "And you're looking at the grandsons of Indian John himself."

"Really? What's your names?"

"I'm Indian Victor and this is Indian Junior."

The white man almost believed them but came to his senses and stormed away with his son in tow.

"What took you so long?" the white man's wife asked.

"Just some Indians," the white man said.

"Just some Indians," the little boy repeated.

Victor and Junior grabbed a free cup of coffee from the stand outside the bathroom. The Veterans of War offered free coffee and donuts in return for donations. Junior dropped a dollar into the box; Victor dropped sugar into his coffee. Both knew it was too warm for coffee, but they drank it anyway and talked about the price of guitar strings and drumsticks. They stood near the coffee stand and dreamed about Seattle.

Chess and Thomas sat on the grass for a long time. Neither wanted to rise and leave the rest stop, because Seattle waited somewhere down the mountain. Seattle. Seattle. The word sounded like a song.

"It's named after an Indian," Chess said. "Seattle is named after a real Indian chief."

"Really?"

"Really. But I guess it was something like Sealth. Chief Stealth. Or Shelf. Or something like that. Something different."

"Seattle was his white name, huh?"

"Yeah, I guess. Jeez, you know his granddaughter lived in some old shack before she died. They name the town after her grandfather, and she lives in a shack downtown."

"Too bad."

"Ain't it awful. You know, I was wondering where your father was. Where'd he take off to anyway? I never even saw him get off the table."

"I don't know."

"You never told us who won that game between your father and the Tribal Cops."

"Who do you think?" Thomas asked. "Who you think won that game?"

5

My God Has Dark Skin

My braids were cut off in the name of Jesus
To make me look so white
My tongue was cut out in the name of Jesus
So I would not speak what's right
My heart was cut out in the name of Jesus
So I would not try to feel
My eyes were cut out in the name of Jesus
So I could not see what's real

chorus:
And I've got news for you
But I'm not sure where to begin
Yeah, I've got news for you
My God has dark skin
My God has dark skin

I had my braids cut off by black robes
But I know they'll grow again
I had my tongue cut out by these black robes
But I know I'll speak 'til the end
I had my heart cut out by the black robes
But I know what I still feel
I had my eyes cut out by the black robes
But I know I see what's real

(repeat chorus)

Chess wondered which member of Coyote Springs most closely resembled the Cowardly Lion as they pulled into the Emerald City, Seattle. The drive from Indian John Rest Area to downtown Seattle took six hours, because the blue van refused to go more than forty miles per hour.

"This van don't want to go to Seattle, enit?" Junior asked.

"Van might be the only smart one," Chess said.

The van drove into downtown and found a Super 8 Motel, right next to the Pink Elephant Car Wash. Coyote Springs all strained their necks to look at everything: the Space Needle, the Olympic and Cascade mountains, the ocean. None of them had ever visited Seattle before, so the sheer number of people frightened them. Especially the number of white people.

"Jeez," Victor said, "no wonder the Indians lost. Look at all these whites."

Thomas parked the van at the motel, and the band climbed out.

"How many rooms should we get, Chess?" Thomas asked.

"How much money we got?"

"Not much."

"Shit," Victor said, "shouldn't those guys at the Backboard be paying for all of this anyway?"

"Yeah, they probably should," Chess said, forced to agree with Victor for the very first time.

Coyote Springs walked into the lobby and surprised the desk clerk. Up to that point, how many desk clerks had seen a group of long-haired Indians carrying guitar cases? That clerk was a white guy in his twenties, a part-time business student at the University of Washington.

"Can I help you?" the clerk asked.

"Yeah," Thomas said. "We need a couple rooms."

"And how will you be paying for your rooms?"

"With money," Victor said. "What did you think? Seashells?"

"He means cash or credit," Chess said.

"Cash, then," Victor said. "What Indian has a goddamn credit card?"

"Okay," the clerk said. "And how long do you plan on staying with us?"

"Three nights," Thomas said. "But listen, I need to use your phone and call the Backboard club. They'll be paying for our rooms."

"The Backboard?" the clerk asked. "Are you guys in a band?"

"Damn right," Victor said. "What do you think we have in these cases? Machine guns? Bows and arrows?"

"What's your name?" the clerk asked, already learning to ignore Victor.

"Coyote Springs," Thomas said.

"Coyote Springs? I haven't heard of you. Got any CDs out?"

"Not yet," Victor said. "That's why we're in Seattle. We're here to take over the whole goddamn city."

"Oh," the clerk said. "Well, here's the phone. Which one of you is the lead singer?"

"I am," Thomas said, and the clerk handed the phone to him.

As Thomas dialed the number, the rest of Coyote Springs wandered around the lobby. Junior and Chess sat on couches and watched a huge television set in one corner. Victor bought a Pepsi from a vending machine. Chess watched him. She knew that kind of stuff tickled Victor. He looked like a little kid, counted out his quarters for pop and hoped he had enough change for a Snickers bar. He just stared at all the selections like the machines offered white women and beer.

"Hey, Victor," Chess shouted. "That's a vending machine, you savage. It works on electricity."

"Hello," Thomas said into the phone. "This is Thomas Builds-the-Fire. Lead singer of Coyote Springs. Yeah. Coyote Springs. We're here for the gig tomorrow night. Yeah, that's right. We're the Indian band."

Thomas smiled at Chess to let her know everything was cool.

"Yeah, we're over at the Super 8 Motel by that Pink Elephant Car Wash. We got a couple rooms, and the clerk wondered how you were going to pay for it."

Thomas lost his smile. Chess looked around the room for it.

"I don't understand. You mean we have to pay for it ourselves? But you invited us."

Thomas listened carefully to the voice at the other end.

"Okay, okay. I see. Well, thanks. What time should we be there tomorrow?"

Thomas hung up the phone and walked over to the rest of the band.

"What's wrong?" Chess asked.

"They said we're supposed to pay for it," Thomas said.

"No fucking way," Victor said.

"What's happening?" Junior asked.

"I guess it's a contest tomorrow," Thomas said. "A lot of bands are going to be there. The winner gets a thousand dollars. The losers don't get nothing. I guess I didn't understand the invitation too well."

"What are you talking about?" Coyote Springs asked.

"It's a Battle of the Bands tomorrow. We have to play the best to get the money. Otherwise, we don't get nothing."

"Jeez," Junior said. "How many bands are there going to be?"

"Twenty or so."

"Shit," Victor said. "Let's forget that shit. Let's go home. We don't need this. We're Coyote Springs."

"We don't have enough money to get home," Thomas said.

"Fuck," Victor said. "Well, let's get the goddamn rooms ourselves and kick some ass at that contest tomorrow night."

"We don't have enough money to get the rooms and eat, too."

"Thomas," Chess said, "how much money do we have?"

"Enough to eat on. But we can't afford the rooms."

"Looks like Checkers was right in staying home," Chess said and missed her sister.

"What are we going to do?" Junior asked.

"We can sleep in the van," Thomas said, feigning confidence. "Then we go and win that contest tomorrow. A thousand bucks. We go home in style, enit?"

Coyote Springs had no other options. Thomas started the van without a word, pulled out of the motel parking lot, and searched for a supermarket. He found a Foodmart and went inside. The rest of Coyote Springs waited for Thomas. He came out with a case of Pepsi, a loaf of bread, and a package of bologna. Silently, Coyote Springs built simple sandwiches and ate them.

† † †

Checkers walked to the Catholic Church early Saturday to meet Father Arnold. She wanted to join the choir. Enough of the rock music. She needed to reserve her voice for something larger. She braided her hair, pulled on her best pair of blue jeans, red t-shirt, and white tennis shoes. Nike running shoes. Checkers always bought expensive tennis shoes, no matter how poor she was.

Go in the supermarket, Luke Warm Water had said to his daughters during one of their shopping visits to Spokane, *and get some eggs, milk, and butter. Oh, and get yourselves some tennis shoes. They're in that third aisle. Try them on first.*

Checkers and Chess slumped into the store, sat in the third aisle, and tried on tennis shoes, those supermarket shoes constructed of cheap canvas and plastic. Other shoppers, white people, stared as the Warm Waters tried on shoes; Checkers saw the pity in their eyes. *Those poor Indian kids have to buy their shoes in a supermarket.* Both sisters cried as they paid for the essential food items and those ugly shoes. Ever since her father had gone, Checkers bought the most expensive pair of shoes she found.

Those shoes felt good on her feet as Checkers walked into the church. A small church. Four walls, a few pews, an altar. Jesus crucified on the wall. Mary weeping in a corner. It felt like home. Checkers crossed herself and kneeled in a pew. She folded her hands into a prayer.

"Please," she whispered. "Let good things happen."

She lost track of time as she prayed. Amen, amen. Coyote Springs entered her mind, and she thought of her sister, tried to send a few prayers over the mountains. She felt a little guilty for leaving the band, but they played well without her. Chess sang and played the piano better than her.

"Thank you, Lord," Checkers whispered as she opened her eyes, surprised to see a priest sitting a few pews in front of her. Father Arnold.

"Hello, Father," Checkers said.

Father Arnold turned and smiled. He was a handsome man, with brown hair and blue eyes. Slightly tanned skin. Even teeth. Checkers smiled back. She believed that every priest should be a handsome man.

"Hello," Father Arnold said. "You're one of those sisters, aren't you?"

"Yes," Checkers said, thrilled. "I'm Checkers Warm Water."

"Checkers? That's an unusual name."

"Well, it's not my real name."

"What is your real name?"

"I don't think I'd even tell you that in confession."

Father Arnold stood, walked back toward Checkers, and sat beside her. He smelled like cinnamon.

"So," Father said. "How is the music business?"

"Not too good. I quit the band."

"Oh, that's too bad. Do you want to talk about it?"

"No, not really."

Checkers thought about Coyote Springs. She already missed the stage. There was something addicting about it. She loved to hear her name shouted by strangers.

"Are you interested in joining our community here?" Father Arnold asked.

"I'm thinking about it," Checkers said. "But I'm from the Flathead Reservation. Is that okay?"

"Are you confirmed?"

"Yeah. Father James over there did that. A long time ago."

Checkers swore she remembered her baptism, though she was only a few months old at the time. Sometimes, she still felt that place on her forehead where Father James poured the water. Once, while fighting fires in her teens, she found herself trapped in a firestorm. Convinced she was going to burn, she suddenly felt the cold, damp touch on her forehead. She felt the water flow down her face, into her mouth, and she drank deeply. Satiated, she

burned down a circle of grass, lay down in the middle, and lived as
the fire crowned the pine trees above her.

"So," Father Arnold said, "tell me about your faith."

"You know," Checkers said, "it's hard to talk about. I
mean, there's a lot I want to talk about."

"I'm sure."

Checkers thought about what she had seen during her brief
time with Coyote Springs. She remembered Junior and Victor
naked in the van with those two white women, Betty and
Veronica, who had disappeared soon after.

"You know," Checkers said, "two of the guys in the
band, Junior and Victor. They've been doing bad things."

"I know them. Are you here to talk about them or you?"

"Both, I guess."

Father Arnold reached for Checkers's hand and held it
gently. Her heart quickened a little.

"You can talk to me," Father Arnold said.

"It's just that everywhere I look these days, I see white
women. We caught Junior and Victor having sex with some white
women. They're always having sex with white women. It makes
me hate them."

"Hate who?"

"White women. Indian men. Both, I guess."

"Are you romantically involved with Junior or Victor?"

"Oh, God, no."

"Well, then, what is it?"

"Those white women are always perfect, you know?
When I was little and we'd go to shop in Missoula, I'd see perfect
little white girls all the time. They were always so pretty and
clean. I'd come to town in my muddy dress. It never mattered
how clean it was when we left Arlee. By the time we got to Missoula, it was always a mess."

"Did you travel with your parents?"

"Yeah, Dad drove the wagon. Can you believe that? We still had a wagon, and Dad made that thing move fast. The horses and wheels would kick up dirt and mud. Chess, my sister, and I always tried to hide under blankets, but it never worked. There'd be mud under our nails, and we'd grind mud between our teeth. There'd be dirt in the bends of our elbows and knees. Dirt and mud everywhere, you know?"

Father Arnold nodded his head.

"Anyway, all those little white girls would be so perfect, so pretty, and so white. White skin and white dresses. I'd be all brown-skinned in my muddy brown dress. I used to get so dark that white people thought I was a black girl.

"I wanted to be just like them, those white girls, and I'd follow them around town while Mom and Dad shopped. Chess was always telling me I was stupid for doing it. Chess said we were better than those white girls any day. But I never believed her."

"How does that make you feel now?" Father Arnold asked.

"I don't know. I just looked at that blond hair and blue eyes and knew I wanted to look like that. I wanted to be just like one of those white girls. You know, Father James even brought his little white nieces out to visit the reservation, and that was a crazy time."

"What happened?"

"Oh, Father James wanted us all to be friends, Chess, me, and his little nieces. So we all sat together in our folding chairs and knelt down on the floor to pray. We even got to help with the candles at mass. I remember I always held onto my candle tight, because I didn't want to drop it. I always thought flames were beautiful, you know?

"All four of us helped with Communion once. It all worked great. It was the best Communion. Then we carried the bread and wine back to the storage closet. While we were in there, those nieces pushed me over, and I dropped the wine and it spilled all over everything. On the floor, on my best dress. Everywhere. Those nieces started laughing. Me and Chess tried to clean it up. Father James came running to see what the noise was all about. When he came into the closet, those nieces started crying like babies. They told Father James that Chess and I'd been messing around and dropped the bottles. Father James really scolded Chess and me and never let us help with Communion for a long time.''

"That's a sad story," Father Arnold said.

"Yeah, it is, I guess. But his nieces could be nice, too. They let me play with their dolls sometimes. They were really good dolls, too. I taught the nieces how to climb trees and watch people walk by. I'd leave Chess at home and stand outside Father James's house and wait for his nieces to come out and play. Sometimes I waited until after dark. I'd walk home in the dark all by myself. But sometimes they came out, and we played.

"And when they left the reservation, Chess and I rode down to the train station with Father James to say goodbye. Chess really didn't want to come, but Mom and Dad made her. We stood there on the train platform, and those nieces wouldn't even look at us. They were in their perfect little white dresses. They looked like angels. I wanted to go with them. I wanted to go live in the big city. I knew I wouldn't get in the way. I'd sleep with their perfect dolls and eat crackers. I wanted to be just like them. I wanted to have everything they had. I knew if I was like them, I wouldn't have to be brown and dirty and live on the reservation and spill Communion wine.

"I wanted to be as white as those little girls because Jesus was white and blond in all the pictures I ever saw of him."

"You do know that Jesus was Jewish?" Father Arnold asked. "He probably had dark skin and hair."

"That's what they say," Checkers said. "But I never saw him painted like that. I still never see him painted like that. You know, we had to hug those little white nieces, too. We're standing there on the platform, and Father James tells us to hug each other. Chess refuses to hug anybody. But I hug those nieces, and the big one pinches my breast, my little nipple. Nobody sees it at all. It hurts so bad, and I start to cry. The nieces get on the train and leave. Father James hugs me because I'm crying. He says it will be all right, he knows how much I'll miss his nieces. I stood there in Father James's arms and cried and cried.''

Checkers cried in the little Catholic Church in Wellpinit. Father Arnold put his arms around her, and she cried into his shoulder, the soft fabric of his cassock. She put her arms around his waist, wanted to look into his eyes, but kept her face hidden.

"Checkers," he whispered. "What's going on? There must be something more. You can talk to me."

Checkers squeezed Father Arnold tighter, until her grip became uncomfortable. But he would not release her.

† † †

Coyote Springs slept fitfully in the blue van. The city frightened them, especially since the thin walls of the van barely protected them. Chess never slept much at all, hadn't slept well for two nights in a row. She sat in the driver's seat and listened to the men stir and moan in their sleep. She recognized the sounds of nightmares but only guessed at the specifics.

Junior dreamed about horses. He rode a horse along a rise above the Columbia River, leading a large group of warriors. They all wanted to attack a steamship, but the boat remained anchored beyond their range. The Indians watched it jealously.

The Indians cried in frustration. Some splashed their ponies into the river and attempted to swim out to the boat. Others fell off their horses and wept violently. Junior slumped, hugged his horse's neck, and closed his eyes. In his dream, he listened for the music. He heard bugles. Cavalry bugles.

From where? a young Indian boy asked Junior.

Junior whirled his horse, looked for the source of the bugle. Everywhere. Junior heard a gunshot, and the young Indian fell dead from his mount. Then the young Indian boy's horse was shot and fell, too. The gunshots came from all angles. The bugles increased.

Where are they? the Indian men screamed as the bullets cut them down. They fell, all of them, until only Junior remained.

Cease fire! a white voice shouted. That voice sounded so close that Junior knew he should have seen the source. But there was nothing in the dust and sunlight.

Drop your rifle! the white voice shouted.

Where are you? Junior asked.

Drop your rifle! the voice shouted again, louder, so loud that Junior dropped his rifle and clapped his hands to his ears in pain. Suddenly he was dragged from his horse by unseen hands. Thrown to the ground, kicked and beaten, Junior heard the labored breathing of the men who were beating him. He could not see anybody.

Where are you? Junior asked again, and he heard only laughter. Then the attackers began to materialize. Soldiers. White men in blue uniforms. They laughed. They spat on Junior. One soldier walked over to Junior's pony, placed a pistol carefully between its eyes, and pulled the trigger. The horse took a long time to fall.

Who are you? Junior asked in his dream.

A large soldier walked up to Junior and offered him a hand. Junior took it and got to his feet.

I'm General George Wright, the large soldier said.

Junior looked at Wright, then down at his dead horse.

You killed my pony, Junior said.

This is war, Wright replied.

A few other soldiers tied Junior's arms behind his back,

dragged him to a table, and sat him down. He sat across from Wright. No voices. Wright drummed his fingers across the table, and it echoed all over the river valley.

What are we waiting for? Junior asked.

General Sheridan, Wright said.

They waited for a long time, until an even larger white man rode up on a pale pony. The larger white man dismounted, walked over to the table, and took a seat next to Wright.

General Sheridan, the larger white man said and offered his hand to Junior. Junior looked at the hand, but his hands were tied. Sheridan smiled at his mistake and pulled out a sheet of parchment.

You've been charged with the murder of eighteen settlers this past year, Sheridan said. *How do you plead?*

Not guilty, Junior said.

Well, well, Sheridan said. *I find you guilty and sentence you to hang by the neck until you are dead.*

The soldiers pulled Junior to his feet and dragged him to the gallows. They hustled him up the stairs and fitted the noose. Junior closed his eyes in his dream. He heard a sportscaster in the distance.

Ladies and gentlemen, we're here to witness the execution of Spokane Indian warrior Junior Polatkin for murder. Eighteen murders, to be exact. Quite a total for such a young man. General Sheridan and General Wright are presiding over the hanging.

In his dream, Junior opened his eyes, and General Sheridan stood in front of him.

I can save your life, Sheridan said.

How? Junior asked.

Sign this.

What is it? Junior asked and looked at the clean, white paper in Sheridan's hand.

Just sign it, Sheridan said.

What am I signing?

Just sign it, and God will help you.

Okay.

Sheridan untied Junior's hands and gave him the pen. Junior looked at the pen and threw it away. The pen revolved and revolved. The sun rose and set; snow fell and melted. Salmon leapt twenty feet above the surface of the Columbia River, just feet from the hanging.

Do you want to say a prayer? Sheridan asked.

I don't pray like that, Junior said.

What do you do?

I sing.

Well, I think it's time for you to sing.

In his dream, Junior started his death song and was barely past the first verse when the platform dropped from under him and the rope snapped tightly.

"Shit!" Junior shouted as he woke suddenly from his dream. Victor rolled over, but Thomas woke up, too.

"What's going on?" Thomas asked, confused.

"Junior's dreaming," Chess said. "Both of you go back to sleep."

Junior flopped over and quickly snored, but Thomas rubbed his eyes and looked at Chess.

"You can't sleep, enit?" Thomas asked.

"No, I'm thinking too much," Chess said.

"About what?"

"About Checkers. About church."

"What about church?"

"Are you a Christian, Thomas?"

"No. Not really."

"Are these two Christian?"

"Junior and Victor? No way. All they know about religion they saw in *Dances with Wolves*."

"Do you pray?" Chess asked but wasn't sure what she wanted to hear. Of course Thomas prayed. Everybody prayed; everybody lied about it. Even atheists prayed on airplanes and bingo nights.

"Yeah, I pray," Thomas said and made the sign of the cross.

"What was that?"

"I'm a recovering Catholic."

"Get out of here."

"No, really. I was baptized Catholic, like most of us on the Spokane Reservation. I think even Junior and Victor are baptized Catholic."

"Those two need a whole shower of the stuff."

"Yeah, maybe. You know, I quit when I was nine. I went to church one day and found everybody burning records and books. Indians burning records and books. I couldn't believe it. Even if I was just nine."

These are the devil's tools! the white Catholic priest bellowed as his Indian flock threw books and records into the fire. Thomas figured that priests everywhere were supposed to bellow. It was part of the job description. They were never quiet, never whispered their sermons, never let silence tell the story. Even Thomas knew his best stories never found their way past his lips and teeth.

Thomas mourned the loss of those books and records. He still mourned. He had read every book in the reservation library by the time he was in fifth grade. Not a whole lot of books in that library, but Thomas read them all. Even the auto repair manuals. Thomas could not fix a car, but he knew about air filters.

Thomas! the priest bellowed again. *Come forward and help us rid this reservation of the devil's work!*

Thomas stepped forward, grabbed the first book off the top of the pile, and ran away. He ran until he could barely breathe; he ran until he found a place to hide. In the back seat of a BIA pickup, he read his stolen book: *How to Fool and Amaze Your Friends: 101 Great Tricks of the Master Magicians.*

"Jeez," Chess said. "That really happened?"

"Yeah," Thomas said. "I still got that book at home."

"That wasn't Father Arnold who did that, was it?"

"No. This happened a long time before he got to the reservation. I don't even know Father Arnold too much. I just see him around."

"Is he a nice guy?"

"Why you want to know?"

"Checkers wants to go to church there, you know? Maybe I'll start going when I get back."

"But I thought you wanted to leave the reservation if we won this contest. You still want to leave, enit?"

"I don't know. Maybe I just want Victor and Junior out of the band. I like your reservation. It's beautiful."

"You haven't seen everything," Thomas said.

† † †

Victor was a hundred miles from home. He was nine years old. He was at the Mission School for the summer. His mother and real father often sent him there for camp. Catholic summers, Catholic summers. Victor mopped the floors.

Victor missed his parents. He cried constantly for the first few weeks away from the reservation. After a while, he cried only late at night, when all the Catholic Indian boys tried to sleep in their dormitories. Victor muffled his cries in a pillow and heard the muffled cries of others.

But on that day when Victor was nine years old and mopped the floors, he lost himself in other thoughts. He remembered picking huckleberries with his family. He remembered climbing trees with his friends, other Indian boys allowed to stay on the reservation. Those Indian boys climbed the limbs off the trees every summer. Victor was still lost in his memories when the priest stormed into the room.

Victor! the priest shouted.

Victor jumped back, frightened, and knocked his bucket of water over. Even more terrified, he mopped frantically and tried to clean up that minor flood.

Stop it! the priest yelled.

Victor stopped, stood at attention, shivered.

What are you afraid of? the priest asked.

Victor was silent.

Are you afraid of God?

Victor nodded his head.

Are you afraid of me?

Victor nodded his head faster. The priest smiled and leaned down.

There's no reason to be afraid, the priest said, taking a softer tone. *Now why don't we clean up this mess together?*

Victor and the priest mopped up the water, mopped the rest of the floor clean, and put the supplies back in their places. The priest touched Victor's newly shaved head.

It's a shame we had to cut your hair, the priest said. *You are such a beautiful boy.*

Victor looked up at the priest and smiled. The priest smiled back, leaned over, and kissed Victor full and hard on the mouth.

† † †

From Checkers Warm Water's journal:

I went to see Father Arnold today and I think I fell in love. He held me closely and I held him back and I think he might love

me, too. He rubbed my back and whispered nice things to me.
No man has ever held me that gently. He listened to me. Really
listened to me. I don't even know what to think or do. I'm
afraid to breathe. I don't want to tell Chess. I don't want to tell
anybody. There's a reason I got in that fight with Victor. I
didn't know why I got so crazy at Victor. Couldn't figure out
what made me so mad. But now I know there's a reason. God
made me stay home so I could meet Father Arnold. God threw
those punches at Victor! God wanted me to meet Father
Arnold. But did God want me to fall in love with his priest? I
don't know what to do. All I know is, I still smell Father
Arnold when I close my eyes. He smells like smoke and
candles.

† † †

Coyote Springs woke, cramped and smelly, in a strange parking lot
in downtown Seattle. The blue van groaned as the band stumbled
out to stretch their backs in the cool morning mist.

"Jeez," Junior said, "what's that smell?"

"It's the ocean," Chess said. "It's wonderful, isn't it?"

"Yeah," Junior said and tried to hide his excitement. "It's
all right."

Thomas breathed deep. He tasted salt.

"So what's the plan today?" Victor asked.

"I don't know," Thomas said. "How about that Pike
Place Market. That's supposed to be cool. What do you think,
Chess?"

"Sounds good."

Everybody climbed back into the van. With Thomas as
driver and Chess as navigator, Coyote Springs soon found the market. Along the way, they noticed there were brown people in Seattle. Not everybody was white. They watched, dumbfounded, as
two men held hands and walked down the street.

"Jeez," Junior said, "look at that."

"Those men are two-spirited," Thomas said.

"They're too something or other," Victor said.

Coyote Springs parked the van and walked around the market, surprised by all of it. The market was old and beautiful, built by wood that had aged and warped. No amount of paint could change the way it looked now. There were flowers and fishmongers, old shops filled with vintage clothing and rare books. The whole market smelled like the ocean, which was just a few blocks away. Coyote Springs was even more surprised by the old Indian men there. Old drunks. Victor kept talking to them. Junior, too. Chess figured drunks talked to drunks like it was a secret club. An Indian liked to talk to anybody, especially another Indian. Chess knew those old Indians were a long way from home, trapped by this city and its freeway entrances and exits. She thought a few of those drunks looked familiar.

"Hey, nephew," one of those old Indians called to Victor. "What tribe you are?"

Indians always addressed each other intimately, even when they were strangers.

"I'm Spokane Indian, uncle," Victor said.

"Oh, yeah, huh? Had a buddy who was Spokane long time ago."

"Who was that?"

"Amos Joseph."

"That was my grandfather."

"No shit. Who you?"

"Victor Joseph."

"Hey, grandson. I'm Eddie Tap Water. Used to be Spring Water. But I'm Urban Indian now."

"Good to meet you, grandfather."

"Yeah, you, too. Where'd you get that shirt anyway? Think your grandfather wore one like that when we was dancing."

The rest of Coyote Springs listened as Victor and Eddie

traded stories, but nobody was all that surprised. The Indian world is tiny, every other Indian dancing just a powwow away. Every Indian is a potential lover, friend, or relative dancing over the horizon, only a little beyond sight. Indians need each other that much; they need to be that close, tying themselves to each other and closing their eyes against the storms.

"Goodbye, grandfather," Victor said and gave him a dollar. Victor talked to most every drunk at the market. He spent all of his time with those old Indians, while the other band members roamed together. Junior left Victor to the drunks. Chess thought those drunks scared Junior. He might have seen himself in their faces. Junior wondered if their disease was contagious. A fall-asleep-on-a-heating-grate disease. Junior was frightened.

Victor should have been frightened. Drunks had always caused him to shake before. But some voice whispered in his ear and pushed him to the old Indians in the market. As a child, each member of Coyote Springs had run from drunks. They all still ran from drunks. All Indians grow up with drunks. So many drunks on the reservation, so many. But most Indians never drink. Nobody notices the sober Indians. On television, the drunk Indians emote. In books, the drunk Indians philosophize.

Lester FallsApart, the most accomplished drunk on the Spokane Reservation, was a tribal hero. Indians run from those tough and angry drunks, but they always flock to the kindest alcoholic on the reservation. One on every reservation, one on every reservation. Everybody on the Spokane Indian Reservation loved Lester so much they showed up at his dog's wake and funeral. A couple hundred Spokanes mourned with Lester.

The market had entranced Coyote Springs and they forgot the time. The little curiosity stores and restaurants pulled them in and refused to let go. Thomas got all wrapped up in the magic store and practiced a few coin tricks.

"Jeez," Thomas said suddenly, "what time is it?"

"About five," Chess said.

"Oh, man. We're going to be late for that soundcheck at the Backboard."

"Where's Victor?"

"Shit," Junior said. "I don't know. Hanging out with those drunks somewhere.."

"Man," Thomas said, "we have to find him quick. We can't be late. They'll kick us out of the contest."

"Okay," Chess said, "let's split up. Thomas and I will look in the market, and Junior, look outside."

"We got to find him," Thomas said again and looked desperate. Coyote Springs was about to break up to search for Victor when the music started.

"Wait," Junior said. "Listen to that."

Coyote Springs listened. They heard the city, the ocean, but something else, too. They heard a beautiful voice, just barely audible. The band couldn't hear the lyrics but picked up the rhythm.

"Who is that?" Chess asked. "That's the most beautiful voice I ever heard."

Coyote Springs walked without talking, searched for the source of that voice. As they got closer, they also heard a guitar accompanying the voice. A nice, simple chord progression, but something hid behind it. Something painful and perfect.

"Shit," Chess said. "I don't believe it."

As Coyote Springs turned a corner, they discovered the magical duo: an old Indian man singer and Victor, the guitar player. In a filthy brown corduroy suit and white t-shirt, the singer looked older than dirt. But his voice, his voice. A huge crowd gathered.

"Look at all the people," Junior said.

Tourists and office workers stopped to listen to this ragged Indian version of Simon and Garfunkel. Those people who usually ignored street people threw money into the old Indian man's hat.

Chess noticed Victor was playing some shoestring guitar and figured it had to be the old man's instrument. Bandaged and bloody, the old man's hands fascinated Chess.

"Why's Victor playing with that guy?" Chess asked.

Thomas also noticed the old man's bandages. That old man could not play the guitar anymore, because he'd played it until his hands were useless. Thomas remembered Robert Johnson's hands; he felt pain in his hands in memory of Robert Johnson's guitar. *Victor's guitar now,* he said to himself.

"Jeez," Chess said. "Victor sounds pretty good on that guitar. That thing's a mess though, enit? Looks like it's made from cardboard."

The old man's guitar *was* constructed of cardboard, but the sound that rose from the strings defied its construction. Thomas watched the money fall into the old man's hat. A hundred dollars, maybe two hundred.

"Thomas, we're going to be late, remember?" Chess said.

"It can wait," Thomas said, frightened, but needing to see the end of that little story in the market.

Victor played with the old Indian man for another hour. The money fell into the hat.

"Thomas!" Chess shouted. "We need to go."

Thomas broke from his trance, rushed to Victor, stole the guitar away, and handed it back to the old man. It burned.

"We need to go," Thomas said to Victor, who briefly reached for the guitar but pulled back. The crowd jeered Thomas.

"Shit," Victor said. "What time is it?"

"After six."

"Man, we got to go."

Coyote Springs ran from the market, but Thomas looked back. The old Indian man picked up the hat full of money and smiled.

"We should've asked that old man to join the band, enit?" Junior asked.

"Maybe," Victor said, and then he smiled at Chess. He really smiled. Chess was frightened. She wanted to go home; she wanted her sister. The blue van rolled down Mercer Street, beneath the Space Needle, and found the Backboard Club. Victor strapped on his guitar, cracked his knuckles, and led the band inside.

† † †

From Thomas Builds-the-Fire's journal:
The Reservation's Ten Commandments as Given by the United States of America to the Spokane Indians

1. You shall have no other forms of government before me.

2. You shall not make for yourself an independent and self-sufficient government, for I am a jealous bureaucracy and will punish the Indian children for the sins of their fathers to the seventh generation of those who hate me.

3. You shall not misuse my name or my symbols, for I will impale you on my flag pole.

4. Remember the first of each month by keeping it holy. The rest of the month you shall go hungry, but the first day of each month is a tribute to me, and you shall receive welfare checks and commodity food in exchange for your continued dependence.

5. Honor your Indian father and Indian mother because I have stripped them of their land, language, and hearts, and they need your compassion, which is a commodity I do not supply.

6. You shall not murder, but I will bring FBI and CIA agents to your reservations and into your homes, and the most in-

telligent, vocal, and angriest members of your tribes will
vanish quietly.

7. You shall not commit adultery, but I will impregnate your
   women with illegitimate dreams.

8. You shall not steal back what I have already stolen from
   you.

9. You shall not give false testimony against any white men,
   but they will tell lies about you, and I will believe them and
   convict you.

10. You shall not covet the white man's house. You shall not
    covet the white man's wife, or his hopes and opportunities,
    his cars or VCRs, or anything that belongs to the white
    man.

† † †

Back on the reservation, Checkers fell asleep on the couch in
Thomas's house. She always slept on couches when houses were
empty. She dreamed of Father Arnold. In her dream, Father Arnold came into her bedroom in the shack in Arlee. Checkers lay
under the covers, naked.

Let me see, Father Arnold said, so Checkers pulled back her
covers.

You're such a pretty girl, Father said.

Father dropped his robe to the floor. Naked. Checkers
studied him. His penis was huge.

Can I lie with you? Father asked.

Checkers patted the sheet beside her, and Father lay down
close to her. She felt his heat, his smell. He smelled like smoke and
Communion wine.

You know I love you, Father said.

Checkers felt his penis brush against her thigh. It was so big she knew it would hurt her. Father touched her breasts, squeezed her nipples, moved his hand down her stomach.

I won't hurt you, Father said. *Not ever.*

Father kissed Checkers gently, flicked his tongue between her teeth. Her jaw ached as he forced her mouth open wider and wider. He tasted strange, old, musty. She cried out as he forced her legs apart.

I forgive you, Father said.

Checkers held her breath as Father climbed between her legs and entered her roughly.

Yes, I forgive you, Father whispered inside her.

† † †

From a live interview on KROK, Seattle's best rock:

Hello, this is Adam the Original, your favorite D.J. in Seattle for six years straight, coming to you live from the Backboard in the shadow of the Space Needle. Tonight, as you all know, was the Tenth Annual Battle of the Bands. After thirty acts, the judges chose a winner. And it's a shocker, folks. The best band tonight happened to be a bunch of Spokane Indians from the Spokane Reservation on the other side of the mountain. The name of the band is Coyote Springs, of all things, and I have with me the lead singer, Thomas Builds-the-Fire. Now, Thomas, tell me about yourself.

Like you said, I'm a Spokane Indian from the Spokane Indian Reservation. I play bass guitar and share vocals with Chess Warm Water. She's a Flathead Indian from Montana, not Spokane.

I've talked to some people here tonight who said they've seen quite a few of your shows. They were really impressed. You're not just a

cover band, are you? When did you make the decision to play orig-inal material? And who writes your songs?
Well, we started out as a cover band. But it was sort of weird, enit? We covered great stuff, like Aretha Franklin and Alex Chilton, but none of those songs were Indian, you know? I mean, some of those songs we covered should've been written by Indians, but they weren't. So I decided to write some songs myself. I write all the songs now. But I was wondering who heard of us before. We mostly played on the reservations. I didn't see no Indians here tonight.

A couple people mentioned they saw you. But seriously, how does songwriting make you feel?
Good.

I've noticed that you had two white women singing backup for the band tonight. That seemed sort of unusual. How do you think other Indians look at that? And how do you think it affects your sound?
I don't even know those women all that well. They were waiting for us when we got here. I've seen them before though. They've been following us for a while, way back on the reservation even, then in Montana. I caught Junior and Victor, the drummer and lead guitarist, all naked with them a while back. They sound really good, enit? We took a quick vote to see if they would sing with us, and the vote was 2–2. So we flipped a coin, and the white women were in. It's kind of tough, though. They only sang backup be-cause they're sleeping with Junior and Victor. I don't know how it affected the music. But we won, didn't we? I don't know what Indian people will think about those white women. But hey, an Indian woman invented the blues a day before Columbus landed, and rock 'n' roll the

next day. We're not stealing those white women or stealing the music. It's not like we're all white because we have
white women in the band.

*Well, if nothing else, the irony is incredible, isn't it? And I was
wondering who voted against the white women. And what are the
white women's names?*
Chess and I voted against them. And their names are Betty
and Veronica.

Really?
Really.

How would you assess their relationship with Junior and Victor?
I'm not like a therapist or something. But I don't think it
has much of a chance. I mean, I think they're all using each
other as trophies. Junior and Victor get to have beautiful
white women on their arms, and Betty and Veronica get to
have Indian men.

*Do you think you could elaborate on that? Our listeners out there
in the rock world would love to know.*
Jeez, I just realized. Them two are the ones who saw us
play before. They must really be following us around. That
Betty and Veronica. Man. They are beautiful, enit?

*Yes, they are. But what do Betty and Veronica have to gain in all
of this?*
Look at them. They got more Indian jewelry and junk on
than any dozen Indians. The spotlights hit the crystals on
their necks and nearly blinded me once. All they talk about
is Coyote this and Coyote that, sweatlodge this and sweatlodge that. They think Indians got all the answers.

How long do you think that relationship will last?
Until the next slow song.

Well, I don't know when that's going to be. That Victor plays a wicked guitar. I've never actually seen a guitar set a table on fire, though. It's a good thing that Chess had fire safety training, isn't it?

We almost lost the whole damn thing because Victor got drunk. How did you know Chess had fire experience?

An amateur would never have put a fire out that quickly. Forgive me for asking, but I noticed that you and Chess seem to have a close relationship.

Jeez, getting personal, enit? She's my partner. We're in love, I guess. No. We are in love. She's pretty amazing. I write songs for her, you know. She's the first Indian woman who ever paid me much attention. That's something special.

Well, I think you'll be getting a lot of attention from all kinds of women now. Especially white women.

I don't need that.

Well, I hope that's true. I also heard that Chess has a sister who used to be in the band. Is that true?

Yeah, Checkers, her sister, stayed home on the reservation. She wants to sing in the church choir instead. They're both Catholic women, you know?

Don't you think that's odd?

I don't think it's odd at all. I mean, I think God loves to dance as much as the rest of us. I think we'd all be better off if we put more rock music into our churches. Chess told me that God is a long ways up, and we need to be loud so God can hear us. What's louder than rock 'n' roll?

Do you believe in God?

Yeah, I do.

Do you believe in the devil?
I don't know. I'm beginning to. Seems there's more proof of the devil than proof of God, enit?

Is God a man or a woman?
God could be an armadillo. I have no idea.

† † †

Checkers stood in the back row of the choir; she was much taller than all the altos, baritones, and sopranos. She was taller than everybody in the church and wondered if Spokane Indian Catholics were short by nature. Easily distracted by the details, she tried to concentrate on the service. Father Arnold led the service with intensity and passion, like he was more Baptist than Catholic. Most priests just went through the motions, recited platitudes by rote, and turned Communion into a Sunday brunch.

"Let us pray together now," Father Arnold said, "in the words Our Father gave us."

Checkers held the hands of the choir members on either side of her, Nina and Maria Christopher. Checkers always loved this part most, the Lord's Prayer, the holding of hands, the circling of the community. She recited the prayer and watched Father Arnold. He glanced around the church, made eye contact with his flock, and smiled.

"Let us now offer each other a sign of peace," Father Arnold said.

"Peace be with you."
"Peace be with you."
"Peace, sister."
"Peace, brother."

The members of the choir hugged as they offered peace to each other. Nina and Maria hugged Checkers, but she held the hugs way past the comfort level of the Christophers.

"Peace to all of you," Father Arnold said, outside the ceremony, and the community responded.

"Peace be with you."

Father Arnold sang his prayers. A beautiful voice. Checkers wondered if he ever sang in a band. Maybe in college. He almost had soul. Catholics were supposed to save souls, not possess them.

"This is the body, this is the blood."

Checkers greedily took Communion, happy to be one of the first. She opened her mouth, offered it to Father Arnold, who placed the bread gently on her tongue. She felt his fingertips, smelled his soft cologne. The ritual, the ritual. She smiled at Father, who smiled back, then looked past her.

"Amen."

Checkers stepped past the Communion wine, though she still smelled the alcohol. She fought back memories of her father's breath after he came home from a long night of drinking.

Checkers? Little one? Are you awake?

Checkers returned to her place in the choir. She hummed the hymn softly because she had forgotten the words. Beautiful, she felt beautiful in her twenty-year-old robe. The fringe was gone, the colors faded, but she knew how beautiful she was. Father Arnold had complimented her before mass.

"Checkers," he said, "you look very nice."

She held those words in her pocket, hidden beneath her robe, and often reached under to touch them. She closed her eyes and let the music enter her body. The organ was older than the church itself and sounded like a train, but that made no difference to Checkers. She just wanted the music to be loud.

"Before we go today, I wanted to make a few announcements," Father Arnold said.

Checkers wanted the service to continue.

"We have a new member of the congregation," Father Arnold said. "She's a new arrival on our reservation, Checkers

Warm Water. Some of you may know her as a member of Coyote Springs, but now she's the newest member of our choir.''

Father Arnold motioned for Checkers to raise her hand. She waved to the church, and they all waved back. Polite applause and a few shouted greetings. Embarrassed, Checkers ducked her head and closed her eyes. She thought the Catholics were celebrating a new member, but they were actually relieved that she had been saved from the hell called Coyote Springs.

"Also, I want you to remember that we have a potluck dinner Tuesday night, right after the elders' meeting. And Bessie, you remember to bring your fry bread.''

The crowd cheered. Bessie Moses had taken third place in the fry bread cook-off for the last ten years, finishing behind only Big Mom and the-man-who-was-probably-Lakota all that time. Since Big Mom and the-man-who-was-probably-Lakota weren't members of the church, Bessie cooked the best Catholic fry bread on the reservation.

"One last thing,'' Father Arnold said. "I know it's really early, but basketball practice starts next week. Wednesday. I'm taking signatures. Remember, we only have room for ten players. We need to start practice early this fall. The Presbyterians and Assembly of God really kicked our butts last year. And remember, no matter what you see on television, God really doesn't care if we win this or not. So, we have to do it by ourselves.''

The Spokane Indian Christian Basketball Tournament was held every November at the Tribal Community Center. The Assembly of God had won the tourney every year since its inception. Last year, the Assemblies had beaten the Catholics 126–105 in a run-and-gun shooting match. The Presbyterians had played a stall game and beat the Catholics 42–30.

"Now, I want you all to go out there, go into the community, and serve God,'' Father Arnold said.

The congregation applauded and quickly filed out of the

church. Catholics exited churches faster than any other denomination, but Checkers took her time because she wanted to have a few minutes alone with Father Arnold. The church was completely empty when Checkers finally came out of the dressing room.

"Checkers," Father Arnold said. "I was wondering what happened to you."

"I was changing," Checkers said.

"Don't change. I like you just the way you are."

Checkers laughed too loudly at his little joke.

"You did really well today," Father Arnold said.

"So did you. But I forgot some of the words to the hymns. It's been a while."

"Yeah, well, things will get better. I have faith in you."

"Thanks."

Checkers played with the hem of her t-shirt.

"Well," she said, "I should get going. The band is coming home tonight. I need to clean up the house."

"Okay, I'll see you next Sunday, right?"

"Yeah, and maybe my sister, too."

"That would be wonderful."

Checkers looked at Father Arnold. He smiled. She kissed him quickly on the cheek and ran away. Father Arnold watched her run, touched his cheek, and smiled.

† † †

Father Arnold fell to the couch in his study, exhausted because of the insomnia he suffered the night before services. On the couch, he closed his eyes and dreamed. In his dream, he stood in front of a huge congregation of Indians. He had come to save them all, his collar starched and bleached so white that it blinded, and was so powerful that he had a red phone at the altar that was a direct line to God.

Listen to me, Father Arnold said, but the Indians ignored him. They talked among themselves, laughed at secret jokes. Some even prayed in their own languages, in their own ways. Eagle feathers raised to the ceiling, pipes smoked, sweetgrass and sage burned.

Please, Father Arnold said, but the Indians continued to ignore him. He preached for hours without effect. He eventually tired and sat in a pew beside an old Indian woman. Suddenly, the church doors opened, and the local missionaries, Marcus and Narcissa Whitman, walked in with black boxes in their arms.

The Indians were silent.

The Whitmans walked to the front of the church, bowed to Father Arnold, then turned to the congregation.

Children, the Whitmans said, *you shall listen to Father and believe.*

Each placed a hand on a black box, and the Indians sat at attention.

You may continue with your sermon, the Whitmans said to Father Arnold.

Father Arnold hesitated, then stood and preached. The Indians' emotions swayed with his words. Whenever an Indian's mind wandered, Marcus and Narcissa threatened to open the black boxes, and the rebellious calmed.

Father Arnold loved his newfound power, although it was the Protestant missionaries who were responsible for it. He delivered the best sermon ever, and he heard God's cash register ring as it added up all the Indian souls saved. But those black boxes distracted Father Arnold. They kept the Indians quiet, but he wondered why. He was curious about them and jealous of the Whitmans' secret power over the Indians.

Amen.

After the sermon ended, the Indians left quietly and respectfully. Father Arnold turned to the Whitmans.

What's in those black boxes?

Faith.

Show me.

The Whitmans opened the boxes. Father Arnold expected to see jewels, locks of hair, talismans, but discovered nothing.

They're empty.

Of course.

What do you mean?

We told the Indians the boxes contained smallpox, and if we opened them, the disease would kill them.

Why would you do something like that?

It's the only way to get them to listen. And you saw how well it works. They listened to you.

But it's wrong. We should teach through love.

Don't be such a child. Religion is about fear. Fear is just another word for faith, for God.

Father Arnold looked at the empty black boxes. In his dream, he stared at them for days, until the boxes closed tight.

Wait, Father Arnold said and noticed the Whitmans were gone, replaced by two Indian women who held the boxes.

These are for you, the Indian women said.

What's in them?

We don't know.

† † †

With a thousand dollars in prize money, Coyote Springs made the trek from Seattle back to the Spokane Indian Reservation. Thomas drove from Seattle to Moses Lake, and Chess drove the rest of the way. Junior and Victor slept the whole time. Betty and Veronica, the new white women backup singers, slept beside Junior and Victor.

"So," Chess asked Thomas as the blue van crossed the reservation border, "are you coming to church Sunday?"

"I don't know. It's been a long time," Thomas said.

"What's that Father Arnold like?"

"He seems pretty nice. He's always hanging around the Trading Post and stuff."

Thomas looked at Chess, looked at the pine trees outside the car window. He looked at the highway, at the deer continually threatening to cross in front of the van.

"Checkers probably has a crush on him by now," Chess said.

"On who?" Thomas asked.

"On Father Arnold."

"Really?"

"Yeah. She always does that. She had a crush on the guy who delivered our mail back home. She stays away from young guys but always gets crushes on older guys, you know?"

They drove for a while in silence.

"You haven't answered my question," Chess said.

"Which question?" Thomas asked.

"Will you go to church with me Sunday?"

Thomas closed his eyes, searched for the answer, and opened them again.

"How can you go to a church that killed so many Indians?" Thomas asked.

"The church does have a lot to atone for," Chess said.

"When's that going to happen."

"At the tipiflap to heaven, I guess."

"I don't know if I can wait that long. Besides, how do we know they're going to pay for it? Maybe we got it all backwards and you get into heaven because of hate."

"You have to have faith."

"But what about Hitler and Ted Bundy? How do you explain George Bush and George Custer? If God were good, why would he create Rush Limbaugh?"

"Sometimes the devil is easier to believe in, enit?"

"Really. How do you explain all of that? How do you explain all of the murdered Indians?"

The van rolled on.

"How do you explain Gandhi and Mother Theresa?" Chess asked. "How do you explain Crazy Horse and Martin Luther King? There's good and bad in the world. We all get to make the choice. That's one of the mysteries of faith."

"Now you sound like Agatha Christie," Thomas said.

"Yeah, and it was God whodunnit."

"Who done what?"

"God created all of this. I mean, how can you look at all of this, all this life, and not believe in God? Look at this reservation. It's so pretty. Do you think the river and the trees are mistakes? Do you think everything is accidental?"

"No," Thomas said, looked at his hands, at the reservation as it rushed by. He loved so much. He loved the way a honey bee circled a flower. Simple stuff, to be sure, but what magic. A flower impressed Thomas more than something like the Grand Coulee Dam. Once he'd stood on the dam for hours and stared at a nest some bird built atop an archway. Thomas looked into himself. He knew his stories came from beyond his body and mind, beyond his tiny soul.

Thomas closed his eyes and told Chess this story: "We were both at Wounded Knee when the Ghost Dancers were slaughtered. We were slaughtered at Wounded Knee. I know there were whole different tribes there, no Spokanes or Flatheads, but we were still somehow there. There was a part of every Indian bleeding in the snow. All those soldiers killed us in the name of God, enit? They shouted 'Jesus Christ' as they ran swords through our bellies. Can you feel the pain still, late at night, when you're trying to sleep, when you're praying to a God whose name was used to justify the slaughter?

"I can see you running like a shadow, just outside the body

of an Indian woman who looks like you, until she was shot by an eighteen-year-old white kid from Missouri. He jumps off the horse, falls on her and you, the Indian, the shadow. He cuts and tears with his sword, his hands, his teeth. He ate you both up like he was a coyote. They all ate us like we were mice, rabbits, flightless birds. They ate us whole.''

Thomas opened his eyes and saw Chess was crying.

"I'm sorry," he said.

"Don't you understand that God didn't kill any of us?" Chess asked. "Jesus didn't kill any of us."

"But they allowed it to happen, enit?"

"They didn't allow it to happen. It just happened. Those soldiers made the choice. The government made the choice. That's free will, Thomas. We all get to make the choice. But that don't mean we all choose good."

"But there's so much evil in the world."

"That's why we have to believe in the good. Not every white person wants to kill Indians. You know most any white who joins up with Indians never wants to leave. It's always been that way. Everybody wants to be an Indian."

"That's true," a voice whispered from the back of the van.

"Who's that?" Thomas and Chess asked.

"It's me, Betty."

"What's true?" Chess asked, irritated at the interruption.

"White people want to be Indians. You all have things we don't have. You live at peace with the earth. You are so wise."

"You've never met Lester FallsApart, have you?" Chess asked. "You've never spent a few hours in the Powwow Tavern. I'll show you wise and peaceful."

"I'm sorry I said anything," Betty said and remained quiet. The other white woman, Veronica, took Betty's hand, squeezed it, and sent a question along her skin: *What are we doing?* Victor and Junior snored away.

"Like I was saying, everybody wants to be an Indian. But not everybody is an Indian. It's an exclusive club. I certainly couldn't be Irish. Why do all these white people think they can be Indian all of a sudden?"

Thomas smiled.

"You know," he said, "I've always had a theory that you ain't really Indian unless, at some point in your life, you didn't want to be Indian."

"Good theory," Chess said. "I'm the one who told you that."

"Oh," he said.

The blue van crossed the Wellpinit city limit.

"Thomas," Chess said, "you know there ain't no such thing as an Indian atheist. And besides, how do you think Indians survived all the shit if there wasn't a God who loved us? Why do you think you and me are together?"

"Because of love."

"That's what faith is. Love."

Thomas was nervous, sweating. He closed his eyes, searched for another one of his stories, but came back to Chess's words instead. He listened to her story.

"Okay," Thomas said. "I'll go to church with you. But I ain't promising nothing."

"Hey," Chess said, "don't make me any promises. I'm an Indian. I haven't heard many promises I believed anyway."

The blue van pulled into Thomas's driveway. Checkers stood in a window. All the house lights blazed brightly in the reservation night. Junior and Victor rolled over in their sleep, only momentarily bothered by the lights and noise, while Betty and Veronica pretended to sleep. Chess jumped out of the van and ran for her sister. Thomas watched Chess and Checkers hug in his front yard. Then he closed his eyes and left them alone.

6

Falling Down and Falling Apart

I know a woman, Indian in her bones
Who spends the powwow dancing all alone
She can be lonely, sometimes she can cry
And drop her sadness into the bread she fries

I know a woman, Indian in her eyes
Full-blood in her heart, full-blood when she cries
She can be afraid, sometimes she can shake
But her medicine will never let her break

chorus:
But she don't want a warrior and she don't want no brave
And she don't want a renegade heading for an early grave
She don't need no stolen horse, she don't need no stolen heart
She don't need no Indian man falling down and falling apart

I know a woman, Indian in her hands
Wanting me to sing, wanting me to dance
She's out there waiting, no matter the weather
I'd walk through lightning just to give her a feather

(repeat chorus)

Robert Johnson sat in a rocking chair on Big Mom's front porch. Big Mom's rocking chair. He had no idea where she had gone. Big Mom was always walking away without warning.

"Robert," Big Mom had said upon his arrival at her house, "you're safe here. Ain't nobody can take you away from this house."

But Johnson was still not comfortable in his safety. He dreamed of that guitar he had left in Thomas Builds-the-Fire's blue van. He couldn't decide if he had left it there on purpose. Certainly, he had tried to leave it behind before, on trains, in diners, on the roadside. He buried that guitar, he threw it in rivers, dropped it off tall buildings. But it always came back to him.

Sometimes, the guitar took weeks to find him. Those were glorious days. Johnson was free to wander and talk to anybody he wished. He never searched for the Gentleman's eyes hidden behind a stranger's face. The Gentleman was just a ghost, just a small animal dashing across the road. When that guitar was gone, Johnson had even considered falling in love. But the guitar would eventually find him. It always found him.

Johnson had to work the minimum jobs, washing dishes, sweeping floors, delivering pizzas, because he could never play music for money. Never again. And just when he began to allow himself hope, he would come home from his latest job to find that guitar, all shiny and new, on the bed in his cheap downtown apartment. Johnson had wept every time. He had considered burying himself, throwing himself into the river, jumping off a tall building. That guitar made him crazy. But he didn't know what would

be waiting on the other side. What if he woke up on the other side
with that guitar wrapped in his arms? What if it weighed him down
like an anchor as he sank to the bottom, a single chord echoing in
his head over and over again?

That guitar would never let Johnson go, until he left it in
Thomas Builds-the-Fire's blue van. Johnson felt free and guilty at
the same time. The guitar would never let go of those Indians now.
It held onto Victor even harder than it ever held Johnson.

Robert Johnson rocked in Big Mom's chair and studied his
hands, scarred and misshapen. All the wounds had healed, but he
could still feel the itching deep down. The itch that can never be
scratched. Sometimes he missed the guitar. Johnson closed his eyes
against the tears and opened his mouth to sing:

Mmmmm mmmm
I's up this mornin'
Ah, blues walkin' like a man
I's up this mornin'
Ah, blues walkin' like a man
Worried blues
Give me your right hand

Then the music stopped. The reservation exhaled. Those
blues created memories for the Spokanes, but they refused to
claim them. Those blues lit up a new road, but the Spokanes pulled
out their old maps. Those blues churned up generations of anger
and pain: car wrecks, suicides, murders. Those blues were ancient,
aboriginal, indigenous.

In his bed, Thomas Builds-the-Fire had recognized Robert
Johnson's voice as those blues drifted down from Big Mom's
mountain. But Thomas also heard something hidden behind the
words. He heard Robert Johnson's grandmother singing backup.
Thomas closed his eyes and saw that grandmother in some tattered
cabin. No windows, blanket for a door, acrid smoke. Johnson's

grandmother was not alone in that cabin. Other black men, women, and children sang with her. The smell of sweat, blood, and cotton filled the room. Cotton, cotton. Those black people sang for their God; they sang with joy and sorrow. The white men in their big houses heard those songs and smiled. *Those niggers singin' and dancin' again,* those white men thought. *Damn music don't make sense.*

Thomas listened closely, but the other Spokanes slowly stretched their arms and legs, walked outside, and would not speak about any of it. They buried all of their pain and anger deep inside, and it festered, then blossomed, and the bloom grew quickly.

† † †

From <u>The Wellpinit Rawhide Press:</u>
Open Letter to the Spokane Tribe
Dear Tribal Members,
As you all know, Coyote Springs, our local rock band, has just returned from Seattle with two white women. They are named Betty and Veronica, of all things. I'm beginning to seriously wonder about Coyote Springs's ability to represent the Spokane Tribe.

First of all, they are drunks. Victor and Junior are such drunks that even Lester FallsApart thinks they drink too much. Second, the two Indian women in the band are not Spokanes. They are Flathead. I've always liked our Flathead cousins, but Coyote Springs is supposedly a Spokane Indian band. We don't even have to talk about the problems caused by the white women.

I know the band was great when it started. I even went to a couple of their practices in Irene's Grocery, but things have gotten out of hand. We have to remember that Coyote Springs travels to a lot of places as a representative of the Spokane Tribe. Do we really want other people to think we are like this band? Do we really want people to think that the Spokanes are a crazy storyteller, a couple of irresponsible drunks, a pair of Flathead Indians, and two white women? I don't think so.

Rumor has it that Checkers Warm Water has quit the band and joined the Catholic Church Choir. We can only hope the rest of the band follows her. They could all use God.

Sincerely,
David WalksAlong
Spokane Tribal Council Chairman

† † †

Nervous and frightened, Thomas walked with Chess and Checkers to church early Sunday morning. He wondered if the Catholics had installed a faith detector at the door, like one of those metal detectors in an airport. The alarms would ring when he walked through the church doors.

"Thanks for coming," Chess said.

Thomas smiled but said nothing and fought the urge to run away.

"Yeah," Checkers said. "This will be great."

When the trio came within sight of the Catholic Church, Thomas was suddenly angry. He remembered how all those Indians bowed down to a little white man in Rome.

"Chess," Thomas said, "no matter what, I ain't ever going to listen to that Pope character."

"Why should you? I don't."

Father Arnold greeted Thomas, Chess, and Checkers at the door. He shook their hands, touched their shoulders, made eye contact that felt like a spiritual strip search.

"Checkers," Father Arnold said, "I'm so happy to see you again. And this must be your sister, Chess. And Thomas, of course. Welcome."

Thomas waved weakly.

"Well," Father Arnold said, "I'm so glad you've all come. I certainly hope you're considering joining our little community. Maybe you'll even sing in the choir?"

"Maybe," Thomas said and looked to Chess and Checkers for help. Checkers stared at Father Arnold and failed to notice Thomas's distress. Chess smiled back at Thomas and grabbed his hand. She held it tightly as they made their way into the church and found seats. Checkers went to the dressing room to change into her choir robe. Father Arnold shook hands up to the front of the church.

"Are you okay?" Chess asked.

Thomas nodded his head and pulled at the collar of his shirt. The church was hot, and he grew dizzier by the second. He nearly fainted as Father Arnold began the service. After all those years, Thomas still remembered the words to all the prayers and whispered along, more by habit than faith. Chess whispered beside him, and he loved the sound of their harmony.

"Lord, hear our prayer."

Checkers sang loudly in the choir. Thomas watched her closely. She watched Father Arnold.

"You're right about her," Thomas whispered to Chess. "She's nuts about him."

"Enit?" Chess said. "I told you so."

Thomas wished for a glass of water as Father Arnold began the homily. At first, Thomas followed the words, something about redemption, but his vision soon faded. He had never felt this way before. When he opened his eyes again, he was in a different, darker place.

*

Thomas, Father Arnold said, although Thomas knew the priest was still back in the church. *Thomas, why are you here?*

Thomas shook his head, tried to wake up, but felt the heat increase instead. He closed his eyes inside his dream, opened them again, and found himself in a sweatlodge. Inside there, it was too dark to see, but Thomas knew the smell and feel of a sweatlodge. He could also sense the presence of others inside the lodge.

The next brother, please, a voice said out of the darkness.

Thomas knew he was supposed to pray next. He could pray silently, and that would be respected. He could pray aloud, scream and cry, and that would be understood. If he sang, his brothers in the sweatlodge would sing with him.

Brothers, Thomas said, *I don't have any traditional songs. I don't even know if I belong here. I don't know if anybody belongs in here. People are listening to us pray. They have come into the sweatlodge to steal from us. We have to keep our songs private and hidden. There is somebody in here now who would steal from us. I can smell him.*

Somebody splashed water on the hot rocks in the middle of the sweatlodge. Steam rose; quiet laughter drifted. Thomas could barely breathe. He saw images of people just beyond his vision, heard strange voices, felt the rustle of an animal beside him. That animal brushed against Thomas and drew blood.

All my relations, Thomas cried out, and the door was opened.

Thomas, a feral voice cried out as Thomas escaped from the sweatlodge. He ran past the campfire, heard the animal crashing through the underbrush behind him. The smell, the smell. He tripped, fell for an immeasurable time, and woke up suddenly in the Catholic Church in Wellpinit.

"Welcome back," Chess said to Thomas as he opened his eyes. "I didn't think Catholics were that boring."

Thomas shook his head, shrugged his shoulders.

"Peace," Chess said as she left the pew.

"Peace," Thomas said at her back.

"Peace be with you," an old Indian woman said to Thomas, but he heard *pleased to meet you.*

"Pleased to meet you, too," he said.

The old woman looked puzzled, then smiled.

"You're that Builds-the-Fire, enit?" she asked.

"Yeah."

"I'm glad to see you here. I'm glad you quit that band. That rock and roll music is sinful."

Thomas nodded his head blankly.

"I can't tell you how happy we were to see that Checkers in here last week. She was saved, she was saved. Now, you've come and her sister, too. People were starting to talk, you know?"

The old Indian woman knelt in the pew. Thomas knelt, with no idea where Chess had gone. Then he saw her with the Communion wafers. Father Arnold worked quickly.

"This is the body, this is the blood. This is the body, this is the blood. This is the body, this is the blood."

"What are people saying about us?" Thomas asked the old woman.

"The Christians don't like your devil's music. The traditionals don't like your white man's music. The Tribal Council don't like you're more famous than they are. Nobody likes those white women with you. We spit in their shadows. We don't want them here."

"But what about Father Arnold? He's white."

"He's a good white man. Those women in your band are trouble."

"But everybody liked us before."

"Before you left the reservation, before you left."

The old woman rose to receive Communion, and Thomas followed her down the aisle. Checkers sang the Communion hymn wonderfully. Thomas knew she had to rejoin the band. Coyote Springs needed two Indian women, not two white women. If Checkers rejoined, Betty and Veronica could be voted out by a majority. Thomas had felt the change in the reservation air but ignored it. At the two rehearsals they'd held since they returned from Seattle, only Lester FallsApart had shown up.

"But we still live here," Thomas said to the old woman.

"But you left. Once is enough."

The old woman opened her mouth to take Communion; Thomas offered his cupped hands. Father Arnold placed the wafer gently in Thomas's hands.

"Amen," Thomas whispered, palmed the wafer, and pretended to eat it. He walked back to his pew but discovered that the old Indian woman had gone. He searched for some evidence of her but found nothing. He knelt in the pew again, made a quick sign of the cross. Then he ran outside, crumbled the wafer into pieces, and let it fall to the earth. The reservation swallowed those pieces hungrily. Not sure why he even took the Communion wafer in the first place, Thomas felt the weight of God, the reservation, and all the stories between.

† † †

Victor and Junior staggered into the Trading Post just a few minutes after the Catholic Church bells rang for the second time that morning. Both had been continually drunk since they returned from Seattle, spending their $200 prize money quickly and efficiently. They were rapidly depleting Betty's and Veronica's cash, too. The-man-who-was-probably-Lakota watched Junior and Victor and shook his head. He also noticed the two white women and offered them a silent prayer.

"Ladies and gentlemen!" Victor shouted. "Elvis is dead. Long live me!"

Victor and Junior stumbled around the Trading Post and searched for the beer cooler. Betty and Veronica gave up and walked back outside.

"What the hell are we doing here?" Veronica asked Betty.

"I don't know."

The white women had left their car in a garage in Seattle. They knew the price to get out rose a little higher with every hour that passed.

"The end of the world is near!" shouted the-man-who-was-probably-Lakota.

"We know," Betty and Veronica said.

Inside the Trading Post, Michael White Hawk watched Victor and Junior stumble up and down the aisles.

"Dose fuckers think they cool," White Hawk said to a loaf of bread as Victor and Junior finally found the beer cooler. They celebrated their discovery and pulled out a case of cheap beer.

"Do we got enough?" Junior asked.

"Enough's enough," Victor said.

"What the hell's that mean?"

"Don't know."

Junior and Victor pooled their change and carried their beer to the cashier.

"We got enough, enit?" Victor asked.

"No sales tax, remember?" Junior said.

They paid for their booze, made their way outside, and shielded their eyes against the sudden sunlight. Michael White Hawk followed them, took advantage of the opportunity, and knocked the beer from Junior's and Victor's arms. A few cans split open and beer fountained out.

"Shit," Victor said. "What's wrong with you?"

"Fuckers!" White Hawk screamed. "Thinkin' you better than us 'cause you fuckin' white women. You ain't shit."

"I ain't shit?" Victor said. "You ain't shit."

Junior picked up a beer can and popped it open.

"Jeez, Michael," Junior said and offered him the can. "If you want a beer, just ask for one."

"Don't want shit from you," Michael said and knocked the beer from Junior.

A crowd gathered suddenly, because people always circle around a potential fight quickly. Betty and Veronica joined the circle, frightened and excited.

"Make them stop," Betty shouted, but nobody paid much attention to her.

"Come on," White Hawk said. "Goin' kick your ass."

"Fuck you," Junior and Victor harmonized.

White Hawk rushed them and knocked both to the ground. He kicked and stomped on Junior and Victor, who were too drunk to fight back. They just curled into fetal balls and waited for it to end. The crowd cheered. A few rooted openly for White Hawk; most celebrated the general violence of it all. Betty and Veronica attacked White Hawk, clawed and punched, but he fought them off. He threw Betty against the phone booth; he backhanded Veronica and broke her nose. White Hawk was blind with rage. He might have beat the shit out of everybody, but the-man-who-was-probably-Lakota stepped through a gap in the crowd and cold-cocked him with a stray two-by-four.

"Jeez," said one of the Android brothers to the-man-who-was-probably-Lakota. "The end of the world is upside White Hawk's head, enit?"

"The end of the world wasn't supposed to start here. Not with me."

The Tribal Police and Emergency Medical Technicians showed up an hour later. The Indian EMTs stuffed Victor, Junior, and White Hawk into the same ambulance and transported them to Spokane for medical attention. All three were unconscious and had concussions. Betty and Veronica were treated on the spot. Betty held a cold pack to her bruised back, while Veronica had two Kleenexes stuffed up her nostrils. She refused to let anybody take her anywhere.

"What the fuck are we doing here?" Veronica asked Betty.

"I don't know," Betty said.

The Tribal Police dispersed the crowd and then went into the Trading Post for lunch. Coffee and microwave chili.

The ambulance ride was an adventure. White Hawk woke up and tried to continue the fight, but the EMT with braids smacked him with an oxygen tank. Reservation emergency medical training covered a lot of situations. White Hawk was bleeding from two head wounds when they pulled into the hospital.

"What happened here?" the emergency room doctor asked the EMT with braids.

"Car wreck," the EMT lied. He had his orders handed down directly from the Tribal Council. The Council always tried to keep white people's laws off the reservation. White Hawk had violated his parole by fighting, but the Council was more interested in maintaining tribal sovereignty than in putting him back in a white jail. Besides, Victor and Junior were drunk, and drunk Indians usually had a way of avoiding serious injury. Above all, White Hawk was Dave WalksAlong's nephew, and that counted for everything.

"Shit," the doctor said. "Car wrecks are an Olympic sport for you Indians."

"Bronze medals all around," the EMT said. "These three lived."

The nurses sterilized and bandaged the Spokanes, kept them overnight for observation, and ignored them until check-out.

"You guys weren't in any car wreck," the white doctor said to the three Spokanes before they were sent back to the reservation.

White Hawk was sentenced only to a few weeks in Tribal

Jail. Junior and Victor moved into Thomas's house the day after they returned to the reservation, because White Hawk's buddies had ransacked their house and stole all the furniture.

"Men with concussions should not sleep on floors," Victor said as he plopped down on the couch in Thomas's house. Junior just lay down in the corner, holding his aching head.

Minutes after Junior and Victor returned from the hospital, Betty and Veronica packed up their bags and waited outside for a ride to Spokane. Thomas stood outside his house with the white women and considered moving, too. He didn't want to live with his lead guitarist and drummer.

"Where the hell you two going?" Chess asked.

"Wherever," Betty said.

"Listen," Veronica said, "we just want a ride to Spokane. We'll catch a Greyhound back home to Seattle. It's nuts here."

"Jeez," Chess said, "I thought you wanted some of our wisdom."

"We didn't want it to be like this," Veronica said. "How were we supposed to know? Everybody always spits on our shadows. What the hell does that mean? I mean, we're walking down the street, minding our own business, and an old Indian woman spits on our shadows. What the hell is that?"

"What?" Chess asked. "Can't you handle it? You want the good stuff of being Indian without all the bad stuff, enit? Well, a concussion is just as traditional as a sweatlodge."

"This isn't what we wanted."

"What did you New Agers expect? You think magic is so easy to explain? You come running to the reservations, to all these places you've decided are sacred. Jeez, don't you know *every* place is sacred? You want your sacred land in warm places with pretty views. You want the sacred places to be near malls and 7-Elevens, too."

"You're nuts," Veronica said. "Just plain nuts. Almonds and cashews. Walnuts and pecans."

"Okay, okay," Thomas said. "That's enough. I'll give you a ride to town."

Thomas, Betty, and Veronica packed up the van and headed off. Chess and Checkers stood in the yard and watched them go.

"I don't know," Checkers said. "Those two women could really sing."

"What?" Chess asked.

"We should've kept them. They could really sing."

"You don't know what you're talking about. Besides, you're not even in the band anymore."

"Well, I might have been. It would have been cool to have white women singing backup for us Indian women. It's usually the other way around."

"Yeah, maybe."

Checkers and Chess went back inside the house to check on Junior and Victor, while Thomas drove the blue van down the driveway.

"Indian men with concussions should not get their own glasses of water," Victor said as Chess and Checkers walked into the house.

"Indian men with concussions should not irritate Indian women with access to blunt objects," Chess said.

The blue van rolled down the highway, past all the pine trees and rocks filled with graffiti. RUNNING BEAR LOVES LITTLE WHITE DOVE. That van rolled past the HUD houses with generations of cars up on blocks, past Indian kids standing idly on the side of the road. Not hitchhiking, not going anywhere at all. Just standing there to watch traffic. One car every ten minutes or so.

"What is it about this place?" Betty asked and waved her arms around.

"What do you mean?" Thomas asked. "What place?"

"She wants to know what's wrong with all of it," Veronica said.

"Wrong with all of what?"

"This reservation, you Indians."

Thomas smiled.

"There's a whole bunch wrong with white people, too," he said. "Ain't nothing gone wrong on the reservation that hasn't gone wrong everywhere else."

Thomas drove off the reservation, through the wheat fields past Fairchild Air Force Base, and into Spokane. The Greyhound Station was, of course, in the worst section of town.

"You sure you'll be all right here?" Thomas asked as Betty and Veronica climbed out of the van.

"What's the difference between here and the reservation?"

"More pine trees on the reservation," Thomas said.

Betty and Veronica walked into the bus station. Thomas was about to drive away when Betty stepped back out of the station. She waved. Thomas waved and drove home.

† † †

Coyote Springs spent most of their time in Thomas's house over the next few weeks. They ventured out for food but were mostly greeted with hateful stares and silence. They didn't go to church. Only a few people showed any support. Fights broke out between the supporters and enemies of Coyote Springs. After a while, the Trading Post refused to let Coyote Springs in the door because there had been so many fights. The Tribal Council even held an emergency meeting to discuss the situation.

"I move we excommunicate them from the Tribe," Dave WalksAlong said. "They are creating an aura of violence in our community."

The Tribe narrowly voted to keep Coyote Springs but deadlocked on the vote to kick Chess and Checkers off the reservation.

"They're not even Spokanes," WalksAlong argued. The Council was trying to break the tie when Lester FallsApart staggered into the meeting, cast his vote to keep Chess and Checkers, and passed out.

Chess and Checkers sat in the kitchen of Thomas's house and chewed on wish sandwiches. Two slices of bread with only wishes in between.

"Jeez," Chess said, "maybe we should go back to Arlee. They like us there. How come all the Indians like us, except the Indians from here?"

"I'm not leaving," Checkers said and thought of Father Arnold. "And besides, we don't have money to leave. What are we going to do when we get to Arlee?"

"We don't have much money left to live here."

The $1,000 prize money from the Battle of the Bands had disappeared. Thomas, Junior, and Victor had each received his monthly stipend of commodity food, but that wouldn't last long. Thomas called small record companies in Spokane, but they weren't interested in the band.

"Indians?" those record companies said. "You mean like drums and stuff? That howling kind of singing? We can't afford to make a record that ain't going to sell. Sorry."

He even called a few companies in Seattle, like Sub Pop. Sub Pop discovered Nirvana and a lot of other bands, but they never returned Thomas's phone calls. They just mailed form rejections. Black letters on white paper, just like commodity cans. U.S.D.A. PORK. SORRY WE ARE UNABLE TO USE THIS. JUST ADD WATER. WE DON'T LISTEN TO UNSOLICITED DEMOS. POWDERED MILK. THANK YOU FOR YOUR INTEREST. HEAT AND SERVE.

The taverns refused to hire Coyote Springs.

"We heard you was causing some trouble," the taverns said. "We don't need any more trouble than we already got."

Coyote Springs shivered with fear.

*

"Shit," Junior said as he ate another mouthful of commodity peanut butter, the only source of protein in reservation diets. Victor strummed his guitar a little; his fingers had long since calloused over. He barely felt the burning. Thomas snuck out of the house to make frantic calls at the pay phone outside the Trading Post. Chess and Checkers sat beside each other on the couch, holding hands. The television didn't work.

Coyote Springs might have sat there in Thomas's house for years, silent and still, until their shadows could have been used to tell the time. But that Cadillac rolled onto the reservation and changed everything. All the Spokanes saw it but just assumed it was the FBI, CIA, or Jehovah's Witnesses. That Cadillac pulled up in front of the Trading Post. The rear window rolled down.

"Hey, you," a voice called out from the Cadillac.

"Me?" the-man-who-was-probably-Lakota asked.

"Yeah, you. Do you know where we can find Coyote Springs?"

"Sure, you go down to the dirt road over there, turn left, follow that for a little while, then go right. Then left at Old Bessie's house. You'll recognize her house by the smell of her fry bread. Third best on the reservation. Then, right again."

"Wait, wait," the voice said. "Why don't you just get in here and show us the way?"

"That's a nice car. But I can't fit in there," the-man-who-was-probably-Lakota said. "I'll just run. Follow me."

"Okay, but this ain't our car anyway. We rented it and this goofy driver, too."

The-man-who-was-probably-Lakota shrugged his shoulders and ran down the road with the Cadillac in close pursuit.

"Can't we go any faster?" the voice yelled from the Cadillac.

"Sure," the-man-who-was-probably-Lakota said and picked up the pace. He ran past a few other cars, which forced the Cadillac to make daring passes. They raced by Old Bessie's house and then made a right.

"Damn, that fry bread does smell good, doesn't it?" one white man in the car said to another.

Thomas's house sat in a little depression beside the road.

"That's where you'll find Coyote Springs," the-man-who-was-probably-Lakota said. He leaned down to look inside the car.

"You sure, Chief?" the voice asked.

"I'm sure. Did you know the end of the world is near?"

"We've been there and back, Chief."

The-man-who-was-probably-Lakota saw two pasty white men sitting in the back seat. They looked small inside the car, but the smell of cigar smoke and whiskey was huge. The driver was some skinny white guy in a cheap suit. Curious, the-man-who-was-probably-Lakota watched for a while, then ran back toward the Trading Post. He had work to do.

The driver stayed in the Cadillac, but the two other white men climbed out of the back of the Cadillac. Both were short and stocky, dark-haired, with moustaches that threatened to take over their faces. Those short white men walked to the front door and knocked. They knocked again. Thomas opened the door wide.

"Hello," the white men said. "We're Phil Sheridan and George Wright from Cavalry Records in New York City. We've come to talk to you about a recording contract."

† † †

From a fax transmitted from Wellpinit to Manhattan:

> Dear Mr. Armstrong:
> We just met with that Indian band we heard about. Coyote Springs. They played a little for us and quite frankly, we're impressed. The lead singer, Thomas Builds-the-Fire, is good, but his female singers, Chess and Checkers Warm Water, are

outstanding. There may be a little dissension in the group because Checkers apparently quit the band earlier. She rejoined when we showed up. I think that shows ambition. Checkers is quite striking, beautiful, in fact, while Chess is pretty. Both would attract men, I think. Sort of that exotic animalistic woman thing.

We had the band play a few sets for us in their home, and we feel confident in their abilities. Builds-the-Fire plays a competent bass guitar, while Victor Joseph is really quite extraordinary on the lead guitar. He is original and powerful, a genuine talent. Junior Polatkin is only average on drums but is a very good-looking man. Very ethnically handsome. He should bring in the teenage girls, which will make up for the looks of Builds-the-Fire and Joseph. Builds-the-Fire is just sort of goofy looking, with Buddy Holly glasses and crooked teeth. Victor Joseph looks like a train ran him over in 1976. Perhaps we can focus on the grunge/punk angle for him.

Overall, this band looks and sounds Indian. They all have dark skin. Chess, Checkers, and Junior all have long hair. Thomas has a big nose, and Victor has many scars. We're looking at some genuine crossover appeal.

We can really dress this group up, give them war paint, feathers, etc., and really play up the Indian angle. I think this band could prove to be very lucrative for Cavalry Records.

We should fly the band out to New York to do a little studio work perhaps. To see what they can do outside their home environment.

Peace,
Phil Sheridan
George Wright

† † †

"Father Arnold," Checkers called, "are you in here?"

She searched the church but finally found Father cleaning graves out in the cemetery. He cleaned the graves of five generations of Spokane Indian Catholics.

"Hello there, Checkers."

"Hello, Father."

"I'm really sorry to hear about Victor and Junior. Are they okay?"

"Yeah, they just got their heads bumped a little. A few bruises here and there. Sore ribs. Might knock some sense into them."

"It might," Father Arnold said and laughed. He leaned against his rake. Checkers studied the rings on his fingers. A college ring, a gold ring. She wanted to kiss his hands.

"What about those two white women?"

"They left. I guess we were too Indian for them."

"Yeah, I know how that is."

Checkers looked around at all the graves. She didn't know anybody buried there.

"So," Father said, "I heard there was some fancy car out at Thomas's place."

"Yeah."

"And?"

"It was some record company guys from New York. They really liked us."

"And?"

"And I rejoined the band."

"Just like that?"

"Yeah, I'm sorry."

Father Arnold dropped the rake, took Checkers's hands. He squeezed her fingers a little, smiled at her. She tried to maintain eye contact but turned her head, ashamed.

"I'm really sorry," she said.

"Are you sure this is what you want?"

"No. But we need the money. We ain't got no money."

"Does everything have to be about money?"

"Of course it does. Only people with enough money ever ask that question anyway."

"There's a kind of freedom in poverty."

That's a lie, Checkers thought and felt worse for contradicting a priest, her priest.

"Jesus didn't have any money," Father Arnold said.

"Yeah, but Jesus could turn one loaf of bread into a few thousand. I can't do that."

"You're right, Checkers. You're right."

Checkers looked down at the ground. She had not wanted to be right. She wanted Father Arnold to forbid her to leave.

"I think we should pray for all of your safety," Father Arnold said.

"Okay," she said.

Both kneeled on the ground, still face to face, holding hands.

"You pray," Father said.

"Dear Father," she began, stopped, started again. She struggled through a brief prayer.

"Amen."

"Amen."

"Checkers," he whispered, "it will be okay."

She leaned forward and kissed him, full on the lips. Surprised, he pulled back. She kissed him again, with more force, and he kissed her back, clumsily.

"Checkers," he said and pushed her away.

She looked up at him; he closed his eyes and prayed.

† † †

Wright and Sheridan sat in the back of the Cadillac. Sheridan was on the car phone. It had taken the driver more than an hour to find a place on the reservation where the reception was good. They sat on top of Lookout Hill, but there was still a lot of static on the line.

"Well," Sheridan said, "what do you think?" He nodded his head, grunted in the affirmative for a few minutes, shrugged his shoulders once or twice. He hung up the phone with a dejected look on his face.

"Oh, shit," Wright said. "He doesn't like the idea, does he?"

"Mr. Armstrong says he got our fax, and he loves our idea," Sheridan deadpanned.

"You're shitting me."

"He wants us to go check out some duo in Seattle first. Couple of hot white chicks, I guess, just started out and already causing a buzz. Then we're supposed to come back here next week and take, as he says, those goddamn Indians to New York."

"Well, this calls for a drink," Wright said.

"A couple drinks," Sheridan agreed.

The horses screamed.

"Well, we should tell them, don't you think?" Wright asked.

"Yeah," Sheridan said. "Driver, take us to Coyote Springs."

The driver carefully drove the car toward Thomas's house. He watched the two record company executives drink directly from a flask. That flask was old, antique, stained. Sheridan and Wright had been drinking from that flask for a century, give or take a few decades. They were never sure how long it had been.

"You've always been a good soldier," Wright said to Sheridan.

"You've been a fine goddamn officer yourself," Sheridan replied.

*

Coyote Springs was sitting in the front yard when the Cadillac pulled up. Drunk, Sheridan and Wright hurried out of the car with the good news. Everybody danced: Junior and Victor tangoed; Thomas two-stepped up a pine tree; Wright and Sheridan dipped Chess and Checkers.

"When do we get to go?" Thomas asked.

"Next week," Sheridan said.

"That long?"

"Well, we have to go to Seattle first. For some other business."

Coyote Springs's stomach growled.

"But we ain't got no money," Thomas whispered.

"No money?" Sheridan asked.

"None."

"Why didn't you say so?" Sheridan asked and opened his wallet. "I've got a few hundred bucks on me. Is that enough?"

Coyote Springs took the money, bribed their way back into the Trading Post, and bought a week's worth of Pepsi, Doritos, and Hershey's chocolate. Victor and Junior bought beer with their share and drank slowly.

"What a fine beer," Victor said. "A wonderful bouquet. Lovely, fruity taste with a slight bitterness."

"Yeah," Junior said, swished a little beer around his mouth, and then swallowed. "Gorgeous, gorgeous beer."

"Even better with corn nuts, enit?" Victor asked.

"You're such a fucking gourmet," Junior said.

Sheridan and Wright left the reservation before Junior and Victor even finished that first beer and barely waved goodbye.

"We'll see you in a week," Sheridan said before they left. "Have all your shit packed. We're flying you over there, so don't take too much."

"Flying?" Thomas asked.

"Of course. What did you think? You'd ride on horses?"

Thomas knew there was no good reason for Indians to fly. Indians could barely stay on the road when they were in cars.

"Well," Chess said after the record company executives had gone.

"Well," Thomas said. "What do we do now?"

Checkers felt dizzy, sat on the ground, and wished for a glass of cold water.

† † †

From a letter received on the day after Wright and Sheridan left:

Dear Thomas Builds-the-Fire,
I've heard you have a chance to audition for a large record company in New York. I don't think you have a chance at landing a contract without my help.

In fact, there are many other complications involved in all of this. Your friend, Robert Johnson, is here. He's been praying and singing for you. Please come see me at my home and bring the entire band. I'm looking forward to your visit.

Sincerely,
Big Mom

7

Big Mom

There's a grandmother talking to me
There's a grandmother talking to you
There's a grandmother singing for me
There's a grandmother singing for you

And if you stop and listen
You might hear what you been missing
And if you stop and listen
You might hear what you been missing

And I hear Big Mom
Telling me another story
And I hear Big Mom
Singing me another song

And she says

I'll be coming back
I'll be coming back
I'll be coming back for you
I'll be coming back
I'll be coming back
I'll be coming back for you
I'll always come back for you

(repeat)

Coyote Springs carried two guitars, a drum set, and a keyboard up the hill toward Big Mom's house. She lived in a blue house on the top of Wellpinit Mountain. She was a Spokane Indian with a little bit of Flathead blood thrown in for good measure. But she was more than that. She was a part of every tribe.

There were a million stories about Big Mom. But no matter how many stories were told, some Indians still refused to believe in her. Even though she lived on the reservation, some Spokanes still doubted her. Junior and Victor once saw Big Mom walk across Benjamin Pond but quickly erased it from memory. Junior and Victor had limited skills, but they were damn good at denial.

"Who the hell is Big Mom?" Victor had asked.

"You know who she is," Thomas said. "You're just pretending you don't know about her. You're just scared."

"I ain't scared of nothing. Especially somebody named Big Mom. What the hell does that mean anyway?"

"She's powerful medicine," Thomas said. "The most powerful medicine. I can't believe she called for us."

"Oh," Victor said, "don't tell me she's some medicine woman or something. That's all a bunch of crap. It don't work."

"Big Mom works."

"And besides, why did she address that letter to Thomas. We're a band, you know?"

"Because he's the lead singer," answered everybody else.

"We have to go there," Thomas said.

"When?" Chess asked.

"Right now," Thomas said. "Everybody grab an instrument and follow me."

"Wait a second," Checkers said. "Can't I say goodbye to Father Arnold?"

"Father Arnold can wait," Thomas said.

"Now," Victor asked again as Coyote Springs climbed up the hill. "Who the hell is this Big Mom?"

"I told you. Big Mom can help us, and she's helped us before," Thomas said. "That's all you need to know."

Coyote Springs walked the rest of the way in silence. They all thought about the help they needed and heard the word *faith* echo in the trees. They all heard the same music in their heads.

"This is spooky shit," Victor said.

"Way spooky," Junior said.

† † †

There were stories about Big Mom that stretched back more than a hundred years. There were a hundred stories about every day of Big Mom's life.

"Ya-hey," Indians whispered to each other at powwows, at basketball games, at education conferences. "Did you know Big Mom taught Elvis to sing?"

"No way," said the incredulous.

"What? You don't believe me? Well, then. Listen to this."

Indians all over the country would play a scratched record of Elvis, Diana Ross, Chuck Berry, and strain to hear the name *Big Mom* hidden in the mix.

"Didn't you hear it? Elvis whispers *Thank you, Big Mom* just as the last note of the song fades."

"Yeah, maybe I heard it. But maybe Elvis was singing to his own momma. He really did love his momma."

But the faithful played record after record and heard singer after singer thank Big Mom for her help. Those thanks were barely audible, of course, but they were there.

Big Mom was a musical genius. She was the teacher of all those great musicians who shaped the twentieth century. There were photographs, they said, of Les Paul leaving Big Mom's house with the original blueprint for the electric guitar. There were home movies, they said, of Big Mom choreographing the Andrews Sisters' latest dance steps. There were even cheap recordings, they said, of Big Mom teaching Paul McCartney how to sing "Yesterday."

Musicians from all over the world traveled to Big Mom's house in the hope she would teach them how to play. Like any good teacher, Big Mom was very selective with her students. She never answered the door when the live Jim Morrison came knocking. She won't even answer the door when the dead Jim Morrison comes knocking now.

Still, Big Mom had her heart broken by many of her students who couldn't cope with the incredible gifts she had given them. Jimi Hendrix, Janis Joplin, Elvis. They all drank so much and self-destructed so successfully that Big Mom made them honorary members of the Spokane Tribe.

Late at night, Big Mom's mourning song echoed all over the reservation. The faithful opened their eyes and took it in, knowing that another of her students had fallen. The unbelieving shut their doors and windows and complained about the birds howling in the trees. But those birds weren't howling. They all stood quietly, listening to Big Mom, too. She didn't teach just humans how to sing. When those birds heard her mourning song, they also wondered which of their tribe had fallen.

† † †

"Who is that?" Chess and Checkers asked as Coyote Springs crested a rise and saw a huge woman standing in the doorway of a blue house.

"That's Big Mom," Thomas said.

Big Mom was over six feet tall and had braids that hung down past her knees. Her braids themselves were taller than any of the members of Coyote Springs and probably weighed more, too. She had a grandmother face, lined and crossed with deep wrinkles. But her eyes were young, so young that the rest of her face almost looked like a mask. Big Mom filled up the doorway of that blue house. She wasn't obese at all, just thick and heavy.

"Ya-hey," Big Mom called out to them, and her voice shook the ground.

"Did we take some bad acid?" Victor asked Junior.

"I hope so," Junior said.

Big Mom walked across her yard to greet the band. She wore a full-length beaded buckskin outfit.

"You're the lead singer," Big Mom said, "Thomas Builds-the-Fire."

"Yes, I am," Thomas said. "Where's Robert Johnson?"

"He's away in the trees, looking for some good wood. He's going to build himself a new guitar."

"What about his old guitar?" Thomas asked.

"That guitar is Victor's responsibility now," Big Mom said. "I just wanted to see it. I just wanted Victor to know he gets to make choices. He can play the guitar or not. I don't think he should, but I won't take it away. If you want, I can throw it away, Victor."

"Shit," Victor said. "I'd like to see you try and take this guitar away."

That guitar nuzzled Victor's neck. Big Mom watched it carefully.

"And you're all going to play for some record company?" Big Mom asked.

"Yeah, we are. How did you know that anyway?"

"Ancient Indian magic."

"Shit," Victor said. "Everybody on the reservation knows about it by now. Ain't no magic in that."

"Well," Big Mom said, "I guess you're right. But gossip can be a form of magic. Enit, Victor?"

"I don't believe in magic."

"Victor," Big Mom said, "you should forgive that priest who hurt you when you were little. That will give you power over him, you know? Forgiveness is magic, too."

"What are you talking about?" Victor asked, but he knew. He still felt the priest's hands on his body after all those years.

"That poor man hasn't even forgiven himself yet," Big Mom said. "He's in an old-age home in California. He just cries all day long."

Victor couldn't talk. He was frozen with the thought of that priest's life. He had prayed for his death for years, had even wanted to kill him, but never once considered forgiveness.

"And you're Junior Polatkin," Big Mom said.

"Yeah, I am," Junior said. "And I'm scared."

Big Mom reared her head back and laughed a thunderstorm. Junior nearly pissed a rain shower in his shorts.

"Don't be scared, Junior," Big Mom said and held out two huge drumsticks. "These are for you."

"I can't use those, I don't think I can even lift them."

"Take them. They're yours."

Junior reached for the sticks, hesitated, then grabbed them quickly. They were too heavy at first, and they dropped to the ground. But Junior reached down and pulled them up. Then he smiled and pounded a little rhythm across the ground.

"Beautiful," Big Mom said.

"Shit," Victor said. "She thinks she's a medicine woman. She thinks she's Yoda and Junior is Luke Skywalker. Use the force, Junior, use the force."

Big Mom ignored Victor.

"And you two are the sisters, Eunice and Gladys Warm Water," Big Mom said. "You're special women. Come sweat with me."

"Eunice and Gladys?" Junior, Victor, and Thomas asked.

Chess and Checkers ducked their heads, hid their faces.

"Eunice and Gladys?" Victor said again. "Jeez, your parents must've been seduced by the dark side of the force when they named you, enit?"

"Eunice?" Thomas asked Chess.

"Yeah, I'm Eunice," Chess whispered.

"Don't be ashamed," Big Mom said. Chess and Checkers each took a hand, and Big Mom led them to the sweatlodge, leaving the men of Coyote Springs to their fears and drumsticks.

† † †

From Checkers (Gladys) Warm Water's journal:

I was so scared when I first saw Big Mom. She was this huge woman with fingers as big as my arms, I think. I kept thinking she could squash me like a bug. But then she called me a special woman. It made me realize Big Mom is really a woman and we could have a good talk.

She took Chess and me into the sweatlodge, and I kept thinking that Big Mom was inside my head. I've always been able to sort of read people's minds, been able to get into their heads a little bit. Even Chess always told me I had a little bit of magic. But there were always people, especially women, who had more magic. I remember I was trying to read this old white lady's mind on a bus ride to Missoula when she turned to me and said "Get out!" Well, she really said it in her head. That old white lady threw me out of her mind, and I had a headache for a week. But that was nothing compared to Big Mom. I kept feeling like she could have made commodity applesauce out of my brain.

Anyway, we took a sweat together, and it was great. Big Mom sang better than anybody I ever heard, even Aretha Franklin. That steam in the lodge felt so good in my throat and lungs. It made me feel like I could sing better. Chess said the steam made her feel that way, too. And Thomas said we could sing better after we came out of the sweatlodge with Big Mom.

But I was also kind of scared that Big Mom would know that I was in love with Father Arnold. She might know that I kissed him and that he kissed me back. I was scared of what she would think of me. How can an Indian woman love any white man like that, and him being a priest besides? Big Mom felt like she came from a whole different part of God than Father Arnold did. Is that possible? Can God be broken into pieces like a jigsaw puzzle? What if it's like one of those puzzles that Indian kids buy at secondhand stores? You put it together and find out one or two pieces are missing.

I looked at Big Mom and thought that God must be made up mostly of Indian and woman pieces. Then I looked at Father Arnold and thought that God must be made up of white and man pieces. I don't know what's true.

† † †

"I'm hungry," Victor said as they all lay on the floor in Big Mom's living room.

"You're always hungry," Chess said.

"Will you two be quiet, please?" Thomas said. "Big Mom is still sleeping."

"Oh," Victor said, loudly. "I didn't think God needed to sleep. I thought God was a twenty-four-hour convenience store."

"She's not God," Thomas said.

"Oh, my," Victor said. "The perfect Thomas admitting that Big Mom ain't God. That's blasphemy, enit?"

"It's not blasphemy," Thomas said. "There is no god but God."

"Well," Victor asked, "who is she then?"

The rest of Coyote Springs looked for the answer, too.

"She's just a part of God," Thomas said. "We're all a part of God, enit? Big Mom is just a bigger part of God."

"Literally," Victor said.

"She's going to teach us how to play better," Thomas said. "She's going to teach us new chords and stuff."

"How?" Victor said. "She's just some old Indian woman."

Just then, Big Mom played the loneliest chord that the band had ever heard. It drifted out of her bedroom, floated across the room, and landed at the feet of Coyote Springs. It crawled up their clothes and into their ears. Junior fainted.

"What in the hell was that?" Victor asked.

Big Mom walked out of the bedroom carrying a guitar made of a 1965 Malibu and the blood of a child killed at Wounded Knee in 1890.

"Listen," Thomas said.

Big Mom hit the chord again with more force, and it knocked everybody to the ground. Everybody except Junior, who was already passed out on the ground.

"Please," Chess said, but she didn't know if she wanted Big Mom to please, quit playing, or please, don't stop.

Big Mom hit that chord over and over, until Coyote Springs had memorized its effects on their bodies. Junior had regained consciousness long enough to remember his failures, before the force of the music knocked him out again.

"Enough!" Victor shouted. "I can't hear myself think!"

"There," Big Mom said to Victor. "Have you learned anything?"

"I've learned that a really big guitar makes a really big noise."

"Is that all?"

"What do you want me to say? I keep waiting for you to call me Grasshopper and ask me to snatch some goddamn pebble from your hand."

Thomas stood up and reached for Big Mom's guitar.

"Patience," Big Mom said and pushed his hand away.

"I can play that chord," Thomas said. "But I need your guitar to do it."

"All Indians can play that chord," Big Mom said. "It's the chord created especially for us. But you have to play it on your own instrument, Thomas. You couldn't even lift my guitar."

"What about Victor?" Thomas asked. "He's got Robert Johnson's guitar. Why can't I have your guitar?"

"That guitar is different," Big Mom said. "That guitar wanted Victor."

"Shit," Victor said. "This is all starting to sound like a New Age convention. Where are the fucking crystals? Well, I know who's got the fucking crystals. Jim Morrison's got the fucking crystals, and he's dancing naked around the campfire with a bunch of naked white people, singing and complaining that his head feels just like a toad."

"Please don't say that name," Big Mom said. "I'm so tired of that name. It's irritating how much I have to hear that name."

"What?" Victor asked. "Which name? Jim Morrison?"

"Stop that," Big Mom said.

"Jim Morrison," Victor said and laughed. "Jim Morrison, Jim Morrison, Jim-fucking-Morrison."

Big Mom shook her head, walked out of the house, and left Coyote Springs alone.

"You're such an asshole," Chess said.

"What's going on?" Junior asked as he finally woke up.

"I know I can play that chord," Thomas said.

"I kind of like the Doors," Checkers said.

"This is the end, my friends, this is the end," Victor said.

† † †

Victor wasn't the first Indian man to question Big Mom's author-
ity. In fact, many of the Indian men who were drawn to Big Mom
doubted her abilities. Indian men have started to believe their own
publicity and run around acting like the Indians in movies.

"Michael White Hawk," Big Mom said to the toughest
Spokane Indian man of the late twentieth century. "Don't you understand that the musical instrument is not to be used in the same
way that a bow and arrow is? Music is supposed to heal."

"But, Big Ma," White Hawk said, "I'm a warrior. I'm
'posed to fight."

"No, Michael, you're a saxophone player, and you need to
work on your reed technique."

Most times, the Indian men learned from Big Mom, but
Michael White Hawk never admitted his errors. White Hawk had
actually been something of a prodigy, an idiot savant, who could
play the horn even though he couldn't read or write.

"I hate white men," White Hawk said. "I smash my sax'-
phone on their heads."

"Michael," Big Mom said, "you run around playing like
you're a warrior. You're the first to tell an Indian he's not being
Indian enough. How do you know what that means? You need to
take care of your people. Smashing your guitar over the head of a
white man is just violence. And the white man has always been better at violence anyway. They'll always be better than you at violence."

"You don't know what you talkin' 'bout," White Hawk
said. "You jus' a woman."

He left Big Mom's house after that and ended up in Walla

Walla State Penitentiary for smashing his saxophone over the head of a cashier at a supermarket in Spokane.

"He tryin' to cheat me for my carrots," White Hawk shouted as he was led away to prison.

"When are Indians ever going to have heroes who don't hurt people?" Big Mom asked her students. "Why do all of our heroes have to carry guns? All Indian heroes have to be Indian men, too. Why can't Indian women be heroes?"

Some of her Indian men students would get all pissed off and leave. They suddenly saw Big Mom as a tiny grandmother without teeth or a life. She shrank in their eyes, until she was just some dried old apple sitting on a windowsill. In their minds, she changed into a witch, bitter and angry.

I'll get you, my pretty, Big Mom said in their heads, although it didn't sound like her at all. *And your little dog, too, because you goddamn Indian boys always got some dog following you around.*

And those Indian men would never play their music right again. You can still see them, standing by the drums at powwows, trying to remember how to sing in the Indian way. *You don't remember, do you?* asks the strange voice in their heads. *Listen to me. I'll teach you.* They attempt to tap their feet in rhythm with the dancers but can never quite get it.

Follow me, that wild voice said. *I'll give you everything you want. Everything.*

All the guitar players cut their fingers to shreds on guitar strings.

Let me fix those wounds for you. There, let me suck the infection out. There, that's good, that's good.

"Forgive us, save us," said those repentant guitar players, with hands bandaged and bloodied, when they crawled back to Big Mom.

"I ain't Jesus. I ain't God," Big Mom said. "I'm just a music teacher."

"But look what you did to us."

"I didn't do anything to you. You caused all this. You made the choices."

"What can we do?"

"You can change your mind."

† † †

"I want you to play that chord again," Big Mom said to Victor.

"I can't play it anymore," Victor said. "I'm tired. I want to go to sleep."

Coyote Springs had been practicing twelve hours a day for nearly a week. They were exhausted but had improved greatly, despite Victor's continual challenges of Big Mom's magic. There wasn't enough room to rehearse in Big Mom's house, so she rigged up some outside lights, which attracted mosquitos and moths.

"Play it again," Big Mom said.

"I can't. My fingers don't even work that way."

Robert Johnson watched from a distance, hidden in the treeline. He held some scrub wood in his hands. It wasn't strong wood. There was no way he could make a desk or a chair. That wood wasn't even good enough to make a broomstick. But somehow Johnson believed that his new guitar waited somewhere in that wood. Proud of his discovery, he was still frightened by his old guitar. Victor's guitar now. Johnson winced when Victor hit the chord.

"Play it," Big Mom said.

"Yeah," Thomas said. "Play it hard."

"Come on, Big Mom, Thomas," Chess said. "We're all tired. Why don't we quit for the day?"

"We'll quit when Big Mom says it's time to quit," Thomas said. "Sheridan and Wright are coming to get us in a couple days. And we just ain't good enough yet."

"Jeez," Victor said. "You sound like we're in some god-damn reservation coming-of-age movie. Who the fuck you think you are? Billy Jack? Who's writing your dialogue?"

Big Mom looked at Thomas as Victor tried once again to play the chord she had requested.

"Will you play that chord again, please?" Big Mom asked again. "Just a few more times, and then we'll all go to sleep."

Victor flipped Thomas off. He needed a drink. He had been up on that goddamn mountain for a week without a drink. He was starting to see snakes crawling around. There were snakes up there, but Victor saw a few too many. Victor breathed deep, flexed his tired hands, and hit the chord a few more times. The rest of the band joined in, and they ran off a respectable version of a new song.

Thomas and Chess whispered in their sleeping bag. After everyone else had fallen asleep, they stayed up to talk.

"I'm scared," Thomas said.

"Scared of what?"

"I'm scared to be good. I'm scared to be bad. This band could make us rock stars. It could kill us."

"Shit, Thomas. That would scare anybody."

Thomas closed his eyes and told this story: "Coyote Springs opens a show for Aerosmith at Madison Square Garden. We get up on stage and start to play. At first, the crowd chants for Aerosmith, heckles us, but gradually we win them over. By the time our set is over, the crowd is chanting our name. *Coyote Springs. Coyote Springs. Coyote Springs.* They chant over and over. They keep chanting our name when Aerosmith comes out. They boo Aerosmith until we come back out. For the rest of our lives, all we can hear are our names, chanted over and over, until we are deaf to everything else."

Thomas opened his eyes and stared into the dark.

"Listen, Chess," Thomas said, "I've spent my whole life being ignored. I'm used to it. If people want to hear us now, come to hear us play, come to listen. Just think how many will come if we get famous."

Chess was just as scared as Thomas, maybe more so. She was scared of the band, scared of Victor and Junior, and of Thomas, too. All her life, she had been measured by men. Her father, her priest, her lovers, her employers, her God. Men decided where she would go, how she would talk, even what clothes she was supposed to wear. Now they decided how and where she was supposed to sing. Now, even sweet, gentle Thomas covered her with his shadow. Even in his dreams and stories, Thomas covered her. She sang his songs; she played his music. She played for Phil Sheridan and George Wright and hoped for their approval. And Thomas still there with his shadow. Chess didn't know whether she should run from that shadow or curl up inside it. She wanted to do both.

"I get scared, Thomas," Chess said. "When I'm up there singing, and I look out at the crowd, sometimes I see a thousand different lovers. All those men. It's not like I love all of them like I love you. I don't. And I know they don't love me like you do. But I still feel all this pressure from them. Sometimes I feel like I have to be everybody's perfect lover and I ain't nobody's perfect nothing."

"So what are we supposed to do?" Thomas asked.

"Sing songs and tell stories. That's all we can do."

Thomas thought back to all those stories he had told. He had whispered his stories into the ears of drunks passed out behind the Trading Post. He had written his stories down on paper and mailed them to congressmen and game show hosts. He had climbed up trees and told his stories to bird eggs. He had always shared his stories with a passive audience and complained that nobody actively listened.

"Thomas," Chess said, "if you don't want to be famous and have your stories heard, then why'd you start the band up?"

"I heard voices," Thomas said. "I guess I heard voices. I mean, I'm sort of a liar, enit? I like the attention. I want strangers to love me. I don't even know why. But I want all kinds of strangers to love me."

The Indian horses screamed.

† † †

Big Mom sat in her favorite chair on the porch while Coyote Springs rehearsed for the last time in her yard.

"You know," Big Mom said, "this is the first time I've ever actually worked with a whole band. I mean, Benny Goodman eventually brought most of his band up here, but that was one at a time."

Coyote Springs played an entirely original set of music now. Thomas still wrote most of the lyrics, but the whole band shaped the songs.

"I think you're as good as you're going to get," Big Mom said. "You have to leave for New York tomorrow, enit?"

"Don't you know?" Victor asked. "I thought you knew everything."

"I know you're a jerk," Big Mom said and surprised everybody.

"Ya-hey," Chess said. "Good one, Big Mom."

The band ran through a few more songs before they packed everything up. Thomas wanted to practice even more, right up until they had to leave, but the rest of the band quickly vetoed that idea. Even Big Mom had had enough.

"But we're not good enough yet," Thomas said.

"Thomas," Chess said, "this is as good as we're going to get. Even you think we're pretty good. You said so yourself."

"Pretty good ain't good enough," Thomas said.

"It's going to have to be."

"But it ain't. We have to come back as heroes. They won't let us back on this reservation if we ain't heroes. Unless we're rock stars. We already left once, and all the Spokanes hate us for it. Shit, Michael White Hawk wants to kill all of us. Dave Walks-Along wants to kick us completely out of the Tribe. What if we screw up in New York and every Indian everywhere hates us? What if they won't let us on any reservation in the country?"

Coyote Springs and Big Mom stared at Thomas. He stared back.

"Don't look at me like that," Thomas said. "We need more help. We need Robert Johnson. We need him. Where is he, Big Mom?"

"He's out there right now," Big Mom said and pointed with her lips toward the treeline. "Watching us."

Thomas scanned the pine for any signs of Johnson.

"Robert Johnson!" Thomas shouted. "We need you!"

Johnson cowered behind a pine tree, covered his ears with his hands, and cried. He wanted to help; he wanted to take back that guitar. Coyote Springs was messing with things they didn't understand. Big Mom couldn't teach them everything. Big Mom couldn't stop them if they were going to sign their lives away. Johnson wondered briefly if he should build his new guitar quickly, hop on the plane with Coyote Springs, and play music with them. A black man and five Indians. It had to work, didn't it? But all Robert Johnson could do was burrow a little deeper into himself.

"He can't help you," Big Mom said. "He's still trying to help himself."

"I mean," Thomas shouted at everybody, "look at all of us! What are any of us going to do if this doesn't work? Robert Johnson's hiding in the woods. What are you going to do, Victor? You and Junior will end up drunk in the Powwow Tavern. You'll go back to ignoring me or beating the crap out of me. Checkers will join some convent. And what happens to us, Chess? What happens if people don't listen?''

Chess took Thomas's hands in hers, and the silence wrapped around them like a familiar quilt.

† † †

From a note left by Junior:

Dear Big Mom,
I just wanted to thank you for your drumsticks and for teaching us how to play better. I know you're probably mad at Victor. He can be a jerk but he's a good guy, too. He's always taken care of me.

I was kind of small and sick when I was little. But I was really smart, too. Nobody liked me, except Victor. He was my bodyguard. If anybody beat me up then Victor would get even for me. He taught me how to fight, too. Once, a bunch of Colville Indians beat me up at a powwow. Victor spent the rest of the powwow finding and fighting all those guys. He beat them up one by one. Really kicked the crap out of them. He was nine years old. He didn't even drink at all during that powwow. He just wanted to get me revenge. Victor's tough that way.

It seems like Victor's always been there for me. After his real dad left and my dad died, we hung out a lot. We took turns being the dad, I guess. Sometimes all we had was each other. I know we both picked on Thomas too much but we didn't really mean it. We never really hurt him too much. I never wanted to really hurt anybody. So I hope you ain't too mad at Victor.

He was the one who came and got me when I flunked

out of college. Victor just borrowed money and his uncle's car and drove to Oregon and got me. He even bought me a hamburger and fries at Dick's. We just sat there at a picnic table outside Dick's and ate. We didn't talk much. Just passed the ketchup back and forth.

You know, I get mad at Victor all the time, but I remember that he's been good to me, too. He's just a kid sometimes, even though he's a grown-up man.

Anyway, I hope you have a good life and I hope we get to see you again. Wish us luck in New York.

                                        Sincerely,
                                        Junior Polatkin

                         † † †

Big Mom watched Coyote Springs walk down her mountain. She had watched many of her students, her children, walk down that mountain. She was never sure what would happen to them. They could become the major musical voice of their generation, of many generations, but they could also fade into obscurity. Her students also fell apart, and were found in so many pieces they could never be put back together again.

"What's going to happen to us?" Chess asked Big Mom just before Coyote Springs left.

"I don't know," Big Mom said. "It's not up to me."

"You sound like a reservation fortune cookie sometimes," Victor said. "You know, you open up a can of commodity peanut butter, and there's Big Mom's latest piece of wisdom."

"Listen," Big Mom said. "Maybe you'll go out there and get famous. I've had plenty of students get famous, really famous. I've had students invent stuff I never would have thought of, like jazz and rap. I've seen it all. But I ain't had many students who ended up happy, you know? So what do you want me to say? It's up to you. You make your choices."

Coyote Springs looked at Big Mom. They sort of felt like baby turtles left to crawl from birth nest to ocean all by themselves, while predators of all varieties came to be part of the baby turtle beach buffet. They sort of felt like Indian children of Indian parents.

"Thank you, Big Mom," Chess and Checkers said, and Big Mom took them in her arms.

Thomas hugged Big Mom; Junior managed a shy smile and wave. Then everybody turned to Victor.

"What?" Victor said. "What do you want? I ain't going to say I had a great time. I ain't going to say you were a tough teacher, Big Mom, and I know we had our differences, but aw shucks, I love you anyway. I was a great guitar player when I came in here and I'm a great guitar player as I walk out. You taught me a few new tricks. That's it."

"Well," Big Mom said, "that may be all I taught you. But you should still thank me for it."

"Fine," Victor said. "Thank you."

"You be careful with that guitar," Big Mom said.

Coyote Springs walked down the hill. Big Mom watched them, for years it seemed, watched them over and over. She watched them walk into Wellpinit, meet up with Sheridan and Wright. She watched them all climb into a limousine and drive off the reservation and arrive suddenly at the Spokane International Airport.

† † †

Coyote Springs waited in the Spokane International Airport for their flight. Wright and Sheridan had already boarded because they were in first class. The flight attendant called for their rows, and Coyote Springs made their way toward the gate.

"Wait a second," Victor said, suddenly understanding that he was getting on an airplane. "I ain't flying in that fucking thing."

"Been in a little bit of denial, enit?" Chess asked him.

Victor refused to board the plane.

"Come on, you chicken," Chess said. "Get on the plane."

"Damn right I'm a chicken," Victor said. "Because chickens don't fly."

"It'll be cool," Junior said. "Don't be scared."

"I ain't scared. I'm being smart."

Everybody looked to Thomas for help.

"Victor," Thomas said, "I brought an eagle feather for protection. You can have it."

"Get that Indian bullshit away from me!"

The crowd at the gate stared at Coyote Springs. They worried those loud dark-skinned people might be hijackers. Coyote Springs did their best not to look middle eastern.

"That ain't going to do nothing," Victor continued, in a lower volume. "It's just a feather. Hell, it fell off some damn eagle, so it obviously wasn't working anyway, enit?"

Victor was being as logical as a white man.

"You can't go to New York if you don't get on that plane," Chess said.

"Please," Checkers said.

Victor stared out the terminal window at the plane. That plane just looked too damn big to fly.

"All right, all right," Victor finally said. "I'll get on that goddamn plane, but I'm going to get wasted. And you're all going to buy me drinks."

"Okay, okay," said all the rest of Coyote Springs, happy for once to be codependents.

"Listen," Thomas said, "you can still have my eagle feather."

"I told you to get that thing away from me," Victor said. "I don't believe in that shit."

Coyote Springs boarded the plane, waved to Wright and Sheridan as they walked back to the coach section. Victor started drinking immediately. He put down shot after shot, closed his eyes as the plane took off.

"Shit," Victor said after the plane reached cruising altitude, "that was easy."

Victor was drunk enough to forget about flying for a while, until the plane hit some nasty turbulence.

"Sorry, folks," the captain said over the intercom. "We've run into some choppy air, and we're going to have to ask you to return to your seats and buckle yourselves in. This is going to be a bumpy ride."

The plane bounced up and down like crazy, and Victor went pale. The whole band turned white.

"Hey, Thomas," Victor slurred, "do you still got that eagle feather?"

"Sure," Thomas said and handed it to Victor, who held it tightly in his hand and whispered some inexpert prayer.

The rest of Coyote Springs looked to Thomas for help, so he produced an eagle feather for each of them.

"Jeez, Thomas," Chess said, "I love you so much."

Thomas just smiled and held tightly to his eagle feather. Chess and Checkers held hands, held their feathers. Junior put his feather in his mouth and bit down to prevent himself from calling out. Coyote Springs was flying to a place they had never been. They didn't know what would happen or how they would come back.

† † †

Meanwhile, the reservation remained behind. It never exactly longed for any Indian who left, for all those whose bodies were dragged quickly and quietly into the twentieth century while their souls were left behind somewhere in the nineteenth. But the reservation was there, had always been there, and would still be there, waiting for Coyote Springs's return from New York City. Every Indian, every leaf of grass, and every animal and insect waited collectively.

The old Indian women dipped wooden spoons into stews and stirred and stirred. The stews made of random vegetables and commodity food, of failed dreams and predictable tears. That was the only way to measure time, to wait. Those spoons moved in slow circles. Stir, stir. The reservation waited for Coyote Springs to fall into pieces, so they could be dropped into the old women's stews.

It waited for the end of the stickgame, one chance to choose the hand holding the colored bone. Those old women always hid the colored bone in one hand and a plain bone in the other. Those old women smelled of stew and pine. If an Indian chose the correct hand, he won everything, he won all the sticks. If an Indian chose wrong, he never got to play again. Coyote Springs had only one dream, one chance to choose the correct hand.

8

Urban Indian Blues

I've been relocated and given a room
In a downtown hotel called The Tomb
And they gave me a job and cut my hair
I trip on rats when I climb the stairs
I get letters from my cousins on the rez
They wonder when they'll see me next
But I've got a job and a landlady
She calls me chief, she calls me crazy

chorus:
I'm walking sidewalks miles from home, I'm walking streets alone
I'm walking in cheap old shoes, I've got the Urban Indian blues
I'm working for minimum, I'm working the maximum
I'm working in cheap old shoes, I've got the Urban Indian blues

I paint the ceilings, I paint the walls
I paint the floors and I paint the halls

That's my job and that's my boss there
He gave me the clothes that I wear
We drink a few in his favorite bar
We drink a few more in his car
He's a friend of the Indian, he says
He's been to the rez, he's been to the rez

(repeat chorus)

I'm saving money for the Greyhound
'Cause I want to be homeward bound
But the landlady raises the rent
The boss don't know where my check went
And the neighbors are lonely
And the neighbors are ghostly
And I watch my television
And I dream of the reservation

Inside the recording studio at Cavalry Records in New York City, Coyote Springs nervously re-tuned their already tuned instruments. Chess and Checkers sang scales. Junior tapped his foot to some rhythm he heard in his head. Victor stroked his guitar gently; the guitar purred.

"Are you folks ready yet?" asked a disembodied voice from the control booth.

"Who are you?" Victor asked.

"Just the engineer," said the voice.

"Where are you?"

"Right here," said a young white woman in pressed denim shirt and blue jeans. She waved at Coyote Springs and grinned.

Phil Sheridan and George Wright sat behind the engineer. They were just as nervous as Coyote Springs.

"What if Mr. Armstrong doesn't like them," Sheridan asked Wright. Thomas watched Sheridan and Wright talk, although he couldn't hear them through the glass.

"He'll like them," Wright said. "He signed that duo from Seattle on just our word, right? He's got to like these guys. Indians are big these days. Way popular, right? Besides, these Indians are good. They're just plain good. They're artists. When was the last time we signed artists?"

"Shit, as if being good meant anything in this business. They don't need to be good. They just need to make money. I don't give a fuck if they're artists. Where are all the executives who signed artists? They're working at radio stations now, right?"

The engineer studied her soundboard. She flipped switches

in patterns that would make the music sound exactly like she wanted it to sound.

"I'm just going to tell Armstrong this was your idea," Sheridan said and laughed.

"Fuck you, too," Wright said.

Sheridan and Wright continued to reassure each other until Mr. Armstrong, the president and CEO of Cavalry Records, arrived.

"Mr. Armstrong," Sheridan and Wright said and stood.

"Where are the Indians?" Armstrong asked.

"Right there," Sheridan said and pointed at the band.

"They look Indian," Armstrong said.

"Of course, sir."

Mr. Armstrong was a small man, barely over five feet, but he weighed three hundred pounds. The weight looked unnatural on him, though, like he had been padded to play a fat guy in a movie. His blond hair was pulled into a ponytail that hung down past his waist. He spoke in short sentences.

"Can they play?" Armstrong asked Sheridan and Wright.

"Yes, sir."

"Can they play?" Armstrong asked the engineer, who just shrugged her shoulders and ran Coyote Springs through a sound check.

"Jeez," Chess said, "that's the big boss man, enit?"

"Yeah, it is," Victor said. "And he's going to sign me up for a solo career after he hears me play. He's just going to send all you losers home."

"Are you ready to run through a song?" asked the engineer.

"Damn right," Victor said.

"Well, let's go for it. Tape's running," said the engineer.

"What do you think we should play?" Thomas asked.

"How about 'Urban Indian Blues'?" Chess asked.

"Makes sense, enit?" Checkers asked.

"Damn right," Victor said.

"Okay," Thomas said. "Count it off, Junior."

The horses screamed.

"One, two, one, two, three, four."

Coyote Springs dropped into a familiar rhythm together. Thomas, Chess, and Checkers sang well. Thomas strummed note by note on the bass; Chess and Checkers both played keyboards. Junior flailed away at the drums, lost a few beats here and there, but mostly kept up. But Coyote Springs needed Victor to rise, needed his lead guitar to define them. Victor knew how important he was. He closed his eyes and let the chords come to him.

At first, the music flowed as usual, like a stream of fire through his fingers and the strings. Victor remembered how much the music had hurt him before. That guitar had scarred his hands, yet he had mastered the pain. He thought he could have placed his calloused hands into any fire and never felt the burning. But then, as the song moved forward, bar by bar, his fingers slipped off the strings and frets. The guitar bucked in his hands, twisted away from his body. He felt a razor slice across his palms.

"Shit, shit!" Victor shouted.

"What's the problem?" asked the engineer.

"Could we start over?" Victor asked.

Sheridan and Wright exchanged a worried look. Mr. Armstrong cleared his throat loudly.

"Whenever you want," said the engineer. "Tape's still rolling."

"What's wrong?" Thomas asked Victor.

"Nothing," Victor said, wiped his hands on his pants, and left blood stains. The rest of Coyote Springs studied those blood stains as Junior counted off again.

"One, two, one, two, three, four."

Checkers could not remember what she was supposed to

play. She looked to her sister for help, but Chess's hands stayed motionless a few inches above the keyboard. Thomas sang half of the first verse before he noticed he was singing alone.

"Hold up a sec," said the engineer. "Where are the keyboards and vocals, ladies?"

"Are you okay?" Thomas asked the sisters.

Chess and Checkers shook their heads. Junior continued to pound the snare drum. Victor's guitar kept writhing in his hands until it broke the straps and fell to the floor in a flurry of feedback.

The engineer let that feedback whine until Sheridan jumped to the intercom.

"What the hell's going on?" Sheridan asked Coyote Springs.

Coyote Springs all stared down at Victor's guitar.

"What the hell's happening?" Sheridan asked everybody in the control booth.

"I don't know," said the engineer. "I think they're just nervous. Give them another chance."

Mr. Armstrong rose from his seat, adjusted his tie and jacket.

"They don't have it," Armstrong said.

"Don't you think you're being a little hasty, sir?" Wright asked.

"No, I don't," Armstrong said and left.

Coyote Springs was still staring at the guitar on the floor when the engineer spoke.

"Hey, that's it, I guess."

Coyote Springs looked up at the engineer, who looked pained behind the glass. Wright and Sheridan were arguing violently, silently. Coyote Springs watched the two Cavalry officers gesture wildly, argue for a few more minutes, and then storm out of the control booth.

"What the hell happened?" Chess asked after a long time.

"I don't know," the engineer said over the intercom. "I thought you were pretty good."

"What the hell happened?" Chess asked Thomas.

"I don't know," Thomas said.

† † †

From *The Wellpinit Rawhide Press:*

Local Skins May Lose Their Shirts

Our local rock band, Coyote Springs, left yesterday for a meeting with Cavalry Records in New York City. Although they've been the center of much controversy on the Spokane Indian Reservation, it seems that white people are still interested in the band.

"We're going to be rock stars," Victor Joseph said before the band left. "And we won't have to come back to this reservation ever again. We'll just leave all of you [jerks] to your [awful] lives."

Lead singer Thomas Builds-the-Fire, however, was a little more guarded about the purpose of the meeting.

"It's an audition," he said. "They haven't promised us anything. You tell everybody that. We ain't been promised anything."

Tribal Chairman David WalksAlong was even more pessimistic about the future of Coyote Springs.

"Listen," he said over lunch at the Tribal Cafe. "Those Skins ain't got a chance in New York City. I've been to New York City, and I know what it's like. My grandfather always told me you can take a boy off the reservation, but you can't take the reservation off the boy. Coyote Springs is done for. I'm happy about that."

But the other members of Coyote Springs seemed to take all the controversy in stride.

"I just want to be good at something," Junior Polatkin said. "I messed up at everything else. I'm not mad at anybody who talked bad about us. I just want them to like us."

Chess and Checkers Warm Water simply gave the thumbs-up as they left the reservation, although some Spokanes thought it was a different finger they raised.

"Listen," Polatkin added, "if we make it big, it just means we won't have to eat commodity food anymore."

† † †

Coyote Springs was still standing in the dark studio when Sheridan and Wright came back. The engineer had already left, so the two record company executives fiddled with the knobs and dials until they found the lights and power.

"Listen," Sheridan said over the intercom. "I don't know what happened to you. But Mr. Armstrong doesn't want to have anything to do with you right now."

"What the fuck are you talking about?" Victor asked.

"Now, you listen closely," Sheridan said. "My ass is on the line here, too. I brought you little shits here. You screwed me over. Now, I'm going to try and fix this. Mr. Armstrong can be a little bit emotional. Maybe he didn't get his coffee or something this morning. Why don't you just head over to your hotel and wait this out. We'll fly you back to the reservation in the morning."

"No fucking way!" Victor shouted. "We can't go back there. Not like this."

"Calm your ass down," Sheridan said. "We'll give Mr. Armstrong a couple months, and then we'll try it again."

"We don't have a couple months," Thomas whispered.

Wright slumped into a chair and wiped his face with a handkerchief just as Victor picked up his guitar and threw it across the studio. Chess and Checkers ducked. Junior continued to beat a quiet rhythm on the drum.

"Goddamn it," Sheridan shouted over the intercom. "That's fucking studio equipment."

"Fuck you," Victor shouted. "You're studio equipment."

"Hey," Sheridan said. "I'm trying to help you. I didn't screw this up. I'm not the goddamn guitar player. Maybe you just aren't ready. Maybe next time. But if you don't calm down, I'll call security."

Victor kicked a music stand over, picked up a studio saxophone and threw it at Sheridan. Sheridan ducked behind the control panel, but the sax just rebounded off the glass and fell to the floor. Angry, Sheridan and Wright stormed into the studio.

"That's it," Sheridan said to Wright. "I'm out of here. I tried to help these goddamn Indians. But they don't want help. They don't want anything."

"I think they want the same things we do," Wright said.

Victor went after Sheridan and Wright then and might have strangled them, but Thomas and Junior tackled him. They pinned Victor to the floor as Sheridan looked down.

"Jesus," Sheridan said. "It isn't that bad. You got a free trip to New York. You aren't leaving until tomorrow. You've got a whole night in Manhattan to yourselves. I'll even treat you to a nice evening. Some dinner, dancing, the sights."

Sheridan pulled out his wallet and dropped a few bills on the floor near Victor. Chess and Checkers quickly picked up the money and threw it in Sheridan's face.

"That's it," Sheridan said. "You're out of here."

"Wait," Wright said, but the security guards arrived quickly and roughly escorted Coyote Springs out of the building. Coyote Springs cried, but no crowd gathered to watch them. Coyote Springs stood in the middle of the sidewalk, and hundreds of people just flowed impassively around them.

"What are we supposed to do?" Chess asked.

"Let's just go home," Thomas said. It was all he knew to say. "Big Mom will know what to do."

"She's just an old woman," Victor shouted. "She ain't magic. And even if she was, she's a million miles away. What the fuck can she do? Everything is a million miles away. It's all lies, lies, lies. All the whites ever done was tell us lies."

Victor roared against his whole life. If he could have been hooked up to a power line, he would have lit up Times Square. He had enough anger inside to guide every salmon over Grand Coulee Dam. He wanted to steal a New York cop's horse and go on the warpath. He wanted to scalp stockbrokers and kidnap supermodels. He wanted to shoot flaming arrows into the Museum of Modern Art. He wanted to lay siege to Radio City Music Hall. Victor wanted to win. Victor wanted to get drunk.

"Let's get the fuck out of here," Victor said to Junior, and they ran off into the crowd.

"Come back," Checkers shouted after them, but they were already gone, swallowed by the river of people.

"I'm so scared," Chess said to Thomas and moved into his arms.

"I am, too," Checkers said and held onto Thomas and Chess.

Thomas felt his whole body shake.

If any New Yorkers had stopped to look, they would have seen three Indians slow dancing, their hair swirling in the wind. The whole scene could have been a postcard. WISH YOU WERE HERE. It could have been on the cover of the *New York Times Sunday Magazine*.

† † †

Chess, Checkers, and Thomas stood in the hotel lobby with no idea what to do about Junior and Victor, who were getting drunk somewhere in Manhattan. But there were thousands of bars, taverns, lounges, and dives in New York. Thousands and thousands. Victor and Junior could be anywhere.

"Jeez," Checkers said, "what are we going to do?"

"I don't know," said Thomas, a reservation storyteller without answers or stories.

"Well," Chess said, "we have to find those two. It's dangerous here. Especially for them."

Thomas was truly frightened. He felt totally out of control. He could only think about the instruments they left in the studio.

"Our stuff," Thomas said.

"What stuff?" Chess asked.

"Our guitars and stuff. They're still in the studio."

"Forget them, it's all over now, anyways. Can't you feel it?"

Thomas touched his body and felt the absence, like some unnamed part of him had been cut away.

"What are we going to do?" Checkers pleaded. She dropped into a chair and held her head between her knees. "I think I'm going to pass out."

Chess watched Thomas and Checkers collapse. She knew Victor and Junior had to be found. There was no time for drama. Victor and Junior, two small-town reservation hicks, were out drunk somewhere in New York City. There were only a few ways to die on the reservation but a few thousand new and exciting ways in Manhattan. All of it felt like a three-in-the-morning movie on television. Some punks would kill Victor and Junior for their shoes and dump their bodies in the Hudson River. And Kojak would never find them.

"Listen," Chess said, but Thomas and Checkers stared off into space.

"Listen, goddamn it!" Chess shouted. Thomas and Checkers looked at her. "Thomas and I will grab a phonebook and hit all the bars in this whole town. Checkers, you stay here in case they come back. How does that sound?"

"That's crazy," Thomas said. "There are thousands of bars."

"I know it's crazy," Chess said. "But what else are we going to do? Who knows what Victor and Junior are going to do? They might get themselves killed."

"Where do we start?"

"With the A's," Chess said. "And work our way from there."

Chess hugged her sister; Checkers wouldn't let her go.

"I've got to go," Chess said.

"Don't," Checkers whispered.

Chess led her sister across the lobby and into the elevator.

"Eleventh floor," Chess said to the elevator man.

"Yes, ma'am."

The elevator doors slid closed. Chess and Thomas left the hotel with a few dozen pages of the phonebook.

† † †

Victor and Junior sat in a smoky lounge with a half dozen empty glasses in front of them.

"Fucking assholes," Victor shouted.

"Be quiet," Junior said. "You'll get us kicked out of here, too."

It was the fourth bar that Junior and Victor had been in since they ran away from the rest of Coyote Springs. The bouncers had tossed them out of the first bar for fighting. The second lounge had closed early, and the third established a new dress code fifteen minutes after Junior and Victor sat down. Still, these bars they visited in New York City weren't all that different from the bars on the reservation. A few tables and chairs, a few stools at the bar, a television, and a pool table. The only difference between bars was the program on the TV.

"Everybody's a liar," Victor whispered. He laughed drunkenly and looked around the bar. The bartender stared at Victor and mentally cut him off.

"Man," Victor said. "Look at all the beautiful white women in here."

Junior looked around the room. He saw beautiful white women in the bar, had seen beautiful white women in all four bars that night, and Victor had made sure to shout about it. There were beautiful women of all colors in those bars and some plain white ones, but Victor and Junior never seemed to notice the plain ones.

"This city's filled up with beautiful white women," Victor said and laughed his drunk laugh. Phlegm rattled in his throat and spit fell from his mouth.

"Victor," Junior said. "Why you like white women so much?"

"Don't you know? Bucks prefer white tail."

Junior didn't feel like laughing. He just ate a handful of peanuts and stared at the television. Victor babbled on about nothing. The bartender cleared the glasses away from Junior's and Victor's area. Victor ordered another beer, but Junior gave the bartender a look that said *He don't need no more*. The bartender gave Junior a look back that said *I wasn't going to give him one anyway*.

Junior knew that white women were trophies for Indian boys. He always figured getting a white woman was like counting coup or stealing horses, like the best kind of revenge against white men.

Hey, Indian men said to white men. *You may have kicked our ass in the Indian wars, but we got your women.*

But that was too easy an explanation, and Junior knew it. He knew he loved to walk around with Betty and Veronica. Especially on the reservation. He loved to have something that other Indians didn't have. He'd had his first white woman back when he was in college in Oregon.

Junior had met Lynn when he had spent a Christmas break in the dorms; neither of them could afford to go home. All during the break, Junior read books and stared out the window into the snow. He watched cars pass by and wondered if white people were happier than Indians.

They met each other while checking their mail the day after Christmas.

"So," Lynn had asked, "what's it like being the only Indian here?"

"It gets pretty lonely, I guess."

"Do you drink much?"

"What do you mean?"

"Well, I see you at parties. You seem to drink a lot."

"Yeah, maybe I do."

Lynn studied Junior's face.

"You know," she said, "you're very pretty."

"You're pretty, too."

They walked around campus for hours, talking and laughing. Then Lynn suddenly stopped and stared at Junior.

"What?" he asked.

"Listen," she said and kissed him. Just like that. Junior had never kissed a white woman before, so he used his tongue a lot, and tried to find out if she tasted different than an Indian woman.

"Irish," said Lynn as she broke the kiss. "I'm Irish."

"Who's Irish?" Victor asked Junior and pulled him from his memories.

"What?" Junior asked.

"What the hell are you talking about?"

"What do you mean?"

"You said you were Irish."

"I didn't say that."

"Yeah, you did," Victor said. "Where the hell were you? On another planet?"

"Yeah," Junior said. "On another planet."

† † †

From the night report, 34th precinct, Manhattan:

12:53 A.M. Two Native Americans, Thomas Builds-the-Fire and Chess Warm Water, reported disappearance of two friends, Victor Joseph and Junior Polatkin. All are from Wellpinit, Washington, and are in a rock band called Coyote Springs, along with a Checkers Warm Water, who is waiting at the band's hotel. The disappeared supposedly took off on drinking binge after confrontation at record company. Took down stats on the missing but informed others that we couldn't do much unless there was some evidence of foul play. Joseph and Polatkin will probably stagger into hotel at dawn. Builds-the-Fire was lead singer of the band.

† † †

Checkers waited in the hotel room and stared out the window, at the clock, at the door. She was afraid for the rest of Coyote Springs, because she knew that Indians always disappeared. She knew about Sam Bone, that Indian who waved to a few friends, turned a corner, and was never seen again.

"Please," Checkers said, her only prayer. She lay on the bed, closed her eyes, and prayed. She prayed until she fell asleep, and then she dreamed.

*

Checkers? asked the voice, like a knock on the door.

Chess, Checkers whispered as she rushed to the door and opened it.

Hello, said Phil Sheridan as he pushed his way into the room.

What do you want? Checkers asked.

I came to apologize, Sheridan said. *Where is everybody?*

They all just left. They'll be back soon.

You're alone?

For just a little while, Checkers said and edged back toward the door. Sheridan stepped around her, shut the door, and locked it. He stared at Checkers. His eyes were wild, furtive.

You guys really blew it, Sheridan said.

What do you mean?

You blew it by acting like a bunch of goddamn wild Indians. I might have been able to talk Mr. Armstrong into listening to you again. He might have given you another chance. But not after that shit you pulled in the studio. You caused a lot of damage.

We didn't start it.

That's what you Indians always say. The white men did this to us, the white men did that to us. When are you ever going to take responsibility for yourselves?

Sheridan paced around the room, lit a cigarette, and waved it like a saber.

You had a choice, Sheridan said. *We gave you every chance. All you had to do was move to the reservation. We would've protected you. The U.S. Army was the best friend the Indians ever had.*

What are you talking about? Checkers asked. *We're not in the army. We're a rock band.*

Checkers made a move for the door, but Sheridan grabbed her.

This is just like you Indians, Sheridan shouted in her face. *You could never stay where we put you. You never listened to orders. Always fighting. You never quit fighting. Do you understand how tired I am of fighting you? When will you ever give up?*

Sheridan threw Checkers to the floor. He pulled off his coat and necktie.

Listen, he said and tried to regain composure. *I don't want to hurt you. I never wanted to hurt anybody. But it was war. This is war. We won. Don't you understand? We won the war. We keep winning the war. But you won't surrender.*

Sheridan kneeled down beside Checkers and tied her hands behind her back with his necktie.

I remember once, he said, *when I killed this Indian woman. I don't even know what tribe she was. It was back in '72. I rode up on her and ran my saber right through her heart. I thought that was it. But she jumped up and pulled me off my mount. I couldn't believe it. I was so angry that I threw her to the ground and stomped her to death. It was then I noticed she was pregnant. We couldn't have that. Nits make lice, you know? So I cut her belly open and pulled that fetus out. Then that baby bit me. Can you believe that?*

I don't know what you're talking about, Checkers said.

You know exactly what I'm talking about. You Indians always knew how to play dumb. But you were never dumb. You talked like Tonto, but you had brains like fucking Einstein. Had us whites all figured out. But we still kept trying to change you. Tried to make you white. It never worked.

Mr. Sheridan, what are you going to do to me?

I don't know, Sheridan said and sat on the floor beside Checkers. *I never know what to do with you.*

Sheridan studied Checkers. He had watched her during the last few centuries. She was beautiful. But she was Indian beautiful with tribal features. She didn't look anything at all like a white woman. She was tall with narrow hips and muscular legs. Large breasts. She had arms strong as any man's. And black, black hair that hung down past her shoulders. Sheridan wanted to touch it. He had always been that way about Indian women's hair.

You know, Sheridan said, *you're more beautiful than your sister.*

She didn't listen. She didn't really care one way or the other. She just wanted help.

I don't care what you think, Checkers said. *I don't believe in you.*

What?

I don't believe in you. I'm just dreaming. You're a ghost, a dream, a piece of dust, a foul-smelling wind. Go away.

Sheridan reached across the years and took Checkers's face in his hands. He squeezed until she cried out and saw white flashes of light.

Do you believe in me now? he asked.

† † †

Thomas and Chess walked into Carson's All-Night Restaurant on the Lower East Side. They had been lost on the subway for hours, sure they were going to be mugged at any time.

"Why aren't we dead?" Chess asked Thomas as they sat in a booth.

"Probably because we looked too pathetic to mug," Thomas said.

"What do you want?" asked the waitress who came to the table. She had an unusually beautiful voice for a waitress, but it was New York. That waitress had been blonde at several different points during her lifetime, even though she was currently redheaded. Still, she was pretty and had even been called back for a few television commercials. She hadn't gotten a role yet, but there was a bathroom cleaner spot in her future.

"Hey," Chess said, "you ain't seen two Indian men come in here, have you?"

"What?" the waitress asked. "What do you mean? From India?"

"No," Chess said. "Not that kind of Indian. We mean American Indians, you know? Bows-and-arrows Indians. Cowboys-and-Indians Indians."

"Oh," the waitress said, "that kind. Shoot, I ain't ever seen that kind of Indian."

"We're that kind of Indian."

"Really?"

"Really."

"Hey, Kit," the waitress yelled back at the fry cook and owner of the deli. "Have you seen any Indians in here?"

"What do you mean?" Kit asked. "You mean from India or what?"

"No, stupid," the waitress yelled. "Indians like in the western movies. Like Geronimo."

"Oh, I ain't seen none of those around for a long time. I saw a few in a book once. You sure there are still Indians around at all?"

"These two right here say they're Indian."

Kit the fry cook came out to look at the two potential Indians. Chess and Thomas saw a fat man in a dirty white t-shirt, although they weren't sure where the shirt ended and the man began.

"Shit," Kit said. "They don't look nothing like those Indians in the movies. They look Puerto Rican to me."

"Yeah," the waitress said. "They kind of do."

"Do you speak English?" Kit asked.

"Let's get out of here," Chess said to Thomas.

"Yeah, let's go home," Thomas said.

"Hey, you speak good English," Kit yelled after Chess and Thomas. "Have a good trip back to Puerto Rico."

† † †

I'm pregnant, Lynn had told Junior after they dated for a few months during that first year in college.

"I'm pregnant," Junior said aloud as he sat with Victor in their sixth bar of the night. After hours. Victor would have been falling down drunk if he had been standing up.

"Who's the father?" Victor asked and laughed.

What do you want to do? Junior had asked Lynn after she told him.

"Am I the father?" Victor asked and laughed some more.

Lynn had just shrugged her shoulders.

Do you want to get married? Junior had asked her then.

"Do you want to get married?" he said aloud in the bar.

"I ain't going to marry you if I ain't the father," Victor said.

I can't marry you, Lynn had said. *You're Indian.*

Junior had turned and walked away from Lynn. He always wondered why they had been together at all. Everybody on campus stared at them. The Indian boy and the white girl walking hand in hand. Lynn's parents wouldn't even talk to him when they came to campus for visits.

Junior walked away from Lynn and never looked back. No. That wasn't true. He did turn back once, and she was still standing there, an explosion of white skin and blonde hair. She waved, and Junior felt himself break into small pieces that blew away uselessly in the wind.

"Nothing as white as the white girl an Indian boy loves," Junior said aloud.

"What the fuck you talking about?" Victor asked. "I ain't white. I'm lower sub-chief of the Spokane Tribe."

Junior walked away from his memories of Lynn and looked Victor square in the face.

"You know," Junior said, "the end of the world is near."

"Shit, I know that. Don't you think I know that? I'm a fatalist."

Spittle hung from Victor's mouth, his eyes were glazed over, and his hair was plastered wetly to his forehead. He smiled a little, a single tear ran down his face, and then he passed out face first onto the table.

"It's time to take you home," Junior said.

Junior picked him up and carried him out the door. The bartender watched them leave, cleaned the glasses they had drunk from, and erased their presence from that part of the world.

† † †

Do you know how many times I've dreamed about you? Sheridan asked Checkers.

It couldn't have been very many, Checkers said. *You haven't known me very long.*

I've known you for centuries.

Jeez, now you're starting to sound like Dracula. And I don't believe in monsters.

I want to kiss you, Sheridan said.

No, Checkers said. *I don't believe in you.*

Sheridan slapped Checkers hard, drew a little blood. A little is more than enough.

Do you believe in me now? he asked.

You ain't nothing, you ain't nothing.

I'm everything.

You ain't much at all. You're just another white guy telling lies. I don't believe in you. All you want to do is fight and fuck. You never tell a story that's true. I don't believe in you.

Sheridan kissed Checkers, bit down hard on her lips. He was pulling at her clothes when there was a knock on the door.

George Wright knocked on the door of Coyote Springs's hotel room. He couldn't sleep at all. He had tossed and turned, worrying about the band. So he jumped into a taxi and came over.

He wasn't even sure why. He knocked on the door again. He heard a woman's voice inside and then her scream.

"Shit," Wright said and threw his shoulder against the door. He was surprised when the unlocked door flew wide open and sent him sprawling.

† † †

From a letter Junior kept hidden in his wallet:

> Dear Junior:
> It's over. I went to the free clinic and it's over. My parents will never know about it. You don't have to worry about it. I'm okay. I barely even felt anything. I just closed my eyes and then it was over. I hummed a little song to myself so I couldn't hear anything and then it was over. My parents will never even know it happened. You don't have to think about it anymore. Just remember that I love you. But that's all over now.
>
> Love,
> Lynn

† † †

Just before sunrise, Thomas and Chess walked into the lobby of their hotel and discovered America. No. They actually discovered Victor and Junior sleeping on couches in the lobby. No. They actually discovered Victor passed out on a couch while Junior read *USA Today*.

"Where've you two been?" Chess asked. "We've been looking for you all damn night."

"We've been here a couple hours," Junior said.

Thomas and Chess looked at each other.

"Didn't the hotel hassle you for being here?" Thomas asked.

"No," Junior said. "I think they figured we was rock stars and didn't want to piss us off."

"Well," Chess said, "we certainly ain't rock stars."

"Why didn't you go up to the room?" Thomas asked.

"I couldn't carry him any farther," Junior said. "And those damn bellboys wanted five bucks to help me."

"Where's Checkers?" Chess asked.

"I don't know," Junior said. "Where is she supposed to be?"

"In the room," Chess said.

"Well, then," Junior said, "she's probably upstairs. You want to help me carry Victor up?"

"Yeah," Thomas said, and all three of them carried Victor into the elevator.

"Oh, man, he stinks," Chess said, and they all agreed.

Chess looked closely at Junior. His eyes were bloodshot, but they weren't glossed over. He didn't even smell like booze. He just smelled like day-old clothes.

"Don't you have a hangover?" Chess asked.

"Nope," Junior said. "I didn't drink none. Just orange juice."

"How come?"

"Somebody needed to stay sober," Junior said. "This is New York City, enit?"

Chess was surprised at Junior's logic.

"You know, Junior," Chess said, "you're always saving Victor from something."

"Yeah, I know."

They dragged Victor to their hotel room and knocked on the door. They were shocked all to hell when George Wright answered.

"What's going on?" Thomas and Junior asked, ready to fight.

"Listen," Wright said, "it's all right. I was just waiting

for you to get back. Checkers asked me to wait. She's sleeping now.''

"What happened?" asked Chess as they dragged Victor into the room. "Where's Checkers? What did you do to her?"

"She's okay, she's okay," Wright said. "I didn't do anything. It was just a nightmare. She just had a nightmare."

"A nightmare?" Chess asked.

"Yes," Wright said, "a nightmare."

Chess went to look in on Checkers. Thomas and Junior surrounded Wright as best as they could. Victor snored on the floor.

"What are you doing here?" Junior asked. "And where's that asshole Sheridan?"

"I don't know where he is," Wright said. "I just came here to apologize."

"Apologize for what?" Junior asked.

Chess walked out of the bedroom.

"How is she?" Thomas asked.

"She's sore, but okay, I guess," Chess said. "She said it was the worst nightmare she ever had."

Junior shivered.

"Checkers said you saved her life," Chess said to Wright.

"I just woke her up," Wright said.

"Why you helping us?"

"Because I owe you."

"Owe us for what?"

Wright looked at Coyote Springs. He saw their Indian faces. He saw the faces of millions of Indians, beaten, scarred by smallpox and frostbite, split open by bayonets and bullets. He looked at his own white hands and saw the blood stains there.

9

Small World

Indian boy takes a drink of everything that killed his brother
Indian boy drives his car through the rail, over the shoulder
Off the road, on the rez, where survivors are forced to gather
All his bones, all his blood, while the dead watch the world shatter

chorus:
But it's a small world
You don't have to pay attention
It's the reservation
The news don't give it a mention
Yeah, it's a small world
Getting smaller and smaller and smaller

Indian girl disappeared while hitchhiking on the old highway
Indian girl left the road and some white wolf ate her heart away

Indian girl found naked by the river, shot twice in the head
One more gone, one more gone, and our world fills with all of our dead

(repeat chorus)

A week after Coyote Springs staggered from Manhattan back onto the Spokane Indian Reservation, Junior Polatkin stole a rifle from the gun rack in Simon's pickup. Junior didn't know anything about caliber, but he knew the rifle was loaded. He knew the rifle was loaded because Simon had told him so. Junior strapped that rifle over his shoulder and climbed up the water tower that had been empty for most of his life. He looked down at his reservation, at the tops of HUD houses and the Trading Post. A crowd gathered below him and circled the base of the tower. He could hear the distant sirens of Tribal Police cars and was amazed the cops were already on their way.

Junior unshouldered the rifle. He felt the smooth, cool wood of the stock, set the butt of the rifle against the metal grating of the floor, and placed his forehead against the mouth of the barrel. There was a childhood game like that, Junior remembered, with a baseball bat. Standing at home plate, you placed one end of the bat on the ground and held your forehead against the other. You were supposed to spin round and round the bat, once, twice, ten times. Then you had to run from home plate to first base, weaving and falling like a drunk. Junior remembered. He flipped the safety off, held his thumb against the trigger, and felt the slight tension. Junior squeezed the trigger.

† † †

The night before Junior Polatkin climbed the water tower, Checkers Warm Water crawled out of a bedroom window in Thomas

Builds-the-Fire's house. She had to climb out of the window because the Tribal Police had ordered the band to stay inside the house. The death threats had started soon after Coyote Springs returned to the reservation, and the Tribal Police weren't taking any chances. Michael White Hawk had been released from Tribal Jail but didn't have much to say about the band. He just walked blankly around the softball field with his huge head still wrapped in bandages, like some carnival psychic. The Tribal Cops kept suggesting that he should go to Indian Health Service, but White Hawk refused to go and just stood for hours at the softball field. He wouldn't say anything at all, but then he would burst into sudden frenetic conversations with himself. He swung his fists at the air and tried to dig up that grave in center field before the Tribal Police calmed him down. White Hawk had been crazy and dangerous before he was knocked twice on the head. Now he had become crazy, dangerous, and unpredictable. Even White Hawk's buddies were afraid.

"He's just acting," White Hawk's friends reassured each other. "He's just trying to fool everybody into thinking he's goofy."

White Hawk was asleep on third base when Checkers slipped out of the window in Thomas's house. Thomas didn't even move, but Chess stirred in bed as Checkers slipped away. Even sound asleep, Chess reached out for her sister. Checkers had not slept well since her return from New York. Phil Sheridan had come back again and again. Sometimes he threatened her. Other times he remained on the edge of her dreams. No matter what she dreamed about, Sheridan sat in a corner with a cup of coffee in his hands. He wore a wool suit or his cavalry dress blues. Sheridan had eventually forced Checkers to abandon her own room and sleep on the floor beside the bed that Thomas and Chess shared.

Wide awake, Checkers climbed out the window and snuck past the Tribal Cops asleep in their cruisers. She avoided the roads and cut across fields. There was no moon on that night, and the walk was treacherous. She stepped in gopher holes, tripped over abandoned barbed wire, heard the laughter of animals. Checkers wasn't afraid of the dark. She was afraid of what waited in the dark. She heard rustling in the brush, the scratch-scratch of unseen animals as they climbed pine trees.

But she made her way through to the Catholic Church. She saw its lights in the distance, and it grew larger and brighter as she approached. Checkers wasn't sure how long the walk had taken. But the church was still lit up, bright as God. She walked boldly through the front door and stepped inside.

Father Arnold kneeled at the front of the church. His whole body rocked and shook. From Checkers's viewpoint, she couldn't tell if he was laughing or crying.

"Father?" Checkers whispered, but he didn't respond.

"Father?" Checkers said louder, and Arnold turned around. He had been crying, was still crying. He wiped his face with a sleeve of his cassock. He stood.

"Father?" Checkers asked. "Are you okay?"

She slowly walked toward him. She had dreamed of this moment. Even as Phil Sheridan floated on the periphery, Checkers had dreamed of taking Father Arnold in her arms. She dreamed of the smell of his hair, washed with cheap shampoo, all that a priest could afford. She dreamed of the kiss they shared just before Coyote Springs left for Big Mom's house, for Manhattan.

Checkers wasn't dreaming as she walked across the church, her muddy feet leaving tracks on the wood floor. She trailed her right hand over the pews, felt the splintered wood. Father Arnold had once told her those pews were over fifty years old. But Checkers didn't really care about the age of that wood. She walked up to Father Arnold and stood just inches away.

"Checkers," Father Arnold whispered.

"Father."

Checkers closed her eyes and expected the next kiss.

"Checkers," Father Arnold said, "this is not going to happen. It can't. I'm sorry."

Checkers looked up at him.

"What are you talking about?" she asked.

Father Arnold led Checkers to a pew and sat beside her.

"I'm leaving the reservation," he said. "I've lost my direction here."

Father Arnold had served the Spokane Indian Reservation for five years and ministered with self-conscious kindness. He effusively praised even the smallest signs of an Indian's faith. He had cried at his first service when Bessie, the oldest Spokane Indian Catholic, presented him with a dreamcatcher. Other priests would have dismissed the dreamcatcher as Indian mysticism or mythological arts and crafts, but Father Arnold was genuinely thrilled by its intricate system of threads and beads. He had laughed out loud when he noticed the dreamcatcher was actually decorated with rosary beads.

"Hang this over your bed," Bessie had said, "and it will catch those Protestant nightmares before they can sneak into your sleep."

"But what about Catholic nightmares?" Father Arnold had asked.

"Protestants are a good Catholic's worst nightmare."

Father Arnold had rushed home and hung it over his bed. Later that night, he stared up at the dreamcatcher over his head. He willed himself to think of the worst possible things. Murders, rapes, loss of faith. Father Arnold imagined that he was nailed to the cross. He heard the dull thud of hammer on nail.

"Come on, nightmares," Arnold had whispered. "You can't touch me now."

*

"Where are you going?" Checkers asked Father Arnold. "Where are they sending you?"

"They aren't sending me anywhere," Arnold said. "I'm leaving the church. I'm letting it all go."

Checkers leaned back in the pew. She felt some winged thing bump against the interior of her ribcage. She felt the slight brush of wingtips as it struggled between her ribs and left her body. She had no name for it. Checkers heard that winged thing flutter against the stained-glass windows. Then it flew so close that she felt a slight breeze. She closed her eyes, and the winged thing was gone.

"But I love you," Checkers said.

"I love you, too," Father Arnold said. "But not like that. It can't work that way."

"But you kissed me."

"I know I kissed you. It was wrong."

"You can't do this. You can't. Not now," Checkers said. She didn't know how much she had left. Coyote Springs had failed, had not even bothered to bring their instruments home from Manhattan. Checkers could see the guitars and keyboards strewn around the studio. Victor's guitar was smashed into pieces, but everything else was just as useless.

"Would you like some headphones?" the attendant had asked Checkers during the flight home from Manhattan. Checkers just shook her head. The rest of Coyote Springs refused the headphones, too.

Checkers sat next to the window, Chess in the middle, and Thomas in the aisle seat. Junior and Victor sat directly across the aisle, one on either side of an empty seat. It was the only empty seat on the plane.

Coyote Springs didn't have much to say on the way home. They all drank their complimentary Pepsis and ate their roasted peanuts. Junior and Victor didn't order any booze. They didn't have the money. They might not have drank anyway, even if given the chance. After they returned home, both just sipped at tall glasses of ice water

"Thomas and I had a talk," Chess whispered to Checkers somewhere over Iowa. "We're going to move back to Arlee. We want you to come with us."

"Why Arlee?" Checkers asked.

"What do you mean? Those are our people. We don't have anywhere else to go anyway."

"We can go anywhere. We can stay on the Spokane Reservation."

"Jeez, Checkers. Will you get your head out of your ass? They don't want us there anymore."

"How do you know that?" Checkers asked. "Besides, it's only that White Hawk causing all the trouble. The people at the church still like me."

"They only liked you because you quit the band," Chess said. "And all you're worried about is Father Arnold anyway."

The plane bounced through rough air, but Coyote Springs barely noticed. Junior looked out his window and wondered how he would feel if the plane lost power and began the long dive to the ground. The oxygen masks would drop from the ceiling while the flight attendants rushed from row to row, speaking in calm and practiced tones.

Remove your eyewear. Remove all jewelry. Make sure the aisles are clear. Buckle yourself in tightly. We're going to make it. We're going to make it. Don't panic. Panic is your enemy. Don't feel guilty that you left college in the middle of an English class. During a boring discussion about the proper way to write an essay. Remember that you had no idea she was going to get an abortion. It's not your fault. You didn't want the baby either. Not really. Not until she didn't want you anymore. Not until she didn't want some half-breed baby. Not until you thought about how much her parents hated you. How they deserved a half-breed grandchild. How would they explain it to their friends? Please, breathe slowly. Hold on to the hand of the person next to you at impact. Don't let them go. Don't let them go even when the flames roll through the cabin and melt you into your seat. She had no other choice. She had no other choice. Our pilot has thousands of hours of flying experience. The whole crew has been trained to deal with these emergencies. No matter what happens, the coroners will be able to identify you from your dental records. Indian Health Service keeps excellent records. And if you do survive the impact, survive the flames and the toxic smoke, then you will hear music. A cedar flute perhaps. Follow that music. Even though you don't deserve it. Follow that thin music.

Junior closed his eyes and listened for the music. He didn't hear anything. He looked over at Victor, who was fighting back tears. Chess, Checkers, and Thomas could not have seen Victor from where they sat. Nobody could have known exactly why he was in mourning. The rest of Coyote Springs might have assumed it was because he had lost his chance to be a rock star. But he mourned for the loss of that guitar. Junior watched his best friend mourn, but he wanted to reach across the seat, touch Victor's arms, and point out the exits.

"You can't leave," Checkers said to Father Arnold. "You can't leave me, us, alone."

"The Bishop will send another priest," Father Arnold said. "They won't have any other option. They can't leave the community alone. I'm sure the new priest will be here soon. They can arrange for a few visitors to conduct the services until he arrives."

"That's not what I mean. You know that's not what I mean."

Father Arnold searched his soul for the right words, the right prayer. He had always had them before. God, he had been sure of the answers. Self-deprecating and modest, he had still believed he was a great priest. He knew he was a great priest, in a quietly arrogant way. On some spiritual scoreboard in his head, he had kept count of the people he was saving.

Checkers had taken all that away. No. That wasn't fair to Checkers. She didn't love him any more than other parishioners had. Father Arnold had resisted advances before. It happened to priests often enough to warrant a few good-natured jokes in the seminary. But Checkers had truly shaken Father Arnold and his vows. He dreamed about her every night. In those dreams, she led him into a tipi, lay down with him on a robe, and touched him. Frightened and aroused, Father Arnold woke and prayed that his dreamcatcher would work. He prayed that his dreams of Checkers would be trapped in the dreamcatcher's web.

"I dream about you," Father Arnold said to Checkers.

"I dream about you, too."

"No," Arnold said. "I don't want to dream about you. I'm a man of God. I belong to God."

Checkers reached for Father Arnold, but he stood and stepped away. He had always loved how his flock kept a respectable distance away, coming closer only with his permission.

"I'm sorry," he said. "But you need to leave. I need to leave."

Father Arnold reached out to Checkers, reconsidered, and then quickly walked out of the church. Checkers didn't follow him. She leaned back in the pew and stared at the crucifix nailed to the wall. Jesus nailed to the cross that's nailed to the wall. She felt a sharp ache deep in her chest. She curled her knees up next to her breasts, wrapped her arms around her legs, and slowly rocked back and forth, back and forth.

† † †

On the day before Checkers made her escape to the Catholic Church, Victor Joseph sat alone on the couch. The rest of Coyote Springs was out on the front lawn, talking to the Tribal Cops. Victor had no use for Tribal Cops, even if they were supposedly protecting him. Victor stared at the space in the room where the television used to sit. Upon their arrival home, Coyote Springs had thrown out the television, which didn't work anyway, three radios, and a pair of squeaky cowboy boots. They didn't want to hear any kind of music. Victor stared at that space until he fell asleep.

In his dream, Victor sat alone in the house and heard a soft noise in the distance. At first, he thought it was the conversation outside, but the noise took shape and became a C chord, then a D, F, and G. He clapped his hands to his ears, but the music would not stop. He stood and looked out the window at his bandmates and the cops, but they just continued, oblivious to the music. He searched the house for the source. The two bedrooms were empty, as were the bathroom and kitchen. The music grew louder as Victor descended the stairs. In the unfinished basement, the blankets that served as walls swayed with the force of the chords.

Victor searched under the stairs, in the bedrooms, and still couldn't find the source. He opened up the downstairs bathroom door and was knocked back by a vicious open chord. The guitar was leaning against the wall.

I think you left something behind in New York, said the guitar. Victor stepped inside the bathroom, shut the door behind him, and reached for it.

Take it easy there, the guitar said. *You can have me back. You can take me and you can be anybody you want to be. You can have anything you want to have. But you have to trade me for it.*

Trade what? Victor asked.

You have to give up what you love the most, said the guitar. *What do you love the most? Who do you love the most?*

Outside, while Victor dreamt, Junior Polatkin thought he heard his name called out. He looked at the Tribal Cops, who just continued to flirt with Chess and Checkers. The Warm Water sisters ignored the Tribal Cops and talked to each other. Thomas sat on an old tire swing. Junior heard his name again and recognized Victor's voice. He looked toward the house, but he was the only one who heard it. Junior heard Victor whisper his name.

† † †

On the night before Victor Joseph dreamed about the guitar, Thomas Builds-the-Fire and Chess Warm Water lay awake in bed. Both assumed Checkers was fast asleep on the floor, but she listened to their whispered conversation.

"Thomas," Chess said, "what are we going to do?"

"I don't know," Thomas said. "What do you want to do?"

"I want to go back to Arlee."

Thomas didn't say anything. He stared up at the stained ceiling. Water stains. He remembered the rain that had pounded his roof, seeped through the insulation, pooled in the crawlspace, and then dripped down onto the bed.

"I want to go back to Arlee," Chess said again. "You said we could go back to Arlee."

Thomas had agreed to go back to Arlee as Coyote Springs waited in Kennedy Airport in New York. He had never felt farther away, never felt more *away* than at that moment. He didn't want to get on the plane for the flight home to Wellpinit. He wanted to get on a different plane and fly to someplace different, somewhere he had never even heard of. Some strange place with a strange name. He wanted to grab a map of the world, close his eyes, and spit. He would live wherever his spit landed on the map. Still, he knew he would probably spit on his own reservation, just a green-colored spot on the map.

"I'll go wherever you want to go," Thomas had said but still knew that every part of him was Spokane Indian.

"Good," Chess had said, but she also saw the doubt in Thomas's eyes. She knew what it felt like to leave her own reservation. She had felt something stretch inside her as that blue van pulled off the Flathead Reservation all those weeks ago. She had looked back and felt a sharp pain, like the tearing of tendon and ligament from bone. She had left her reservation because of that goddamn guitar, that sudden fire it had lit inside her. But that fire had consumed almost everything, and despite her years of firefighting experience, she had not been able to stop it. She had not dug fire lines, had not provided herself with a quick escape route. She loved the music, she loved Thomas, she loved the fire. But Thomas was all that she had left, and the Spokane Indian Reservation was threatening to keep him.

"Thomas," she had said just before their flight number was called.

"What?" he asked.

She had taken his hand in hers, studied the way their fingers fit together, and almost wanted to stay there in the airport forever. She had almost wanted to stay suspended between here and there, between location and destination. She squeezed Thomas's hand and waited.

"There's nothing left here for us," Chess said to Thomas in bed. "There's nothing left here for you."

"I know," Thomas said. "But they're my people. They're my Tribe."

"Of course. But the Flatheads are my people. And they ain't threatening to kill us."

"Not everybody wants to kill us. Nobody wants to kill us. They're just talking. We just let them down."

"Don't make excuses for them. You don't need to make excuses for them."

Checkers rolled over on the floor. She knew her movement would make Thomas and Chess stop talking. She didn't want to go back to the Flathead Reservation, and she didn't want Chess to convince Thomas to move. Even if Chess and Thomas left, Checkers knew she would remain behind. Indians were always switching reservations anyway. For love, for money, to escape jail time. Checkers was still thinking of Father Arnold.

"Thomas," Chess said after a long silence. "Are you still awake?"

"Yeah."

"We don't have to go to Arlee. I mean, I really want to go home. But mostly, I just want to leave here. I don't want to be here anymore."

"Where would we go?"

"I don't know. Anywhere but here. Maybe we should go west. All the white people did and look what they got."

"What's west of here?"

"Everything's west of here, Thomas. Everything. We could move to Spokane. Is that west enough?"

Spokane, a mostly white city, sat on the banks of the Spokane River. Spokane the city was named after the Tribe that had been forcibly removed from the river. Spokane was only sixty miles from the reservation, but Thomas figured it was no closer than the moon.

There was nobody waiting for Coyote Springs in the Spokane International Airport when they deboarded the plane. They had crossed three time zones and still had no idea how they worked.

"It's like fucking time travel," Victor said.

Coyote Springs had waited at the baggage carousel until all the passengers had picked up their luggage. All except Victor. All the other passengers on the plane had been greeted by family and friends who took the luggage from their hands. All the other passengers had already left the airport. Coyote Springs waited for Victor's bag.

"Shit," Victor said. "What happened?"

Coyote Springs was just about to abandon the bag when a guitar case slid down onto the carousel. The rest of Coyote Springs took a quick step back, but Victor reached for it and grabbed the handle. He pulled the guitar case off the carousel and turned back toward the rest of the band.

"It's my guitar," Victor said. "It's my guitar, goddamn it. We can start over. We can get the band going again. We don't need those fucking guys in New York City. We can do it ourselves."

A young white man with a white shirt and dirty jeans came running back into the baggage area. He was in a panic but relaxed visibly when he saw Victor holding the guitar case.

"Oh, God," said the white man. "I can't believe I almost forgot it."

Coyote Springs looked at him blankly. He stared back.

"That's mine," the white man said and pointed at the guitar case. "I almost forgot it."

Victor pulled the guitar up close to his body.

"That's mine," the man repeated. "That's my name there on the side."

Coyote Springs looked at the black guitar case with "Dakota" written in white paint.

"Your name ain't really Dakota, is it?" Chess asked.

"Yeah, my dad is way into the Indian thing. He's part Indian from his grandmother. She was a full-blood Cherokee."

"If he was Cherokee," Chess said, "then why did he name you Dakota?"

"What do you mean?"

"Cherokee and Dakota are two different tribes, you know?"

"I don't understand what you're trying to say."

Coyote Springs took a deep breath, exhaled.

"You ain't supposed to name yourself after a whole damn

tribe," Victor finally said. "Especially if it ain't your tribe to begin
with."

"Well," said the white man, "it's my name. And that's
my guitar."

Victor had known the guitar inside the case wasn't his. He
had only wanted to be close to any guitar.

"Here," Victor said. "Take the damn thing."

The white man took the guitar from Victor and walked
away. Coyote Springs watched him. Then he turned back after a
few steps.

"You know," he said, "you act like I'm stealing something from you. This is my guitar. This is my name. I didn't steal
anything."

Chess and Thomas finally agreed to leave the Spokane Indian Reservation for anywhere else. There was no doubt that
Checkers would come with them, but she lay on the floor, fuming.
She didn't want to leave. She was still angry when she fell asleep.
After Thomas had fallen asleep too, Chess climbed out of bed and
walked quietly into the kitchen. She sat at the table with an empty
cup. She kept bringing the cup to her lips, forgetting it contained
nothing.

She rubbed her eyes, brought the cup to her lips again, set
it back. She cleared her throat, thought about the cup again, and
then the sun rose so suddenly that she barely had time to react.

"Good morning," Thomas said when he walked into the
kitchen. "You're up early."

Checkers shuffled in a few minutes later, while Victor and
Junior slept on. Those two found it was easier to just sleep, rather
than wake up and face the day.

"Morning," Checkers mumbled. She poured powdered
commodity milk into a plastic jug and added water. She stirred and
stirred. She stirred for ten minutes, because that powdered milk

refused to mix completely. No matter how long an Indian stirred her commodity milk, it always came out with those lumps of coagulated powder. There was nothing worse. Those lumps were like bombs, moist on the outside with an inner core of dry powdered milk. An Indian would take a big swig of milk, and one of those coagulated powder bombs would drop into her mouth and explode when she bit it. She'd be coughing little puffs of powdered milk for an hour.

"Do you want some breakfast?" Checkers asked Chess and Thomas. Neither of them was very excited about the milk, but they had to have something for breakfast.

"Okay," Chess and Thomas said.

Checkers poured milk into their cups and into a cup of her own. The three sat at the kitchen table, took small sips, then a big drink, and coughed white powder until Victor and Junior could not sleep through the noise.

† † †

The day before Chess and Thomas decided to leave the Spokane Indian Reservation for good, Robert Johnson sat on the porch at Big Mom's house while she sat in her rocking chair. Johnson's vision had improved tremendously during his time on the reservation. Back in his youth in Mississippi, he saw everything blurred. White spots clouded one eye. His sister bought him glasses when he was ten years old, but he never wore them much. But now he could see the entire Spokane Indian Reservation when he looked down Wellpinit Mountain. He watched Michael White Hawk march dumbly around the softball diamond. From home to first base, second, third, and back to home.

"Home," White Hawk whispered to himself. Then he marched around the bases again.

"What's wrong wit' him?" Johnson asked Big Mom.

"Same thing that's wrong with most people," Big Mom said. "He's living his life doing the same thing all day long. He's just more obvious about it."

"What d'y'all mean?"

"Well, think about it. Most people wake up, have breakfast, go to work, come home, eat dinner, watch television, and then go to sleep. Five days a week. Then they go see a movie, go to church, go to the beach on weekends. Then Monday morning comes, and they're back to work. Then they die. White Hawk's just doing the same thing on a different level. He's a genius. It's performance art."

"Well, I guess. You pos'tive 'bout that? Maybe he just got hisself knocked too hard on the head. Like a fighter. I seen how fighters end up gettin' slugged too much."

"Maybe."

"You ain't serious 'bout that, are you?"

"Maybe."

Robert Johnson and Big Mom sat for hours in silence. Big Mom thought about the young Michael White Hawk, who had come to get help with his saxophone. She remembered that version of White Hawk, who had nearly believed in Big Mom once, before he went to prison for assaulting that grocery store cashier. But Johnson had never known that White Hawk. Johnson watched him walk circles around the softball diamond. Home, first, second, third, home again.

"It happens that way," Johnson whispered. "It really does happen that way."

Son House, preacher and bluesman, had been a star in Robinsville, Mississippi, way back when. Robert Johnson was just a teenager when he started to follow House from juke joint to joint. Johnson only played harmonica then, but he was good enough to join Son House on stage every once in a while. Johnson loved the stage. He only felt loved when he was on stage, singing and blow-ing his harp. But it still wasn't enough. Johnson wanted to play guitar.

"Oh, God," Son House said to Johnson after he let him play guitar at a juke. "I ain't lettin' you play no more. I ain't ever heard such a racket. You was makin' people mad."

Ashamed, Johnson packed up his clothes and guitar and left town. He just disappeared as he walked north up Highway 61. Just vanished after the first crossroads.

Robert Johnson looked over at Big Mom. She was carving a piece of wood. Johnson had given up on carving a new guitar out of that scrub wood he had gathered when Coyote Springs was still practicing at Big Mom's house. That wood was still in a pile out there in the pine trees. He barely remembered his dreams of a new guitar.

"What's you makin' there?" Johnson asked Big Mom.

"None of your business," she said.

"That a good piece of wood?"

"Good enough."

Johnson looked down the mountain and watched a group of Spokane Indians carrying picket signs and marching in circles around the Tribal Community Center. The very traditional Spo-kanes carried signs written in the Spokane language and chanted things in the Spokane language, too. But they all sounded pissed off. The Indian Christian signs read COYOTE SPRINGS NEEDS TO BE SAVED and REPENT, COYOTE SPRINGS, REPENT! while the nonsecu-lar signs said COYOTE SPRINGS CAN KISS MY BIG RED ASS.

"What's goin' happen down there?" Johnson asked Big Mom. "What's goin' happen to Coyote Springs?"

"I don't know. It ain't up to me to decide."

"That's what you always say."

"I say it because it's true. What do you want me to say?"

*

"What do you want, Mr. Johnson?" asked the Gentleman. A handsome white man, the Gentleman wore a perfectly pressed black wool suit in the hot Mississippi heat. He leaned against the crossroads sign, picking at his teeth with a long fingernail.

"I want to play the guitar," Johnson said.

"But you already play the guitar."

"No. I mean, I want to play the guitar better."

"Better than what?"

"Better than anybody ever."

"That's a big want," the Gentleman said. His lupine eyes caught the sunlight in a strange way, reflecting colors that Johnson had never seen before.

"I want it big," Johnson said.

"Well, then," said the Gentleman after a long pause. "I can teach you how to play like that. But what are you going to give me in return?"

"What you mean?"

"I mean, Mr. Johnson, that you have to trade me. I'll teach you how to play better than anybody ever, but you have to give me something in return."

"Like what?"

"Whatever you love the most. What do you love the most, Mr. Johnson?"

Johnson felt the whip that split open the skin on his grandfathers' backs. He heard the creak of floorboard as the white masters crept into his grandmothers' bedrooms.

"Freedom," Johnson said. "I love freedom."

"Well, I don't know," the Gentleman said and laughed. "You're a black man in Mississippi. I don't care if it is 1930. You ain't got much freedom to offer me."

"I'll give you all I got."

The horses screamed.

The Gentleman leaned over, touched Johnson's guitar with the tip of a fingernail, and then smiled.

"It's done," said the Gentleman and faded away. Johnson rubbed his eyes. He figured he'd been dreaming. The hot summer heat had thrown a mirage at him. So he just turned around and walked back toward Robinsville. He'd only been gone for a few hours. Nobody would even notice he'd left, and he was foolish for leaving. He'd forget about the guitar and play the harp with Son House. Johnson vowed to become the best harp player that ever lived. He'd practice all day long.

"Where you been?" Son House asked when Johnson walked into the juke joint. House sat in a chair on stage.

"What you mean?" Johnson asked. "You act like I been gone forever. I just walked out to the crossroads. Then I changed my mind and came back."

"You been gone a year! Do you hear me? You been gone a year!"

Stunned, Johnson slumped into a chair on the floor below House and laid his guitar on his lap. He heard an animal laughing in his head.

"Don't you know where you been?" House asked.

"Been at the crossroads," Johnson said. He looked down at his guitar. He looked at House.

"Well, boy," House said, "you still got a guitar, huh? What do you do with that thing? You can't do nothing with it."

"Well," Johnson said, "I'll tell you what."

"What?"

"Let me have your seat a minute."

House and Johnson exchanged seats. Johnson sat onstage, tuned his guitar, while House sat on the floor, the very first audience. Johnson pulled out a bottle, a smooth bottle, and ran it up and down the fretboard. He played a few songs that arrived from nowhere. Son House's mouth dropped open. Robert Johnson was suddenly the best damn guitar player he had ever heard.

"Well, ain't that fast," House said when Johnson finished.

Big Mom carved her wood while Johnson stared blankly at the Spokane Indian Reservation. He watched Victor sleeping. He could see Victor's dreams. That guitar, that guitar.

"I feel bad," Johnson said.

"About what?" Big Mom asked.

"About that guitar of Victor's. I mean, my guitar. I mean, that Gentleman's guitar. I mean, whose guitar is it?"

"It belongs to whoever wants it the most."

"Well, I guess it don't belong to nobody anymore. It's all broken up back in New York, ain't it?"

"If you say so."

Johnson knew the guitar had always come back to him. Sometimes it had taken weeks, but it always found its way back into his arms and wanted more from him at every reunion. That guitar pulled him at him, like gravity. Even though Victor had owned it for months now, Johnson could still feel the pull. Johnson wondered if he'd ever really be free again.

† † †

The day before Big Mom carved a good piece of wood into a cedar harmonica while Robert Johnson watched the reservation, Father Arnold stood in the phone booth just outside the Trading Post. He had dialed the Bishop's phone number a dozen times but hung up before it rang. Father Arnold just held the phone to his mouth and pretended to talk as Spokane Indians walked in and out of the Trading Post.

"The end of the world is near!" shouted the-man-who-was-probably-Lakota as he stood in his usual spot.

Father Arnold dialed the Bishop's number again.

"Hello," answered the Bishop.

Father Arnold held his breath.

"Hello," said the Bishop. "Is there anybody there?"

"Hello, Father," Father Arnold said. "It's Father Arnold. Out on the Spokane Indian Reservation."

"Father Arnold? Oh, yes. Father Arnold. How are you?"

"I'm good. Well, no. I'm not. I have a problem."

"What ever could that be?"

"I don't think I'm strong enough for this place. I'm having some doubts."

"Really? Tell me about them."

Father Arnold closed his eyes, saw Checkers Warm Water singing in the church choir.

"I don't know if I'm being effective out here," Father Arnold said. "I think we might need a fresh perspective. Somebody younger perhaps. Maybe somebody with more experience."

Silence.

"Are you there?" Father Arnold asked, his favorite prayer.

"Father Arnold," the Bishop said, "I know it's never easy ministering to such a people as the Indians. They are a lost people, God knows. But they need you out there. We need you out there."

"Please."

"Father, we have no one to send out there. We have a shortage of priests as it is. Let alone priests to serve the Indian reservations. Father John has to serve three separate reservations, did you know? He has to drive from reservation to reservation for services. No matter the weather. Did you know that, Father?"

"No, I didn't."

"If Father John can serve three communities, I think you can serve just one."

"Yes."

"For better or worse, you and those Indians are stuck together. Do you understand?"

"Yes."

"Well, perhaps you need some more time in study. More prayer. Ask for strength and guidance. Quit worrying so much about the basketball out there and worry more about your commitment to God."

"Yes."

"Well, then. Is there anything else?"

"No," Father Arnold lied.

"Okay, then. I'll talk to you soon."

Dial tone.

Father Arnold felt the connection break, hung up the phone, and opened the phone booth. He couldn't face Checkers again. He was ashamed and had to leave the reservation, no matter what the Bishop said.

"I'm leaving," Father Arnold said. "I'm leaving."

"The end of the world is near! It's near! The end of the world is near!"

† † †

On the day after Coyote Springs returned to the reservation, just a day before Father Arnold decided to leave the Catholic Church entirely, Betty and Veronica sat in Cavalry Records's recording studio in Manhattan.

Betty and Veronica had already heard the story of Coyote Springs's disaster in the studio and weren't all that surprised. The white women had been truly shocked when Wright and Sheridan showed up at their very first show in Seattle.

What a coincidence, Veronica had said to Sheridan. *I can't believe you're going to sign Coyote Springs. We just left them. Did they tell you about us? Is that how you heard about us?*

No, Coyote Springs doesn't know anything about this, Sheridan had said. *And we'd like to keep it that way. A little bird landed on my shoulder and told me about you. Told me to bring you to New York City. What do you think?*

"These the girls from Seattle?" Armstrong asked Wright and Sheridan in the control booth. Betty and Veronica shifted nervously on their stools in the studio.

"Yes, sir, they are," Sheridan said. "We think you're going to love them. They have a unique sound. Sort of a folk sound."

"Folk doesn't sell shit."

"Yes, sir, folk hasn't been much of a seller for us," Sheridan said. "But I think these girls might change all of that."

"What do you think?" Armstrong asked Wright.

"They're talented," Wright said. He felt sick.

"You said those Indians were talented, too," Armstrong said.

"Listen," Sheridan said to Armstrong, "these two women here are part Indian."

"What do you mean?" Armstrong asked.

"I mean, they had some grandmothers or something that were Indian. Really. We can still sell that Indian idea. We don't need any goddamn just-off-the-reservation Indians. We can use these women. They've been on the reservations. They even played a few gigs with Coyote Springs. Don't you see? These women have got the Indian experience down. They really understand what it means to be Indian. They've been there."

"Explain."

"Can't you see the possibilities? We dress them up a little. Get them into the tanning booth. Darken them up a bit. Maybe a little plastic surgery on those cheekbones. Get them a little higher, you know? Dye their hair black. Then we'd have Indians. People want to hear Indians."

"What do you think?" Armstrong asked Wright.

"I don't have to have anything to do with it," Wright said and left the room.

Wright walked out of Cavalry Records and hailed a cab. The driver was an old white woman. She had beautiful blue eyes.

"Where you going?" asked the driver.

"I just want to get home," Wright said.

The driver laughed and took Wright to a cemetery in Sacramento, California.

"How much I owe you?" Wright asked when he climbed out of the cab.

"You don't owe me anything," the woman said. "Just go on home now. Just go on home."

The cab pulled away. Wright watched it disappear in the distance, then he walked through the cemetery to a large monument. He studied the monument, remembering the ship that went down in the Pacific and the water rushing into his lungs. He read the monument:

Gen. George Wright, U.S.A.
and his wife
died
July 30, 1865
Lovely and pleasant in their lives,
and in their death they
were not divided

"Margaret," Wright said as he lay down on top of his grave. "I'm home. I'm home. I'm so sorry. I'm home."

Margaret Wright rose wetly from her place and took her husband in her arms. She patted his head as he wept and remembered all those horses who had screamed in that field so long ago. He remembered shooting that last colt while Big Mom watched from the rise.

"I was the one," Wright said to his wife. "I was the one. I was the one who killed them all. I gave the orders."

The horses screamed in his head.

"Shh," Margaret whispered. "It's okay. I forgive you."

Wright closed his eyes and saw the colt standing still in that field. He remembered that he had taken a pistol from a private.

This is how it's done, he had said as he dismounted from his own horse. He pressed the pistol between the colt's eyes, pulled the trigger, and watched it fall.

"Oh, God," Wright sobbed to his wife on their graves. The grief rushed into his lungs. "I'm a killer. I'm a killer."

"You've come home," Margaret whispered. "You're home now."

Betty and Veronica watched Armstrong and Sheridan talking in the control booth.

"What do you think they're talking about?" Betty asked.

"The assholes are probably wondering how our asses will look on MTV," Veronica said.

"Hey, girls," Sheridan said over the intercom.

"Yeah," Betty and Veronica said.

"Could you come in here?"

Betty and Veronica set their guitars down, walked into the control booth.

"Listen," Sheridan said, "Mr. Armstrong and I have been talking about your potential. Well, you see, there's a market for a certain kind of music these days. It's a kind of music we think you can play, given your heritage. But there's a whole lot of marketing we have to do. We have to fine tune your image."

"What do you mean?" Veronica asked. "What's our heritage?"

"Well," Sheridan said, "there's been an upswing in the economic popularity of Indians lately. I mean, there's a lot of demographics and audience surveys and that other scientific shit. But I leave that to the boys upstairs. What I'm talking about here is pure musical talent. That's you. Pure musical talent shaped and guided by me. Well, I mean, under the direction of Mr. Armstrong, certainly."

Veronica looked at Betty.

"Now," Veronica said, "what the hell are you talking about?"

"Well," Sheridan said, "our company, Cavalry Records, has an economic need for a viable Indian band. As you know, Coyote Springs self-destructed. We were thinking we needed a more reliable kind of Indian. Basically, we need Indians such as yourselves."

"But we ain't that much Indian."

"You're Indian enough, right? I mean, all it takes is a little bit, right? Who's to say you're not Indian enough?"

"You want us to play Indian music or something?"

"Exactly," Sheridan said. "Now you understand."

Mr. Armstrong shifted in his seat. He was bored.

"Cut to the chase," Armstrong said.

"Okay," Sheridan said. "What it comes down to is this. You play for this company as Indians. Or you don't play at all. I mean, who needs another white-girl folk group?"

"But we want to play our music," Betty protested.

"Listen," Sheridan said, "you do things for us, we can do things for you. It's a partnership. We want you to have everything you ever wanted. That's the business we're in. The dream business. We make dreams come true. That's who we are. We just ask for a little sacrifice in return. A little something in exchange for our hard work. What do you think?"

Betty and Veronica looked at each other. They could hear drums.

† † †

Coyote Springs staggered onto the reservation a couple of hours after they left the Spokane International Airport. Actually, they were hiding beneath a tarp in Simon's pickup. Coyote Springs had managed to walk only a few miles on Highway 2 before Simon pulled up. He'd been back on the reservation for just a few days after his visit with relatives on the coast. He only drove his truck in reverse, using the rearview mirror as guide, even on white people's highways. He'd never been caught.

"Jeez," Simon said, "I thought you guys were in New York City."

"We were," Thomas said. "But everything went wrong."

"Oh, man," Simon said. "I don't know if you want to go back to the reservation. Ain't nobody too happy with you up there. I can't believe it. It's like the Spokane Indian Reservation has become Republican or something."

"Enit?" Chess asked. "What are you?"

"Shit," Simon said. "I'm a Communist. A goddamn plnko redskin. Joe McCarthy would have pissed his pants if he ever saw me."

"Well," Thomas said, "we have to go back there. We ain't got any money. We ain't got no place to go."

"Well," Simon said, "if you insist. Climb in the back and get under that tarp. I don't want nobody seeing you."

"What if they do?" Victor asked.

"Any problems," Simon said as he patted the rifles hanging in his gun rack, "and I'll have to take care of business."

"Are those loaded?" Junior asked.

"You bet your ass," Simon said.

Coyote Springs climbed under the tarp and pulled it over them. They had no idea where they were at any given time. They could only guess by certain curves in the road, the sudden stops, the sound of water rushing over Little Falls Dam as they crossed onto the Spokane Indian Reservation.

10

Wake

I saw ten people die before I was ten years old
And I knew how to cry before I was ever born

Wake alive, alive, wake alive, alive

Sweetheart, I know these car wrecks are nearly genetic
Sweetheart, I know these hands have been shaking for generations
And they shake and shake and shake and shake
Sweetheart, I know these suicides are always genetic
Sweetheart, I know we have to travel to the reservation
For the wake and wake and wake and wake
And sweetheart, all these wakes for the dead
Are putting the living to sleep

I can't bury my grief
Unless I bury my fear

I can't bury my fear
Before I bury my friend

Wake alive, alive, wake alive, alive

Sweetheart, I know this cirrhosis is nearly genetic
Sweetheart, I know this heart has been shaking for generations
And it shakes and shakes and shakes and shakes
Sweetheart, I know these suicides are always generic
Sweetheart, I know we have to travel to the reservation
For the wake and wake and wake and wake
And sweetheart, all these wakes for the dead
Are putting the living to sleep

And I think it's time for us to find a way
Yeah, I think it's time for us to find a way
And I think it's time for us to find a way
Yeah, I think it's time for us to find a way

To wake alive, to wake alive, to wake alive, to wake alive

There wasn't much of a wake for Junior Polatkin. Coyote Springs just laid Junior in the homemade coffin and set it on top of the kitchen table in Thomas's house. Coyote Springs didn't have the energy to sing or mourn properly, and the rest of the reservation didn't really care, although a few anonymous Indians did send flowers and condolences. Simon, whose rifle had been used in the suicide, felt so bad that he drove his pickup backwards off the reservation, and nobody ever saw him again.

"Assholes," Victor said when another reservation bouquet arrived. He kept thinking of the guitar he saw in the bathroom, in his dream. "Why the fuck they sending flowers now?"

"Well," Chess said, "at least they sent something."

"Yeah," Victor said, holding his hands close to his body, trying to hide the scars. "But nobody gave a shit when he was blowing his brains out. They were all cheering him on."

"That ain't true," Chess said. "Nobody cheered."

Lester FallsApart showed up then and gave Coyote Springs three dogs. It was an unusual gift at a wake, but Lester didn't have anything else to offer. He owned a dozen dogs. That's to say, a dozen dogs followed him all over the reservation. Thomas wanted to name those three dogs Larry, Moe, and Curly. Chess wanted to name them John, Paul, and Peter. Checkers didn't care what they were named. But Lester said he'd already named them the Father, the Son, and the Holy Ghost. Those dogs sniffed at Junior's coffin and began to howl.

On top of Wellpinit Mountain, Big Mom sat on her porch and cried. She could hear the dogs howling down below. She'd had no idea that Junior was going to kill himself but still felt like she could have saved him. If she had only known, if she had only paid attention.

"Big Mom," Robert Johnson said, "what you goin' to do? You're scarin' me."

Big Mom felt a weakness in her stomach, in her knees. She didn't know if she could even stand, let alone walk down her mountain. Another one of her students had fallen, and Big Mom had felt something fall inside her, too. Maybe all those bodies, those musicians, those horses had been stacked too high inside her.

"I don't know if I can do this anymore," Big Mom said. "I just don't know."

"They need you," Johnson said. "We all need you."

Big Mom looked at Robert Johnson, noticing how he had changed since his arrival. He had gained weight, his eyes were clear, his hands had healed.

"I saved you," Big Mom said.

"Yes, you did."

Big Mom stood, breathed deep, and began the walk down her mountain. She turned back, dug through her purse, and threw a small object back at Robert Johnson. He caught it gently in his hands.

"What is this?" Johnson asked.

"It's yours," Big Mom said.

Johnson held a cedar harmonica. He could feel a movement inside the wood, something familiar.

"Why this?" Johnson asked.

"You don't need that guitar anymore," Big Mom said. "You were supposed to be a harp player. You're a good harp player. All by yourself, you can play a mean harp."

"Thank you."

"You're welcome," Big Mom said and walked down the mountain.

*

Father Arnold, wearing a t-shirt and jeans, had just loaded his last box into his yellow VW when Big Mom walked up to him.

"Holy cow," Arnold said. "You scared me."

"I'm sorry," Big Mom said and then noticed the boxes. "So, you really are leaving then?"

"I have to," Arnold said. "The Bishop reassigned me."

"That's not true."

Father Arnold was ashamed. He pulled at the neck of his t-shirt.

"You're right," he said. "It's because of Checkers."

"Do you love her?"

"Yes. No. I mean, I love her. But it's not like that."

Father Arnold leaned heavily against the VW.

"Listen," he said, "I don't know what to do. I think about her. I dream about her. Sometimes I want to give it all up for her. But I don't even know why. I haven't known her very long. I mean, she's beautiful and smart and funny. She's got a tremendous faith. I just don't know."

"What are you supposed to know?" Big Mom asked.

"Everything, I guess. Don't you know everything?"

"No, I'm just as scared as you are."

"What am I supposed to do?"

Big Mom closed her eyes. She listened to the wind, the voices of the reservation. She heard the horses.

"I'm not sure," Big Mom said. "But it's up to you, no matter what, enit?"

Arnold nodded his head, pulled the car keys from his pocket, and looked down the road. Big Mom touched his arm, smiled, and then started to walk away.

"Wait," Arnold said. "Where are you going?"

"Those kids need me," Big Mom said. "They lost somebody, and they need help to say goodbye."

Father Arnold swallowed hard. He ran his hand along his neck.

"Well," Big Mom said, "are you coming or not?"

"I don't know. I mean, what about Checkers? What about all of it? You're not even Catholic, are you?"

"Listen," Big Mom said, "you cover all the Christian stuff; I'll do the traditional Indian stuff. We'll make a great team."

"Are you sure?"

"No, I'm not sure," said Big Mom as she grabbed Father Arnold's hand. "Come on."

"But what about my collar, my cassock?" Arnold asked.

"You don't need that stuff. That's a very powerful t-shirt you have on."

"Really?"

"Really," Big Mom said and led the way toward Coyote Springs.

† † †

From *The Spokesman-Review's classified ads:*

Help Wanted

Western Telephone Communications seeking opera-
tors for entry-level positions. Must have good commu-
nication skills, ability to type 45 wpm, and experience
with computers. Please send resumes to P.O. Box
1999, Spokane, WA 99204.

† † †

Coyote Springs buried Junior in the Spokane Tribal Cemetery, in the same row with his mother and father. Big Mom and Father Arnold took turns leading the service, while Checkers, Chess, Victor, and Thomas stood at the graveside. Lester FallsApart and the three dogs kept a polite distance. No other Spokane Indians showed up.

Ashes to ashes, dust to dust.

Father Arnold finished the ceremony and asked if anybody had any final words for the dearly departed.

"Final words?" Chess asked. "I don't know if I'll ever be able to stop talking about this."

The Father, the Son, and the Holy Ghost howled. Lester tried to quiet them, but Big Mom had to walk over. She knelt down beside the dogs, whispered to them, and stroked their fur. The dogs whimpered and kissed Big Mom.

"What are their names?" Big Mom asked Lester and laughed when he told her.

"Well," she said, "I think we should change their names. That isn't exactly respectful."

"Well," Lester said, "they ain't my dogs no more. I gave them to Coyote Springs."

"Ya-hey," Big Mom called out. "What are you going to name your dogs?"

Thomas looked at Chess.

"I don't know," Thomas said. "It's not really up to us to decide. We're going to let Victor have the dogs. We've got other plans."

"How come I get the dogs?" Victor asked.

Big Mom wondered about Thomas's and Chess's plans but knew they had something to do with leaving the reservation.

"Is there anything anybody wants to say about the departed?" Father Arnold asked.

"Junior never hurt anybody, not on purpose," Victor said and surprised everybody. He was lying, of course, but he wanted to make sense of Junior's life.

"He hurt himself the most," Big Mom said.

"He tried to be good," Thomas said. "He tried really hard."

Big Mom sang under her breath, a quiet little mourning song. Coyote Springs trembled with the music. They didn't sing along.

"Did you know that Junior had a kid?" Victor asked.

Everybody on the Spokane Indian Reservation had heard the rumors, but nobody had known the truth except Junior. After Junior killed himself, Victor found that note in Junior's wallet and learned the whole story. Lynn, the little romance, the abortion.

"Yeah, a half-breed little boy," Victor lied, trying to make more significance out of his best friend's life and death.

"How old is the kid?" Chess asked.

"Almost ten years old now. Named him Charles."

"Wow," Chess said. "Where did all this happen?"

"When Junior was in college," Victor said. "In Oregon."

"It was a white woman, enit?" Chess asked.

"Yeah, what about it?" Victor said and continued the lie, feeling the guilt that he was responsible for the suicide, that he'd sold his best friend's life. "Her parents didn't like it either. And sent that baby away. Junior never saw him. Just heard about him once in a while."

Big Mom sang another mourning song, a little louder this time.

"Jeez," Chess said. "Now I know why he never talked about it."

Checkers whispered a prayer to herself.

Chess looked around the graveyard, at all the graves of Indians killed by white people's cars, alcohol, uranium. All those Indians who had killed themselves. She saw the pine trees that surrounded the graveyard and the road that led back to the rest of the reservation. That road was dirt and gravel, had been a trail for a few centuries before. A few years from now, it would be paved, paid for by one more government grant. She looked down the road and thought she saw a car, a mirage shimmering in the distance, a blonde woman and a child standing beside the car, both dressed in black.

*

Look, Chess said and ran down the road toward the woman and child. She had so many questions.

Why did you love him, that broken Indian man? Chess asked the white woman. *Why did you conceive him a son?*

Chess wanted to tell the white woman that her child was always going to be halfway. *He's always going to be half Indian,* she'd say, *and that will make him half crazy. Half of him will always want to tear the other half apart. It's war.* Chess wanted to tell her that her baby was always going to be half Indian, no matter what she did to make it white.

All you can do is breed the Indian out of your family, Chess said. *All you can do is make sure your son marries a white woman and their children marry white people. The fractions will take over. Your half-blood son will have quarter-blood children and eight-blood grandchildren, and then they won't be Indians anymore. They won't hardly be Indian, and they can sleep better at night.*

Chess ran down that road toward the white woman and her half-Indian son, because she wanted to save them from the pain that other Indians would cause.

Your son will be beaten because he's a half-breed, Chess said. *No matter what he does, he'll never be Indian enough. Other Indians won't accept him. Indians are like that.*

Chess wanted to save Indians from the pain that the white woman and her half-Indian son would cause.

Don't you see? Chess asked. *Those quarter-blood and eighth-blood grandchildren will find out they're Indian and torment the rest of us real Indians. They'll come out to the reservation, come to our powwows, in their nice clothes and nice cars, and remind the real Indians how much we don't have. Those quarter-bloods and eighth-bloods will get all the Indian jobs, all the Indian chances, because they look white. Because they're safer.*

Chess wanted to say so much to the white woman and her half-Indian son. She closed her eyes, opened them again, and the white woman and her son were gone. They'd never been there.

*

"What is it?" Thomas asked Chess. The rest of Coyote Springs, Big Mom, and Father Arnold had already begun the walk away from the cemetery. Lester FallsApart and the three dogs followed closely behind. Chess still stood at the graveside, staring into the distance.

"Chess?" Thomas asked again. "What is it?"

"Thomas," Chess said and took his hand, "let's get married. Let's have kids."

Thomas was surprised. He couldn't respond.

"Really," Chess said. "Let's have lots of brown babies. I want my babies to look up and see two brown faces. That's the best thing we can give them, enit? Two brown faces. Do you want to?"

Thomas smiled.

"Okay," he said.

† † †

Checkers went straight to bed when they returned to Thomas's house after the burial. Thomas and Big Mom sat in the kitchen and talked about making lunch. Victor jumped in the blue van and drove away. Father Arnold stood alone outside on the front lawn, feeling unwelcome.

"Checkers?" Chess asked her sister. "Are you okay?"

"Yeah," Checkers said. "I'm just tired. I haven't been sleeping well."

"Those nightmares, enit? Does Sheridan keep coming back for you?"

"It ain't Sheridan anymore. It's Dad who comes every night now."

"What?" Chess asked. Luke Warm Water rarely entered her dreams.

"Yeah," Checkers said. "He stands in the doorway of the bedroom. Just like he used to. He's been drinking. I can smell him. He doesn't say nothing. He just stands there in the doorway, holding his arms out to me. Then I wake up."

"Do you think it's really him?" Chess asked.

"Yeah, it's him."

"How do you know?"

"Because he's crying the whole time."

The sisters sat for a long while in silence. They held hands; they cried.

"We're leaving soon, you know," Chess said after a while. "Thomas and I are leaving for Spokane. Are you coming or not?"

"What are we going to do about money?" Checkers asked.

"I got a job. At the phone company. As an operator."

"Enit?"

"Enit. It'll hold us over until you and Thomas find jobs."

"Does Victor know?"

"No."

"Does Big Mom know?"

"Probably. You should tell Father Arnold."

"I don't want to talk to him," Checkers said. "I don't care what he does."

A knock on the door.

"Who is it?" Chess asked.

"It's me, Big Mom."

"Come in."

Big Mom stepped in, and Father Arnold was right behind her.

"He wants to talk to you," Big Mom said to Checkers. "Alone."

Checkers shook her head.

"Okay," Big Mom said. "How about if Chess stays?"

Checkers looked at her sister. Chess nodded in the affirmative.

"Good," Big Mom said and left the room. "I've got some lunch to make."

Arnold closed the door, sat in a chair at the foot of the bed.

"Hello," he said.

Checkers looked at Chess.

"Hello," Checkers said to Arnold.

"How are you?" he asked. He looked scared.

"I'm okay."

Arnold looked at Chess, then back at Checkers.

"Can we talk?" he asked.

"About what?" Checkers asked.

"About us."

"Yeah, I guess so."

The three all looked uncomfortable, exchanged glances, stared at the floor, walls, and ceiling.

"I'm sorry for everything," Arnold said.

"You should be."

"This is all my fault. I led you on."

"Well," Checkers said, "none of that matters much now. We're leaving the reservation. So you don't have to worry about me. I'm leaving and you can stay."

"You're leaving?" Arnold asked, feeling a combination of sadness and relief.

"We're moving to Spokane. Chess got a job as a telephone operator."

"When are you leaving?"

"Soon," Checkers said and reached under the bed. "And here's a bottle of your Communion wine. I stole it because I was mad at you."

"Why'd you steal that?" Chess asked, shocked at her sister.

"I was going to get drunk. But then Junior shot himself."

Arnold took the bottle. There was a long silence.

"Do you forgive me?" Checkers asked Arnold.

"Yes, do you forgive me?"

"I don't know. Am I allowed to?"

"Yes, you're allowed to."

"Well, then. I don't think I do. Not yet. I mean, I still love you. I still feel that, you know? It ain't like that changes. But I can still tell you to shove your God up your ass. But I don't know if I mean it. I don't know what I mean. I don't know nothing, and you don't know any more than I do."

Arnold didn't say anything. He agreed with Checkers. He'd been just all of the other performers in the world. He'd wanted to be universally loved. He wasn't all that different from Victor, Thomas, or even Junior. They all got onstage and wanted the audience to believe in them. They all wanted the audience to throw their room keys, panties, confessions, flowers, and songs onstage. They wanted the audience to trust them with all their secrets. But Victor, Thomas, and Junior had fallen apart in the face of all of that. Arnold had fallen apart, too. Junior could never be put back together again, but maybe the rest of them could.

"Discipline," Father Arnold said with much difficulty. It was only one word, but he needed to find the one word that would make Chess and Checkers understand. "I knew how to pray with discipline. I can do it again."

Chess and Checkers both understood but still felt suspicious. They'd grown up with priests and their churches. The sisters had loved them all. The sisters had loved to kneel in the pew and pray in exactly the way they'd been taught. For years, the sisters said those same prayers over and over, as if sheer repetition could guarantee results. As if their little prayers had a cumulative effect on God, adding one on top of another, until all of their prayers were as tall as a priest's single prayer.

"Checkers," Father Arnold said, "I can't believe you stole the Communion wine."

"Enit?" Checkers asked. "Not very original, was it?"

"No," Father said. "And that stuff is awful anyway. How did you ever think you could drink it?"

"Discipline," Checkers said and laughed. Chess and Father Arnold laughed, too. But it was forced, awkward, as if everything depended on it.

† † †

After Victor left Thomas's house in the blue van, he drove around for a few hours before he finally parked at Turtle Lake. There was nobody else around. He turned on the radio and heard Freddy Fender.

"Junior," Victor said. "What the fuck did you do?"

Victor closed his eyes and saw Junior sitting in the passenger seat when he opened them. Junior looked exactly like someone who had shot himself in the head with a rifle.

"Happy reservation fucking Halloween," Junior said, and Victor screamed, which made Junior scream, too. They traded screams for a while.

"So," Junior said after the screams had stopped, "are you happy to see me?"

"Jesus," Victor said. "What do you think this is? An American Werewolf in London? You're supposed to be a ghost, not a piece of raw meat."

"Ya-hey," Junior said. "Good one."

"I don't believe this," Victor said and closed his eyes. He heard a rifle blast. He was shaking.

"Are you going to miss me?"

Victor opened his eyes and looked at Junior. He didn't know what to feel.

"I'm going to miss getting drunk with you," Victor said.

"Oh, yeah, enit? We had some good times, didn't we?"

Victor smiled. Junior pulled a silver flask out of his coat and offered it to Victor.

"Hey, look," Junior said, "somebody put this in my coffin during the wake. Was it you? Must be worth fifty bucks. Maybe you can hock it. I don't really need it where I'm going."

Victor took the flask, opened it, and sniffed.

"It's whiskey," Victor said. "It must've been Father Arnold. You know those priests."

"Sure. Take a drink."

"I don't know, man. I've been thinking about going on the wagon."

"Since when?"

"Since you killed yourself. I ain't drunk any since then, you know?"

Junior and Victor stared at the silver flask.

"It's pretty, enit?" Junior asked.

"Yeah," Victor said. "I wonder if Father Arnold really gave it to you."

"Maybe."

Victor was nervous. He'd never talked to the dead before. It felt like a first date.

"This feels like a first date, enit?" Junior asked.

"Yeah, it does."

"So," Junior said, "am I going to get lucky?"

Both laughed. There was silence. They laughed at the silence. There was more silence.

"Why'd you do it?" Victor asked.

"Do what?"

"You know, shoot yourself. In the head."

"You know," Junior said, "I heard some people talking at the Trading Post after I did it. They thought I couldn't hear them. But I could. They said I didn't mean to kill myself. That I was just looking for attention. Assholes."

"Some people sent you flowers, though, did you see?"

"Yeah, the assholes."

Silence.

"You know," Junior said, "I really am going to miss getting drunk with you. Remember when we used to go out chasing white women? Before you got fat and ugly."

"Fat and ugly, my ass. Those white women loved me."

"Do you remember Betty and Veronica?"

"Of course."

"Those two weren't bad," Junior said. "Maybe we should've held on to them."

"Yeah, maybe. Junior, why'd you do it?"

"Do what?"

"Kill yourself."

Junior looked away, watching the sunlight reflecting off Turtle Lake.

"Because life is hard," Junior said.

"That's it?"

"That's the whole story, folks. I wanted to be dead. Gone. No more."

"Why?"

"Because when I closed my eyes like Thomas, I didn't see a damn thing. Nothing. Zilch. No stories, no songs. Nothing."

Victor looked down at the silver flask of whiskey in his hands. He wanted to take a drink. He wanted that guitar back, still dreamed about it every night.

"And," Junior added, "because I didn't want to be drunk no more."

Victor rolled down his window and threw the flask out into Turtle Lake. It sank quickly.

"I don't need that no more," Victor said. "I'm going on the wagon."

"Here," Junior said and handed Victor another flask. "You better throw this one out, too."

"How many of these you got?"

"A whole bunch. We better get to work."

"What are we going to do after this?" Victor asked.

"Well, I've got other places to go. But I think you should go get yourself a goddamn job. I ain't going to be around to take care of your sorry ass anymore."

Like some alcoholic magician, Junior pulled flask after flask from his clothes and handed them to Victor, who threw them out the window into Turtle Lake. Those silver flasks floated down through the lake rumored to have no bottom, rumored to be an extinct volcano, and came to rest miles below the surface.

† † †

Big Mom lit the sage, and Chess, Checkers, and Thomas bathed themselves in the smoke. They pulled the smoke through their hair, over their legs and arms, into their open mouths.

"Who do you want to pray for?" Big Mom asked.

"Everybody."

Big Mom picked up a 45 record with her huge hands and gently placed it on the turntable. She placed needle to vinyl, and they all waited together for the music.

† † †

Spokane Tribal Chairman David WalksAlong sat in his office, thinking about his nephew Michael White Hawk, when Victor came looking for a job. His nephew had been getting progressively worse, going from wandering around the football field in confused circles to drinking Sterno with the Android Brothers behind the Trading Post. All those half-crazy Sterno drunks talked some kind of gibberish to each other that only they understood. WalksAlong was wondering if he should just shoot his nephew in the head and end his misery, just like that Junior Polatkin ended his own misery.

"What the fuck do you want?" WalksAlong asked Victor when he walked into the office, pushing open that warped door.

Victor'd worked up all the courage in the world to come to Walks-Along.

"They said you're the one who decides who gets to work. I want a job," Victor said. "Please."

"Look what you did to the reservation, and you want me to give you a job?"

"I'm sorry about your nephew," Victor said, but he wanted to tell WalksAlong that his nephew never had a chance.

"Well," WalksAlong said, "what the hell can you do?"

Victor handed him a piece of paper.

"What the hell is this?" WalksAlong asked.

"It's my résumé."

"Your résumé?" WalksAlong asked, in complete disbelief. "What do you think this is, Wall Street?"

"I thought this was the way it worked," Victor said. "Enit?"

WalksAlong read the résumé, crumpled it up, and threw it at Victor.

"Get the fuck out of here," WalksAlong said.

Victor picked his résumé off the floor, smoothed it out, then folded it neatly into a small square, and tucked it into his pocket. His hands were shaking.

"Listen," Victor said, his voice breaking. "I thought this was the way it worked."

WalksAlong turned his back. Victor tried to think of something to say, some words that would change all of this.

"I want to drive the water truck," Victor said. "Just like Junior used to. I want to be like Junior. It was his last wish."

WalksAlong didn't respond, and Victor left the office, feeling something slip inside him. He stole five dollars from Walks-Along's secretary's purse and bought a six-pack of cheap beer at the Trading Post.

"Fuck it, I can do it, too," Victor whispered to himself

and opened the first can. That little explosion of the beer can opening sounded exactly like a smaller, slower version of the explosion that Junior's rifle made on the water tower.

† † †

From <u>The Wellpinit Rawhide Press</u>:

Father Arnold Leads Catholics to Championship

Father Arnold scored 33 points Tuesday night, including the game-winning free throws with no time left on the clock, to lead the Catholic Church to a thrilling come-from-behind 111–110 win over the Assembly of God in the championship game of the Spokane Indian Christian Basketball Tournament.

"I wasn't sure those free throws were going in," Father Arnold said, "but I sure prayed for them. Who knows? Maybe God was listening this time."

Randy Peone, minister of the Assembly of God, had no official comment about the game, but was reported to have said that Father Arnold had probably spent more time away from the church than with his church, and that explained all the time he had to practice.

"He just didn't play like a Catholic," one spectator said. "Especially not like a Catholic priest."

"Hey," responded Bessie, the oldest Catholic on the reservation, "what the hell do any of you know about being Catholic? You have no idea how hard it is."

† † †

A few days after Junior's burial, while Chess and Checkers were taking a sweat with Big Mom, Thomas Builds-the-Fire heard a scratching on his roof. At first, he wondered which ghost had come to haunt him. But then he heard a knock on the back door.

"Who is it?" Thomas asked. He was still worried about Michael White Hawk.

"Package," the voice said.

Thomas opened the door just a bit and saw the FedEx guy standing on the back porch, with rappelling gear.

"Jeez," Thomas said. "It's just you."

"Mr. Builds-the-Fire, I presume," said the FedEx guy.

"You know who I am."

"We can never be too sure. Sign here."

Thomas signed the form. The FedEx guy handed him a package and then climbed back onto the roof and scampered away. Thomas closed the door, took the package inside, and set it on the kitchen table. It was a small package, barely weighed anything at all. The return address said Cavalry Records. He didn't want to open it and almost threw it in the garbage, but curiosity got the best of him. Inside, there was just a letter and a cassette tape.

> Dear Coyote Springs,
> We just heard about Junior, and we wanted to tell you how sorry we are. We'll miss him.
> Things are going well for us. We signed a deal with Cavalry Records, thanks to your help, and we're currently working on our debut CD, which will be out next summer. We recorded our first song the other day, and there's a copy on the tape enclosed.
> We both think that Junior is in a better place now.
>
> Sincerely,
> Betty and Veronica

Thomas read the letter over a few times. He held the cassette tape in his hands. He didn't know what to do and was shocked that Betty and Veronica had signed with Cavalry Records. Should he throw that cassette away and never listen to it? That wouldn't do any good, because the CD would be all over the place next summer. He'd hear it played on the radio. Betty and Veronica would have a Platinum Album, a number one hit, and videos on MTV. Thomas wanted to protect Chess and Checkers from the music on this cassette tape. He held it in his hands for a while, studied its design, then walked over to the tape player he'd hidden away, dropped the cassette into place, and hit the play button. Thomas heard a vaguely Indian drum, then a cedar flute, and a warrior's trill, all the standard Indian soundtrack stuff. Then Betty's and Veronica's beautiful voices joined the mix.

Can you hear the eagle crying?
Can you hear the eagle crying?
I look to the four directions
And try to find some connection
With Mother Earth, Mother Earth

I offer you tobacco and sweetgrass
I offer you tobacco and sweetgrass
I pray to the four directions
And try to find some connection
With Father Sky, Father Sky

And my hair is blonde
But I'm Indian in my bones
And my skin is white
But I'm Indian in my bones
And it don't matter who you are
You can be Indian in your bones

Don't listen to what they say
You can be Indian in your bones

Can you hear the buffalo dying?
Can you hear the buffalo dying?
I look to the four directions
And try to make the corrections
For Mother Earth, Mother Earth
I'll smoke the pipe with you
I'll smoke the pipe with you
I pray to the four directions
And try to make the corrections
For Father Sky, Father Sky

And your hair is blonde
But you're Indian in your bones
And your skin is white
But you're Indian in your bones
And it don't matter who I am
I am Indian in my bones
I don't listen to what they say
I am Indian in my bones

Thomas hit the eject button, threw the cassette on the floor, and stomped on it. He pulled the tape ribbon from its casing until it spread over the kitchen like pasta. Using a dull knife, he sliced the tape ribbon into pieces. Then he ran around his house, grabbing photos and souvenirs, afraid that somebody was going to steal them next. He had photographs of his mother and father, a Disneyland cup even though he'd never been there, a few letters and cards. He gathered them all into a pile on the kitchen table and waited.

† † †

Victor Joseph
Wellpinit, WA 99040

Jobs I had before.

Leed Gitar Player Coyote Springs
Viceprezidant Senior Class Wellpinit High School.
Mowd lawns and shuveled snow.

Edgeucation.

Graguatid Wellpinit High School 1978.
Watched Jepordee a hole bunch on tv.

Skills.

Drive water truck & rode with best friend Junior alot.
Am strong & fast.

Refrences.

Thomas Buildsthefire & Big Mom.

† † †

Coyote Springs was gone. Thomas, Chess, and Checkers packed all
their stuff into the blue van and left Coyote Springs behind in the
house. Victor didn't want anything to do with Coyote Springs, either. He just wandered around the reservation with his three dogs.
He hadn't taken a shower in a week. Everybody figured he'd be
drinking Sterno before too long. They all worried about the dogs.

*

"We're leaving," Thomas had said to Victor earlier that morning.

"For where?"

"Spokane."

"When you coming back?"

"We aren't," said Thomas and then reluctantly asked if Victor wanted to come along. He shook his head and walked away.

Thomas stood in the driveway, studying his HUD house, the familiar angles and weathered wood. It had never been painted. Thomas closed his eyes and saw his mother and father standing on the front porch, waving. When he opened his eyes, Chess was standing beside him.

"Are you going to say goodbye to your dad?" Chess asked.

"I don't even know where he is," Thomas said. "Besides, he's got Indian father radar. He'll show up at our place in Spokane, knocking on the door at three in the morning."

"Really?" Chess asked, impressed and not altogether happy about it.

"Yeah, he's amazing that way."

"Well, I guess I'll go get Checkers."

Chess walked into the house, found Checkers in a back bedroom, and both soon came out.

"Do you want some time alone?" Chess asked Thomas.

Thomas looked at his house.

"No," he said, "it's time to go."

The trio climbed into the blue van. Thomas drove. Chess sat in the front passenger seat, and Checkers sat in the back. Thomas put the car into drive, and they pulled away from his house. There was a tightness in Thomas's chest that he could not explain; he took a deep breath. The blue van rolled down the reservation road.

"Look," Chess said and pointed. Big Mom was standing

on the roadside with a big thumb sticking up. Thomas pulled up beside her. Checkers rolled down her window.

"Where you headed, sweetheart?" Checkers asked Big Mom.

"Over to that feast at the Longhouse," Big Mom said. "You should come with me."

"Nah," Thomas said. "We'll give you a ride over there. But those people don't want us around."

"Well," Big Mom said as she climbed into the van. "I think you should eat before you go."

"Those people will eat us alive," Checkers said in the back.

"Where's Robert Johnson?" Thomas asked.

"Oh," Big Mom said, "he's up at the house, I guess. He's getting better every day. He'll probably be leaving us soon."

"That's good," Chess said.

"I suppose," Big Mom said.

They were quiet until they arrived at the Longhouse. There were a few dozen reservation cars parked at random angles.

"Jeez," Checkers said. "The whole Spokane Tribe must be here."

"There are quite a few," Big Mom said. "Are you sure you don't want to eat? You can't leave on an empty stomach. It's bad luck to travel on an empty stomach."

"Where did you hear that?" Thomas asked.

"I just made it up."

"I don't know," said Checkers, obviously frightened. "They might try to hurt us."

"I won't let them hurt you," Big Mom said. "Hey, do you have any money?"

"A little," Thomas said.

"Well," Big Mom said, "I have a few bucks I've saved up. Here. And maybe we can take up a collection inside."

"They ain't going to give us any money," Chess said.

"Maybe not," Big Mom said, "but at least you can get some food."

Thomas's stomach growled loudly.

"I guess Thomas has made up his mind," Chess said.

"Let's go, then," Big Mom said and led Chess, Checkers, and Thomas toward the Longhouse. They could hear laughter and loud conversation inside, but everybody fell into silence when they walked in. All the Spokane Indians stared at Big Mom and her co-dependents. Big Mom waved, and the crowd gradually resumed their conversations.

"Jeez," Chess said. "I thought they were going to scalp us."

Chess, Checkers, and Thomas sat at a table with Big Mom. They all waited for the feast to officially begin. But the term *feast* was a holdover from a more prosperous and traditional time, a term used before the Indians were forced onto the reservations. There was never a whole lot of food, just a few stringy pieces of deer meat, a huge vat of mashed potatoes, Pepsi, and fry bread. But the fry bread made all the difference. A good piece of fry bread turned any meal into a feast. Everybody sat at the tables and waited for the cooks to come out with the meal, the fry bread. They waited and waited. Finally, when there was no sign of the meal, Big Mom stood and walked into the kitchen.

"What's taking so long?" Big Mom asked the head cook.

"There's not enough fry bread," said the head cook.

"You're kidding. How much do we have?"

"We have a hundred pieces of bread and two hundred Indians out there waiting to eat."

"Do we have enough venison and potatoes?" Big Mom asked.

"Yeah."

"How much Pepsi do we have?" Big Mom asked.

"Enough."

"Well, you take the deer, potatoes, and Pepsi out there. I'll bring the fry bread."

"But there's not enough bread," the head cook said. "There'll be a fry bread riot. And you remember what happened during the last fry bread riot."

Big Mom remembered.

"Just serve the meal," Big Mom said.

The head cook and her helpers served the Pepsi and the rest of the meal, but that only made the Indians more aware of their fry bread deficiency.

"Fry bread, fry bread," chanted the mob.

Chess and Thomas looked at each other; Checkers and Chess looked at each other. They were ready to run.

"It's going to be a fry bread riot," Thomas whispered.

Just as the feast was about to erupt into a full-fledged riot, Big Mom walked out of the kitchen with a huge bowl of fry bread. The crowd, faithful and unfaithful alike, cheered wildly.

"Listen," Big Mom said after the crowd had quieted a little. "There's not enough fry bread."

Indians angrily rose to their feet.

"What are you going to do about it?"

"There are only one hundred pieces of fry bread," Big Mom said, "and there are two hundred of us. Something needs to be done."

The crowd milled around, stared each other down, picked out the opponent they would fight for their piece of fry bread. More than a few people had planned on jumping the surviving members of the band. Thomas, Chess, and Checkers ducked under their table.

"But there is a way," Big Mom said. "I can feed you all."

"How?" asked somebody.

Thomas, Chess, and Checkers peered from under the table, listening for the answer.

"By ancient Indian secrets," Big Mom said.

"Bullshit!"

"Watch this," Big Mom said as she grabbed a piece of fry bread and held it above her head. "Creator, help me. I have only a hundred pieces of fry bread to feed two hundred people."

Big Mom held that fry bread tightly in her huge hands and then tore it into halves.

"There," Big Mom said. "That is how I will feed you all."

The crowd cheered, surging forward to grab the fry bread. There was a complete feast after all.

"Big Mom," Thomas asked later as they were eating, "how did you do that? What is your secret?"

Big Mom smiled deeply.

"Mathematics," Big Mom said.

Robert Johnson was walking toward the Longhouse when he saw the-man-who-was-probably-Lakota sitting on a rock beside the road.

"Ya-hey," Robert Johnson called out. He was learning.

"Ya-hey," answered the-man-who-was-probably-Lakota. "Where you headed?"

"Over to the feast. I'm getting hungry."

"Enit? I guess I'll come with you."

Johnson and the old man walked toward the Longhouse. They didn't say much. Johnson carried his cedar harmonica, and the old man carried a hand drum. They arrived at the Longhouse just as Big Mom tore the fry bread into halves.

"Ya-hey," Thomas said when Johnson and the old man walked into the Longhouse. "Look who it is."

"Thomas," Johnson said as he sat at the table, "it's good to see you."

"You look great," Thomas said, could scarcely believe this was the same man he had met at the crossroads all that time ago.

"Big Mom's been good for me," Johnson said as a means

of explaining his appearance. "She even made me this ribbon shirt."

Johnson was wearing a traditional Indian ribbon shirt, made of highly traditional silk and polyester.

"So, what are you doing here?" Thomas asked. "Do you want to leave with us?"

Johnson looked up at the-man-who-was-probably-Lakota, looked to Big Mom.

"I'm goin' to stay here," Johnson said. "On the reservation. I think I jus' might belong here. I think there's been a place waitin' at this Tribe's tribal for me. I think this Tribe's been waitin' for me for a long time. I'm goin' to stay right here."

Big Mom smiled.

"Why do you want to do that?" Checkers and Chess asked.

"I don't know. Seems like the right thing to do. I think these Indians might need me. Maybe need my music. Besides, it's beautiful here. And Thomas, I *have* seen everythin'."

Johnson took Thomas's hands in his own.

"We both have places we need to be," Johnson said.

"Yeah, Thomas," Chess said, "we have places to be. We need to get going. It's late."

Thomas looked at Big Mom.

"We have to go," he said.

"Okay," Big Mom said. "But hold on a second. You need some start-up money. That operator job won't pay you much. And you need first month, last month, and deposit to move into an apartment."

"We'll manage," Chess said.

"You'll do more than that," Big Mom said and stood. She cleared her throat, and the feast crowd turned all their attention to her.

"Listen," Big Mom said. "Thomas, Chess, and Checkers are leaving the reservation today. They need some money. We need to have a collection."

"Bullshit!" shouted somebody.

"Now, I know some of you aren't happy with how this all turned out," Big Mom said, "but think of poor Junior Polatkin. Think of how hard these kids worked. Think of your tribal responsibilities."

"Think of getting them off the goddamn reservation," shouted a voice in the back. It was David WalksAlong. He threw a hundred dollar bill into his cowboy hat and sent it around the room. "We'll never have to see their faces again. We won't have to hear any of their stink music."

The cowboy hat made its way around the room. Some Indians gave money out of spite; some gave out of guilt; a few gave out of kindness. There was a few hundred dollars in the hat when it finally made its way to Big Mom.

"There you go," Big Mom said and dumped the cash in front of Chess, Checkers, and Thomas. "It ain't a whole lot. But that should be enough to get you started."

"You better take care of it," Thomas said to Chess. She stuffed the bills into her pockets.

"Well," Big Mom said, her voice breaking a little, "I guess this is it."

"Jeez," Chess said, "we ain't going that far. Just to Spokane. It's an hour away."

"Anywhere off the reservation," Thomas said, "is a long ways from the reservation."

Thomas, Chess, and Checkers left the Longhouse. A few Indians waved goodbye. Big Mom, Robert Johnson, and the-man-who-was-probably-Lakota followed them outside.

"We'll see you soon," Thomas said but knew he was lying.

"Just call information," Chess said, "and maybe I'll be your operator."

Checkers climbed quietly into the van.

"Goodbye," Big Mom said. "You can always come back."

Robert Johnson pulled out his harmonica and blew a few

chords. The-man-who-was-probably-Lakota played along on his hand drum. The blue van pulled away.

"The end of the world is near! The end of the world is near!"

† † †

They drove away from the Spokane Indian Reservation in silence, Chess, Thomas, and Checkers all struggling with the silence and wanting to find something to say. They smiled at each other and tried to read each other's mind. Chess could feel Thomas and Checkers trying to read her mind, but she wouldn't let them in. She tried to read their minds, but they wouldn't let her in. What were they all thinking? What did they think was going to happen in Spokane? Would Thomas be ignored in the city, would those Urban Indians try to hurt him? Would some friend of David WalksAlong or Michael White Hawk come running out of the crowd with a knife, a gun, or a razor-sharp piece of a broken dream? Was Checkers still thinking about Father Arnold? Did she think she'd come running back to the reservation? And what about Victor? Would he still be trying to drink himself to death when he was eighty years old, a complete failure at everything he ever did?

"I'm scared," Chess said to Thomas.

"Chess," he said, "we're all scared."

They all held their breath as they drove over the reservation border. Nothing happened. No locks clicked shut behind them. No voices spoke, although the wind moved through the pine trees. It was dark. There were shadows. Those shadows took shape, became horses running alongside the van.

Chess, Checkers, and Thomas all looked at each other with fear and wonder. A shadow horse was running so close to the van that Chess could have reached out and touched it. Then she rolled down her window and reached out to touch that shadow, that horse. It was hot and wet. Checkers reached out of her window and touched a horse of her own, while Thomas drove the van, illuminating more shadows galloping down the road in front of them.

Those horses were following, leading Indians toward the city, while other Indians were traditional dancing in the Longhouse after the feast, while drunk Indians stood outside the Trading Post, drinking and laughing. Robert Johnson and the-man-who-was-probably-Lakota played a duet. Big Mom sat in her rocking chair, measuring time with her back and forth, back and forth, back and forth there on the Spokane Indian Reservation. She sang a protection song, so none of the Indians, not one, would forget who they are.

In a dream, Chess, Checkers, and Thomas sat at the drum with Big Mom during the powwow. All the Spokane Indians crowded around the drum, too. They all pounded the drum and sang. Big Mom taught them a new song, the shadow horses' song, the slaughtered horses' song, the screaming horses' song, a song of mourning that would become a song of celebration: we have survived, we have survived. They would sing and sing, until Big Mom pulled out that flute built of the bones of the most beautiful horse who ever lived. She'd play a note, then two, three, then nine hundred. One for each of the dead horses. Then she'd keep playing, nine hundred, nine thousand, nine million, one note for each of the dead Indians.

In the blue van, Thomas, Chess, and Checkers sang together. They were alive; they'd keep living. They sang together with the shadow horses: we are alive, we'll keep living. Songs were waiting for them up there in the dark. Songs were waiting for them in the city. Thomas drove the car through the dark. He drove. Checkers and Chess reached out of their windows and held tightly to the manes of those shadow horses running alongside the blue van.